"What happened?" ... whisper issuing fro... a deep breath and p... ...silver flask away.

"You fainted. I am not sure why." Everett's deep voice had a beautiful timbre and his eyes held sympathy. Or she thought they did. But perhaps that was only wishful thinking.

Venetia sat up. "I never faint. I must have tripped."

He frowned. "I offered you my room and you fell into my arms."

And she hadn't even known what it felt like to be held by him. She quelled the feeling of disappointment. She was being ridiculous. She was confused, that was all. By his arrival. By the news she was a marchioness, along with her worry for Mary. It was like being thrown into a maelstrom after years of calm waters.

"I must have caught my foot in the frayed edge of the carpet. I must see about its repair."

"Do not bother. We return to London immediately."

"We? London?" She stared at him in shock. The very thought of London, of Society, made her feel ill. And what about Mary? "I am not going to London."

An expression of annoyance crossed his face. "You are my wife. You will."

Author Note

Venetia and Everett's journey to happiness reminds us that the path to love is not always smooth or even particularly quick. We are also reminded that love has many forms, especially love for our family.

It is hard to believe that it's been two hundred years since the end of the official Regency era—George IV became king in 1820 upon the death of his father. In that historically short space of time, women have accomplished much in regard to equality, even if more remains to be done. Nowadays, it is difficult for me to imagine a time when women were considered their husbands' property. Nevertheless, women have always been strong and resilient, and no matter the era, they found ways to make their voices heard as Venetia does in this story.

If you wish to learn more about me and my books, please go to my website at annlethbridge.com.

ANN LETHBRIDGE

The Wife the Marquess Left Behind

HARLEQUIN
HISTORICAL

HARLEQUIN®
HISTORICAL™

Recycling programs
for this product may
not exist in your area.

ISBN-13: 978-1-335-72324-6

The Wife the Marquess Left Behind

Harlequin Enterprises ULC
22 Adelaide St. West, 41st Floor
Toronto, Ontario M5H 4E3, Canada
www.Harlequin.com

Printed in U.S.A.

In her youth, award-winning author **Ann Lethbridge** reimagined the Regency romances she read—and now she loves writing her own. Now living in Canada, Ann visits Britain every year, where family members understand—or so they say—her need to poke around every antiquity within a hundred miles. Learn more about Ann or contact her at annlethbridge.com. She loves hearing from readers.

Books by Ann Lethbridge

Harlequin Historical

It Happened One Christmas
"Wallflower, Widow...Wife!"
Secrets of the Marriage Bed
Rescued by the Earl's Vows
The Matchmaker and the Duke
The Viscount's Reckless Temptation
The Wife the Marquess Left Behind

The Widows of Westram

A Lord for the Wallflower Widow
An Earl for the Shy Widow
A Family for the Widowed Governess
A Shopkeeper for the Earl of Westram

Visit the Author Profile page
at Harlequin.com for more titles.

I would like to dedicate this book
to all the members of my family who have
supported me in my love of writing stories.

Chapter One

The Lasalle London town house was as familiar to Everett, Marquess of Gore, as his own face, and as strangely foreign as the words running through his head. *Familia casa.* Home. Or at least one of many homes. Through years of service to the Crown, along with strategic marriages, the marquisate had acquired many holdings. None of which he had set foot in for five years.

The demise of Everett's older brother, Simon, had come as a shock. Simon had been in the prime of life when Everett had chosen to go to India in a vain attempt to encourage his brother to be more responsible. Disenchanted by his older brother's reckless behaviour, Everett had decided it was time Simon stood on his own two feet, instead of leaning on Everett to get him out of trouble.

He'd also become jaded by the way some of the marriageable females thought to use him as a stepping stone to the most eligible bachelor in Town, his brother, never minding whether they trampled on his heart to do so.

No, he'd been excited to leave, had been looking forward to carving out his own future and becoming more than the spare for a marquess.

Looking back, he could only shake his head at his younger self's naivety. Letting his guard down, drinking more than he should have, while he and Simon celebrated his last night in England, had been stupid. He should have guessed Simon was up to something when he dragged Everett along to that ball.

Trusting his brother had led to Everett being duped into marrying a fortune hunter the day before he left for India. Like all the others in Simon's orbit, the girl hadn't wanted Everett. She had thought she had done what no other female had managed. She thought she had trapped the heir to the Marquess of Gore.

Instead, she had accosted Everett, who had passed out in the garden. A error that had cost Everett dear on the eve of his departure. He'd been forced to wed the girl the morning before he boarded his ship to India. Hungover and furious, he'd stormed off the moment the knot was tied. He hadn't seen the woman from that day to this.

Knowing she'd failed in her attempt to trick his brother into marriage had been Everett's only consolation. Until he'd received word of his brother's demise.

How happy she must be, to discover that after all these years she was now the marchioness.

And he was stuck with a wife he didn't know and didn't want. Had been stuck with her for five years. She had, willy-nilly, put an end to his bachelorhood, never mind how often he had told himself he owed her nothing. Every time he was tempted to forget his vows, he recalled the skinny, blotchy-faced, glowering girl he'd been forced to wed. And for some reason, his stupid sense of honour and duty had stopped him short.

He hoped she'd been equally faithful.

Before his brother died, he had been able to keep his vow he would never see the woman again. Now, he would hold his nose and fulfil his duty to the marquisate and take up the mantle of marriage.

He handed his outer raiment to the grey-haired balding butler who had greeted him at the door. 'How are you, Potter?'

Potter bowed. 'In excellent health, my lord. It is good to see you home again, though I regret the need.'

Potter had a mouthful of platitudes for every occasion. 'Thank you.'

Everett glanced around him. After the exotic surroundings of India, the house seemed austere and exceedingly cold. He shivered. A reaction to England's chilly climate. Nothing to worry about. To be sure, however, he would take some of the horrible concoction he'd been given by the physician in Calcutta.

'And Lady Gore?'

Potter looked confused. 'I...er... Her Ladyship... But, my lord, she died—'

His heart seized. A pair of angry brown eyes set in a narrow angular face with heavy dark brows and pinched lips floated across his vision. Not a pretty face. Was his famous luck at work in this matter also? Was he rid of a wife he never wanted? 'My wife died? Why was I not informed?'

'Your w-w-wife, my lord? I thought you were speaking of your grandmother.'

Everett stared at his butler. 'My grandmother died before I left for India, Potter. You know this as well as I do.'

Potter looked miserable. 'I forgot you were married, my lord.'

What the devil? Yes, he'd left right after the ceremony, but he had been wed. That was not a figment of the wild dreams he had when the fever took him down. Those imaginings were full of other events. Never of his 'wife.'

On the other hand, he had treated his 'wife' rather badly when he'd realised who had been standing in church beside him. In his drunken haze the night before, he hadn't realised that rather than the pretty sister who had been in relentless pursuit of Simon for weeks, it was the older sister who had ended up beneath him in the bushes.

Not that he cared which sister it was. He'd been legshackled against his will.

No doubt his ungentlemanly behaviour at the altar was why she had not replied to any of his letters these past many years, despite that she had happily been pocketing the small fortune he sent her every month for her keep.

So why was she not here at the town house to greet him? Had she hidden herself away for some reason? Did she fear his reprisal for her trick to catch his brother in marriage? Or might she be ashamed? Did the sort of woman who would dupe a man into marriage have a conscience?

He had been so angry on the morning of his wedding. And so very hungover. He'd stormed off after a few choice words.

Well, his wife, Venetia was her name, though he rarely thought of her as anything but the woman whom he had been forced to marry, was likely thrilled at her elevated status.

'Someone must know where the devil she is.'

Potter wrung his hands in a rare show of emotion. 'Perhaps Mr Week, my lord. Your late brother's man of business. He will know, I am sure.'

'Week?' Everett frowned. 'My grandfather's man of business was Bucksted, surely?'

'His late Lordship preferred his own man for some of his business dealings, as I understand it, my lord. After your grandfather's death, the estate's business matters were dealt with by Mr Bucksted and those of a more personal nature handled by Mr Week.'

Everett winced. Given some of Simon's wild excesses, he had likely decided Bucksted's disapproval would cramp his style. It would be typical of Simon to try to avoid taking responsibility for his misdeeds. Though in the matter of Everett's wife, he could not see the reason he would hand her care off to this other fellow. But with Simon, one never exactly knew what was going on in his mind.

'Very well. Locate this Week fellow and arrange for me to meet with him.'

'Yes, my lord. Will you dine as your grandfather did, at five, or would you prefer a later time?'

In his latter years, his grandfather had preferred the earlier hours of the country for his dinner, no matter where he was in residence. Everett had become accustomed to dining later, in the cool of the Indian evening. 'I prefer dinner at nine, Potter, but since you were not expecting me until tomorrow, I believe I will dine at White's this evening.'

Potter bowed his acceptance.

Perhaps that was why his wife was not here to greet him, Everett mused. In his last letter, he had told her to expect his arrival tomorrow, but the ship had docked one day early.

While he certainly did not expect her to welcome him with effusion, he did expect her to be civil. He would bet a pound to a penny she would be in eager anticipation of his arrival, since his brother had passed away some six months before. The Marchioness of Gore had always been a leader in Society and no doubt this one would be champing at the bit to take up her role.

Unlike himself. The last thing he had ever wanted was the title.

Simon had done him one favour by not getting married. There was no widow to console and care for. Though if Everett could have had his way, Simon would have married and produced his own heir and a spare, instead of landing Everett with the title.

'I will have your carriage brought around at eight, then, my lord.'

'No need. I will walk.' The air of London was so different to the heat of Calcutta. He wanted to breathe it in and know he was home. He had not realised just how much he had missed England.

He climbed the stairs to what had once been his grandfather's chamber and, for a year or two, that of his older brother. Another shiver ran through him.

Dammit he would not be ill.

Venetia, Lady Everett Lasalle, shivered and pulled her shawl closer around her. The fire was dying but she did not dare use up any more of her little store of coal. She had pulled the shabby curtains closed against the draughts that seeped through the ancient windows, but it did little good.

She put her embroidery aside and smiled across at her companion, a blonde pretty young thing reading out loud from Sir Walter Scott's *Waverly*.

They used the glow from the fire to augment the light from the candles which were in short supply. 'It is time to retire, my dear. You will not wish to ruin your eyesight.'

Her companion, Mrs Smith, nodded and set aside the book. The last woman had been called Mrs Brown. And their first names were given as Mary. It was safer for them that Venetia did not know their real names. This new one had been with her for almost two weeks and any day now a messenger would come with the details of her departure for Italy. She would be the second wife Venetia had helped escape from an abusive husband.

Venetia envied the woman her upcoming freedom. Once or twice she had thought of going to Italy herself, dreamed of becoming plain Mrs Smith or Mrs Brown and fleeing to the Continent to live her life out in peace and contentment.

But she was at peace and contented. She had not heard a word from her husband, Lord Everett Lasalle, younger brother of the heir to the Marquess of Gore, for many years. He had taken one look at his new wife and run off to India, leaving his brother to summarily deposit her here at Walsea on their wedding day. She had lived in this draughty old house on a tiny pension ever since, while he no doubt enjoyed the fleshpots of foreign climes.

She had made the best of her situation. It was only in the depths of winter that she found the house and its environs close to untenable. Even that had changed after she took in her first runaway. The company of the other woman made it bearable. The knowledge that she was able to aid another to break free of cruel tyranny gave her a deep sense of satisfaction.

To hell with Everett Lasalle. May he never return.

The fire was almost out. She picked up the poker, intending to make sure it was safe.

Mary Smith shot to her side. 'Let me do that.'

She let the other woman take her place at the hearth. Venetia tried to ignore the girl's awkward left-handed wielding of the poker. Her right arm had been dislocated at the shoulder by her husband during their last argument and had not yet healed properly. Grateful for the help she had received, she said it eased her mind to feel as if she was giving something back and tried her best to be helpful. She was a nice young thing and did not deserve the misery she had endured at the hands of her husband.

At a knock on the front door, Mary swung around. From cheerful and confident, Mary's expression became one of terror. She swallowed. 'Is it him?'

'I very much doubt it,' Venetia said more calmly than she felt, given the hour and the fact that she never had callers at any time of day. 'But be ready to go to the hiding place I showed you.'

They were prepared for irate husbands or fathers.

Her heart picked up speed. Could it be this Mary's husband? Had he somehow discovered his wife's whereabouts? Or worse yet a constable? A man with the power of the law on his side, who could whisk them both off to prison.

John, the young man who served as her man of all purpose, a servant she could ill afford but whom she had discovered she could not manage without, arrived a few moments later bearing a calling card.

Her heart knocked wildly against her ribs. Was this

the end of her life? Mary's stricken expression likely mirrored her own.

'I told the gentleman how, as you wasn't receiving, my lady,' John said. 'The way you said I should.' He was a son of one of the local farmers and a strong and sensible young man. 'He insisted I give you this.'

She glanced at the name on the card. The fear roiling in her stomach was replaced by utter astonishment.

Why on earth would the Marquess of Gore come to call? And at this time of night? How very odd. Not one of Lasalle's relatives had called on her since she arrived here. And she received little news from her own family either. That had not surprised her.

She and her father had never got along. He had been very glad to wash his hands of her. She was far too outspoken and too much of a bluestocking to conform to his view of what a young lady should be. Meek, docile, uncomplaining, like her poor mother. Or pretty and decorative like her younger sister.

She glanced at Mary. 'All is well. It is my brother-in-law. Show him in, please, John.'

A reflex action made her hands smooth her skirts. As if anything could improve their worn state. She did have a better gown that she wore to church on Sundays, but there was never enough money to waste on new clothes, especially when those who came to her had so little and their need was so much greater than hers. This one had arrived with nothing but what she was wearing.

One thing was certain: she did not want the marquess taking an interest in Mary Smith and, given the time of night and the remoteness of the house, she was bound in duty to offer him a bed for the night. 'Retire to your room right after I make the necessary introductions. We must avoid any awkward questions. I will do my best to be rid of him in short order.'

So far as Venetia was aware, the marquess remained a bachelor, though she rarely got a glimpse of a newspaper these days. She couldn't afford a subscription.

Mary stood beside the hearth as if frozen, her eyes wide and scared.

Venetia wanted to reassure her, but it was too late for further conversation. The fair-haired, blue-eyed strikingly handsome marquess strolled in. Thinner than she recalled. Less arrogant. And tanned? He looked about him with a frown.

The low lighting made it difficult to see his features, reminding her of the night she had tried to rescue Florence from causing a scandal and had ended up being the brunt of one instead.

She had been fooled in the dim light in the garden into thinking the man she had come to berate was the Marquess of Gore. Instead, it was the marquess's younger brother into whose arms she had fallen. It had been like one of those farces that audiences loved to mock when one went to the theatre. Her blood ran hot then cold at the recollection of the events that had changed her life.

The embarrassment. Her husband's obvious distaste at the sight of his bride. The humiliation as he stalked away. Her chest squeezed painfully.

An odd sensation tickled behind her breastbone.

This was not... This was...her husband? But his card...

His gaze went from Mary to her and back to Mary, no doubt because of the young woman's beauty. For a moment, he seemed puzzled, then his glance rested firmly on Venetia.

'Madam,' he said in icy tones.

Her brain whirled with disbelief and yet she could not doubt the evidence of her eyes. She dipped a curtsey. Mary followed suit. 'My lord. How can this be? Your brother...'

His eyes widened a fraction. 'My brother died six months ago. I wrote to you of this. Informing you of my date of arrival.'

Confused, she shook her head. 'I received no communication. I was unaware...'

He looked at her in obvious disbelief. 'Someone must have written to you. Not to mention the account of his accident was in all the newspapers.'

The shabby state of her apparel made her want to cringe under that cold stare. She straightened her shoulders. 'I do not take a newspaper. I care nothing for the doings of others. Why have you come?'

He seemed taken aback by her words. 'It is time we spoke, do you not think?'

He had not communicated with her for five years—what on earth did they need to speak about now? 'I cannot say I have given the matter much thought at all.'

He frowned. 'Nevertheless, talk we will—in the morning. I am too weary for discussions this evening. The road in this area is exceedingly bad.'

A bad road and its nearness to the coast made it ideal for her purposes, as it happened, though she had been horrified by its remoteness from the nearest town on the day she arrived.

'You will stay the night, then?'

At best she sounded grudging, but he did not seem to notice.

'I will.' He rubbed his hands together as if he felt cold.

Well, that was hardly her fault. If she had more money, she would love to have a blazing fire. 'I will arrange a chamber for you. Give me a few moments, if you please.' She would have to give him her room and take the only other available bedroom. 'Would you like a cup of tea? Something to eat?' She inventoried the leftovers in the pantry. 'Meat pie?'

'Nothing, thank you. I ate earlier.'

Thank goodness for that. 'Very well, please make yourself comfortable while I see to your room. I shall be but a few minutes.'

Mary was staring at the marquess with an expression of awe and Venetia hoped her own face did not mirror that expression. Her husband was a far too handsome man to be saddled with such a plain wife, but for that wife to act like a besotted schoolgirl would put her at a terrible disadvantage.

'Mrs Smith, perhaps you could give me a hand,' she said with a smile, but at Mary's little start realised she had spoken with a little more asperity than she had intended.

Outside the room, she turned to the young woman. 'Go to bed, my dear. I will get John to assist me with preparing a room for the marquess. We shall soon be rid of him, I am sure.'

How she was to accomplish his departure if he decided, for some obscure reason, he preferred to stay, she wasn't quite sure.

After his wife's departure from the room, Everett crossed the room to stand near the hearth's meagre warmth. Since his arrival in England it seemed as if he was always chilled to the bone. Hopefully he would become acclimatised soon. God, he hoped the bedroom they were preparing for him would be warmer than this.

Not only was the fire mean and small, the room itself had seen much better days. The rug needed replacing, the upholstery was worn and patched. The only bright spot was a boldly embroidered cushion on the sofa.

He frowned. First, she had sequestered herself in an out of the way part of the country and then she allowed the place to go to rack and ruin. Very strange.

It did not bode well for the future.

And the other young woman, who was she? For a brief second, he had thought she was his wife's younger sister. But despite being pretty, the blonde blue-eyed young woman had been nowhere near as lovely as Florence.

And his wife, whom he only recalled seeing once on his wedding day, was as unlike her sister as it was possible to be. He still could not believe the way she had schemed to take her sister's place. Seeing her blotchy cheeks, her scowling glare, after the ceremony had nigh on sent him to his knees. But it was water under the bridge. They both had to make the best of it.

It was almost a half hour before his wife returned carrying a tray. 'I thought you might like a cup of tea while we wait for your chamber to be made ready.'

Why was the Marchioness of Gore carrying her own tea tray? And had likely made the tea herself, if he wasn't mistaken. There was something very wrong here.

He took the tray from her hands and placed it on the table beside one of the chairs.

A brief smile of thanks changed her face entirely.

While her features were angular, her nose prominent, her chin firm, taken as a whole, her face had a stern kind of beauty he had not remembered from their wedding day. But when she smiled, she became radiant, almost beautiful. Or perhaps it was the low light in the room. Or his increasingly fuzzy vision.

Dammit, he was surely not going to experience another bout of fever so soon after the last.

'Do not go to a great deal of trouble on my account. However, a good fire in my chamber would be most welcome.' Indeed, it would be a necessity. Even better would be if she invited him to her bed.

He stilled. Where had that thought come from? Well, she was his wife, after all. And he had kept his marriage vows all these many years. A place in her bed was his right. An unwelcome longing caught at his heart.

He scoffed at his foolishness. From her reactions so far, he would bet his considerable personal fortune that no such offer would be forthcoming. Not tonight anyway.

'John has his instructions.'

'John?'

'The fellow who opened the door to you. My man of all work. He has not valeted before, so please be patient with him. I do not receive many visitors.'

No butler, no footman and possibly no maids? Merely a man of all work? What the devil was she doing with all the money he sent? The woman must be shockingly nipfarthing. A penny-pincher.

The idea of years of future discomfort loomed in his mind.

She poured tea and handed him a cup. One taste and he relaxed. Darjeeling and perfectly brewed. He sipped appreciatively as it warmed him through. At least she wasn't stinting on the tea. Or reusing previously brewed leaves. A horrifying thought, but common practice among those less well-heeled.

'Will you be here long?' She winced slightly. 'I mean, was it your intention to visit for a day? Or more? I would like to know how to plan the household arrangements.'

She sounded as if she wanted to be rid of him. Well, that was not going to happen, but he certainly didn't want to remain at this ghastly mansion a moment longer than necessary.

What on earth had made her pick such an uncomfortable situation when there were so many more pleasant houses belonging to the estate, he could not imagine. The air here was damp. The countryside, what he had seen of it, flat and unappealing, and according to his map, the North Sea lay only a quarter of a mile away. It seemed to be the last place in England anyone would want to live.

When he'd given Bucksted the address he'd obtained from Week, Walsea House, it had taken the bailiff a half an hour combing the estate records to discover it was located near a village on the coast called St Oswych not far from Colchester.

If he wasn't so damned exhausted after the journey, he would have liked to converse with her about these matters, but the last bout of fever on board ship had robbed him of stamina. Tomorrow would be soon enough for long discussions.

Hopefully she could be packed up and ready to move back to London in short order. 'Not more than two days, I should think. I am sure we can organise everything in that length of time.'

An expression of extreme relief passed across her face. A reaction she immediately tried to hide. A reaction he did not understand and needed to get to the bottom of. But not tonight. He put down his cup. 'Thank you for the tea. If my room is ready, I should like to retire.'

She rose gracefully to her feet. She was above average height for a woman and her slender figure gave her elegance. The first time he had seen her through the haze of too much brandy, courtesy of Simon, he'd thought she looked like a stick, all bony and pointy elbows. If that impression had been correct then, time had softened the angles and filled out the curves somewhat. Thank goodness.

'Then let me not keep you from your bed,' she said briskly. 'I am sure your room is ready.'

Grateful she was not bombarding him with questions, which was something he had expected at this their first meeting in years, he followed her up the stairs. Tomorrow would be soon enough to go into the details of his history. And hers. He definitely needed an explanation of why she was living in such dreadful circumstances. Tomorrow. They would talk tomorrow. Right now, he was simply too weary to think.

The door she led him to was on the first floor, to the right of the landing. She threw it open for him to pass inside.

Thank God. A fire blazed merrily in the hearth. A couple of candelabra filled the room with a soft light. And yet the air had an edge of chill. The fire needed time to do its work.

He looked about him. As was the case downstairs, the furnishings were heavy and old, purchased in a previous century. No doubt the bed ropes would creak every time he moved. He recalled his grandfather unwillingly discarding a similar bed he and Simon had bounced on until it broke.

Still, the covers were drawn down, revealing pristine white sheets. With any luck they would not be damp.

His valise had been brought up and placed on a chest at the end of the bed.

'I hope this will do,' she said. 'It is the best I can offer at short notice.'

The strain in her voice tugged at his conscience. He had arrived unannounced and while any wife ought to have expected her husband's arrival at some point, clearly she had not.

He had come home to England expecting calm and quiet. He certainly needed it after the rough passage from India, but it seemed he had caused quite a deal of consternation in this house.

He put his hands out, intending to take hers in his, to offer her reassurance. 'Venetia—'

She stepped back, thrusting her hands behind her, looking startled. 'Ring the bell for John if there is anything you need. I will bid you goodnight, my lord. We will talk more in the morning.'

She sped from the room, leaving his mouth agape.

Devil take it, what on earth was wrong with the woman?

He sank on to the edge of the bed. He frowned at the frayed edge of the carpet.

From the time he had walked in the door she had been treating him like a guest in his own home. He was the head of this household, not some stray she had taken off the streets.

Some old advice he had heard from his grandfather to Simon years ago crept into his mind. *'When a man takes a wife, he must establish his position as the lord of his domain right away, or he will regret it for the rest of his days.'* He had not done so with his wife. Time had not permitted since his ship for India left the same day as he was wed.

Another adage also arose to guide him. *Do not let the sun go down on an argument.* It wasn't quite an argument, but he had the instinct that there was some sort of misunderstanding going on.

He looked about him and saw the odd hint of a female presence. The flowery counterpane, the embroidered stool before the dressing table, the patterned ewer and jug, all hinted at a woman's taste. Dammit. She had given her room up to him.

Guilt that he had displaced her gave him a little pang. But then she could have stayed, could she not? The fact that she did not want to was not a surprise, even if he did feel an unwelcome sense of disappointment.

What? Had he expected her to welcome him with open arms? Perhaps he had. But he should not be surprised that she had not, he supposed. They didn't know each other. Apart from the debacle in the garden, something he scarcely recalled at all, they had only met once. On their wedding day. And then only for as long as it took to get the knot tied.

And now he had put her out of her room. A matter he really ought to rectify.

He pushed to his feet and shook off his exhaustion.

Chapter Two

The moment she was out of earshot of his door, Venetia ran for her bedchamber. The only word in her mind a resounding, *No!*

She burst through her chamber door and turned the key on the lock, panting. She covered her face in her hands. *What was the matter with her?* When he had reached out to her, she'd had the strangest idea that she should run into his arms.

As if she had suddenly lost her wits. Forgotten the years of hardship and neglect at the first sign of kindness. Surely, she was long past acting like a schoolgirl at the sight of a handsome face and a smile, even if he was her husband?

On her wedding day, she had longed for that smile. Instead, he'd taken one look at her, and told her he would be happy never to see her again.

The sharp pain of his words had been dulled by time, and yet the memory of his look of distaste still had the power to cause her stomach to fall away.

Never in her wildest dreams had she imagined or wanted his return. She was quite happy as she was, especially now she had begun helping other women on their way to make a new start.

Why had no one let her know that her brother-in-law had died or that her husband had inherited the title? Perhaps it was a case that everyone assumed someone else had passed the information along.

One thing was certain, Mary Smith would need to keep her wits about her. Did she even realise the danger she was in now the Marquess of Gore was under the roof? The opportunity for conversation had been limited from the moment John put the calling card in her hand. Perhaps she ought to pay Mary a quick visit and clarify the situation. Indeed, it would be wise to insist she remain in her room for the remainder of his time here.

She opened her door. And found her husband, back against the wall opposite, staring at her in surprise.

She gasped. 'What—?' Words tumbled around in her brain. 'I— There— Oh, good heavens—'

He raised an eyebrow. 'I was trying to decide if I should knock or barge right in,' he said with a mildness that held an edge of steely resolve.

She took a deep steadying breath. 'Is there a problem with your room?'

He raised an eyebrow. 'I have no wish to evict you from what is clearly the chamber you have been using.'

Was he saying what she thought he was saying? Did he actually mean he wanted her to share the room with him? That he wanted to share her…bed? Like husband and wife?

Her mouth dried. Her vision darkened and—

She came to her senses in her room, on the small sofa beside the hearth. Someone was pressing something to her lips. The fumes made her choke and then cough. A large warm hand patted her back.

She looked up into the face of…her husband.

Her husband…oh, good Lord, her husband…was kneeling beside her. He must have carried her in.

'What happened?' Horrified by the whiney whisper issuing from her lips, she drew in a deep breath and pushed the silver flask away.

'You fainted. I am not sure why.' His deep voice had a beautiful timbre and his eyes held sympathy. Or she thought they did. But perhaps that was only wishful thinking.

She sat up. 'I never faint. I must have tripped.'

He frowned. 'I offered you my room and you fell into my arms.'

And she hadn't even known what it felt like to be held by him. She quelled the feeling of disappointment. She was being ridiculous. She was confused, that was all. By his arrival. By the news she was a marchioness, along with her worry for Mary. It was like being thrown into a maelstrom after years of calm waters.

'I must have caught my foot in the frayed edge of the carpet. I must see about its repair.'

'Do not bother. We return to London immediately.'

'We? London?' She stared at him in shock. The very thought of London, of Society, made her feel ill— And what about Mary? 'I am not going to London.'

An expression of annoyance crossed his face. 'You are my wife. You will—' He cut off his words and shook his head. 'These are matters I will discuss with you in the morning.' He rose and bowed slightly. 'Since you will not accept my offer to exchange our rooms, I will bid you goodnight.'

Heat rushed up to her hairline. Exchange. He had offered an exchange, not to share. Well, of course that was all he had offered. What man would want to share his bed with her? Her chest tightened. But if he wanted an heir, at some point they would have to…

Her heart picked up speed. No. There had to be something she could do. Some way out of this mess. When he said he never wanted to see her again, she had taken him at his word. She had made a life for herself, and now here he was, back, making demands, ordering her about. It was unacceptable.

She swallowed. 'Yes. We will discuss this tomorrow.' Meanwhile, she would think of some way to remind him of his avowed intent to cut her out of his life. Was not a gentleman supposed to keep his word?

At the door, he hesitated and turned back, his eyes narrowed. 'Where were you going?'

Her stomach dipped. 'I beg your pardon?'

'Just now. You were going somewhere.'

The man was no fool, clearly. 'I needed a word with John. I recalled something I forgot to tell him. About where to serve breakfast in the morning.'

Heat rose up her neck to the roots of her hair. She always blushed when she lied. It was why she never saw the point of doing so. Except now there was more at stake than herself. She had to think of Mary's well-being.

He gave her a wolfish smile that implied he did not believe her. 'Perhaps I can relay the message, since he will be on hand to attend me.'

He had noticed her colouring up? Of course he had. And was now calling her bluff.

'Please tell him to serve breakfast in the dining room since we have a guest.'

'Oh,' he said, very quietly. 'I am not a guest, my dear. This is *our* home. I shall tell him to serve it in the usual room.' With a grim smile, he bowed. 'I look forward to the resumption of our conversation when we are both rested.'

Her heart quickened at his masterful tone. He was not a man to be easily managed. But manage him she must. For Mary's sake.

But after that, what on earth was she going to do? She did not want to be a marchioness and she certainly did not want a husband. Did she?

Irritation buzzed in Everett's veins. He returned to his room feeling thoroughly out of sorts.

What the devil was wrong with him? Was his annoyance because he had expected to squash the pretensions of a woman ready to take Society by storm? But instead he had found a woman both alluring and independent-minded who cared nothing for the title. Or him.

He entered his room.

Their conversation tomorrow was clearly not going to go as easily as he had expected. What did she mean, she did not want to go to London? And what the devil had she done with all the money he had sent for her keep?

He was tired nigh unto death. His brain was no longer functioning as it ought. Tomorrow morning would be time enough to get to the bottom of things.

John came out of the dressing room with an expression of relief. 'Here you be, my lord. I thought mebbe the bell was broken when you didn't ring. There be quite a few things that need mending around here.'

It was pretty close to a where-have-you-been? question as a servant could get. Everett certainly wasn't going to answer it. 'Help me out of this coat, please, John, and then you can be on your way to bed. I can manage the rest.'

The young man nodded and eased him out of his fashionably tight-fitting tailcoat. 'I brought up some hot water for washing. Will you been needing me to shave you in the morning, my lord?'

Everett rubbed his chin and grinned. 'What time do the ladies eat in the morning?'

'Around seven, my lord.'

Good Lord. So early. 'I assume you will be busy preparing breakfast. Just bring the hot water. I will do the rest.'

The young man placed the coat carefully on the chest at the foot of the bed, bowed and left.

After a wash down, Everett hopped into the bed which was surprisingly comfortable and actually warm. John must have used the bed warmer in Everett's absence.

His wife knew how to run a household, even if she spent as little money as possible doing it.

He stared up at the canopy. Where had his wife been headed when she opened that door?

Not to the kitchens as she had said. She had definitely not been telling the truth about that. He'd seen the lie in her face. Simon had made him very adept at spotting a lie. Though with Simon, he rarely ever spoke the truth about anything that mattered. So, if his wife was not off to the kitchen, then where?

Clearly, his arrival had not been a source of pleasure. Was it possible she had a lover tucked away somewhere? Was that why she had decided to live so far from civilisation?

His wife had lied to him. He'd had enough of Simon's lies; he was not going to tolerate it in his wife.

His wife.

She was a far more attractive woman than he remembered from when she lifted her veil on her wedding day. She wasn't what most would describe as pretty. Her looks were better than that, and likely more enduring, feminine and aesthetically elegant. Definitely nothing like her popular younger sister.

Looking back with a mature eye, he realised her sister, Florence, had been lovely but completely bird-witted. And truth to tell, Simon had been almost as bad. Maybe worse. Because Simon's jokes often had an edge of malice.

No, Venetia was nothing like her sister in the brains department She was clever. And underhanded, as shown by the way she had tried to trick Simon into marriage. Tomorrow he would have the truth about everything.

To Everett, the next morning, the breakfast room looked like an architect's afterthought. It jutted out from the house's east flank into the formal garden and was surrounded by windows on three sides.

He entered to find Venetia already seated at the table eating a boiled egg. The morning light flooded into the room, and the severe style of her hair accentuated the angles and planes of her features. A strong face. Uncompromising. The contrasting delicate luminosity of her skin reminded him of the marble statues he had seen on his travels.

She glanced up with a surprised expression. Not expecting him to be up and about so early, no doubt.

'Good morning, my lord.'

She sounded stiff and formal. He sighed. Clearly, a night's rest had not softened her feelings towards him. Last night he had been too tired to deal with her. Today, his resolve to put his house in order had strengthened.

'Good morning.' He took in the view of the flat uninspiring scenery beyond the windows. 'The day appears pleasant enough.'

At least it wasn't raining, though the clouds were scudding along as if propelled by a brisk wind.

'It does indeed,' she said. 'May I offer you a cup of tea? Or do you prefer coffee? Please help yourself to food from the sideboard.'

Five years of marriage and she knew nothing about him. Nor he about her. What a tragedy. For them both. Now they would have to make the best of it. Duty and responsibility would have to guide them for the rest of their lives. They owed it to their position to do their best. 'Tea, please.'

He filled his plate. The food was plain English fare, scrambled eggs cooked to perfection, bacon curling at the edges and sliced to just the right thickness, along with sausages and toast. All served on plain white china. John, apparently, had unexpected talents.

She ate. He ate. The silence seemed full to bursting with unspoken questions.

'Mrs Smith is not joining us?' he finally asked.

'She broke her fast earlier. She has some errands to run today.'

She sounded calm, but a telltale rush of pink to her cheeks had him thinking she was lying. Again. Why would she lie about the whereabouts of her friend?

He pretended not to notice and forked up the scrambled eggs. Delicious and delicately seasoned. 'My compliments to John. He is an excellent cook.'

Her eyes widened a fraction. Her lips parted. Then she gave a slight shake of her head and picked up her cup and took a sip.

She didn't need to say anything. Understanding came to him. 'John did not cook breakfast, did he? You did.'

She hid her face behind her teacup for a moment. 'I did.' She put the cup down. 'Is that a crime?'

Did she have to be so dashed prickly? 'Then my admiration is for you, not for John.'

'Thank you.'

She didn't sound terribly grateful.

'Why don't you hire a cook?'

'Cooks are expensive.'

Just as he surmised, she was a nipfarthing. 'Not that expensive, surely?'

She stared at him in astonishment. 'If you wish to hire a cook for the time you are here, my lord, please, feel free. Now if you will excuse me, I have some household duties that require attention.'

Apparently in high dudgeon, she headed for the door.

'We have things we need to discuss.'

'I have things I need to do right at this moment.'

He held on to his patience with difficulty. 'Very well. We will meet in one hour. In the library... I assume there is a library?'

She inclined her head. 'There is.'

'Then we will meet there. I hope that will provide enough time for your duties.'

'I will arrange to be there.'

He was still none the wiser what her duties were and

he presumed he was supposed to be grateful that she had agreed to give him any of her time.

He took a deep breath.

Becoming angry would not serve his purpose.

The hen house was a cacophony of cackles and the overwhelming musty and acrid smell of chicken. Amid the straw, Venetia discovered a lovely clutch of brown eggs, a little mucky and still warm. She added them to her basket. She really liked her hens.

The cockerel was another story. He eyed her askance as she emerged into the sunshine. Hopefully, he would not attack her today. She'd put out plenty of corn to keep him busy while she looked for eggs. He went back to his pecking, and she breathed a sigh of relief.

She left him to it and headed for the kitchen garden. Dinner for a marquess would stretch her meagre repertoire.

She forked up a dozen new potatoes and put them beside the eggs, then started snipping off the herbs she would need. The scent of sage and then rosemary perfumed the air. Those and a little parsley should be all she needed.

Fortunately for her, she had a leg of mutton coming from the butcher today, or she would have had to kill one of her lovely hens. Next, she would send John off to visit his father's farm to see if they could spare a ham hock. It would be enough for three people for dinner, surely? And if His High and Mightiness the Marquess wasn't pleased, she didn't care.

Except she did. She wanted him to see that she had risen above his neglect and managed very well alone.

At breakfast, in the bright light of morning, he had

looked pale beneath his tan, as if he had not slept well.
And thin, as if food had been scarce for months. Which
seemed unlikely. Was he ill? What sort of life had he
led in India?

She had longed to ask questions, having only travelled from her home in Kent to London and then here
to Essex. Little more than a hop, skip and jump, really.

But to show any interest would only make him linger,
or worse yet, think that he was welcome in her home.
He wasn't.

'So, this is your "matters of importance."' The deep
voice sounded disgruntled.

She jumped.

She had been head down snipping parsley and so
busy with her thoughts she hadn't heard his approach.

She slowly rose to her feet and glared at him. 'There
is no need to be following me about, my lord.'

He gave her a quizzical stare. 'I decided to take some
air and saw you scurry back here and came to see what
you were about.'

She tipped up the brim of her gardening bonnet the
better to see his face. 'I do not scurry.'

He sighed. 'You were very intent on your purpose
else you would have seen me.' He reached out to take
her basket. For a moment, she held it fast, then realised
she was being foolish. She laid the parsley on top of the
other items and relinquished her hold.

He grasped her bare hand and turned it over. His hand
was bare and warm and terribly strong. He rubbed his
thumb over her palm and shame washed over her. Her
skin was rough and calloused in spots because half the
time she forgot to wear her gloves.

A shiver ran down her spine at the rasp of his skin over hers.

Oh, mercy, why had she forgotten them today of all days? She snatched her hand back.

He frowned.

Had she annoyed him? Too bad. Besides, she didn't care what he thought of her hands, or anything else for that matter. He was the one who had left her struggling to make her own way. And she had done it too.

Her brother, Paris, had offered to help, but her family wasn't wealthy enough to support themselves and her as well. And then the marquess, the previous one, Simon, had warned Paris off.

Her brother had retreated as ordered, but then she had never told him just how financially badly off she had been left by her dear husband. She had been ashamed of the way she had been rejected.

'Thank you for your help. I will take these to the kitchen and then I will attend you in the library.' She reached to take back the basket.

'Why don't we go together?'

What? Did he think she was going to try to avoid meeting him? She wasn't afraid of anything he might have to say. Not in the least. If he decided to become ugly about things, she would join Mary on the next boat.

Only then there would be no one to help any more wives who wanted to escape.

They entered the house through the back door. John was already there, getting the kitchen fire going, ready for her to bake bread.

He glanced up at their entry and touched his forelock. 'All the fires be lit, my lady. I was intending on doing a little fishing before I run the rest of the errands if 'n that suits you, my lady?'

'That would suit me very well, John. Fish would be an excellent addition to dinner.'

'Fishing?' Gore's face lit up. 'Do you have a boat?'

Oh, mercy, did he think she ran a sporting lodge here? 'We do not have a boat. He is talking about river fishing, from the bank.'

'We only have one rod,' John said. 'If 'n you wants to fish, my lord, I can leave you to it and I'll do my errands.'

'Good idea,' she said.

Gore gave her a piercing look. 'If I go fishing, we will have to postpone our meeting until later this afternoon.'

That suited her perfectly well. Indeed, he could put it off for ever as far as she was concerned. And while he was out of the way, she could get a message off to her contact in London warning her of the added complication of a marquess under her roof.

'Please yourself. If you don't go, then John will.'

He huffed out a breath. 'I will go.'

'I do hope you catch something,' she said sweetly. A little too sweetly. 'Dinner will depend upon your success. Perhaps you could also try to dig up some clams on the beach.'

He looked so appalled she almost laughed. No doubt he thought himself above such a mundane task. A tap at the door and the butcher's boy entered with the joint on his shoulder.

Gore gave her a cheeky grin. 'I guess I am safe. If the fish don't bite, a bit of mutton will be equally tasty.'

She smiled wryly and nodded.

'This way, my lord,' John said. They left together, talking about bait and deep pools and brackish water.

Men. They always had all the fun. Neither of them had thought she might like to do a bit of fishing.

Still, Gore looked as though some fresh air would do him good and it would keep him out of her hair, since he seemed intent on following her around and poking his nose where it was definitely not wanted.

Chapter Three

Everett tramped up to the kitchen door feeling pleasantly exhausted instead of drained. His doctor had been right. The air in England would aid in his recovery from the ague that plagued so many Englishmen in India. In addition, the fishing proved to be excellent. He'd thoroughly enjoyed the peace of the past few hours and had used the time to give some serious thought to how he should approach the situation of *his wife*.

Venetia. Her name was Venetia. Her brother was named Paris and her young sister Florence. Their parents must have had a liking for city names or the cities themselves. He would ask her about it one day.

He left his rod and reel leaning against the wall beside the back door and carried his basket through the scullery and into the kitchen.

The meat cooking on the stove smelled delicious.

With her back to him, his marchioness was making pastry at the long wooden table. With each roll of the pin across a circle of dough her body moved to and fro in a steady rhythm. The delicate fabric of her navy-blue gown emphasised the curve of her derriere each time she bent forward and, devil take it, her wide stance had him thinking wicked thoughts.

She spun around, rolling pin upraised.

He leaped back. He must have made some sort of sound. Hopefully not a lustful one. With the back of her hand, she brushed aside a tendril of hair that had fallen free. A dusting of flour appeared on her forehead.

Adorable. Flour smudged and pink from effort, she looked good enough to eat.

She frowned and spoiled the effect.

'Oh, it is you. Did you manage to catch anything?' Her tone was far from welcoming.

'I did.'

She went back to her rolling. He moved around her to the sideboard across the other side of the kitchen to avoid staring at her rear end. But the view from this side was almost as enticing, particularly the way her gown hugged her breasts. He put his basket on the sideboard. 'Two nice perch.'

'Thank you.' She did not look up.

There was no sign of anyone else in the kitchen. John really was her only servant, then, and he'd been sent off on an errand.

'I will take them outside and prepare them for cooking.'

The rolling stopped. She straightened. The frown remained. It was the drawing down of her unusually dark eyebrows that made her look so disapproving and unapproachable.

An expression that made him feel like a schoolboy caught with a bag of illicit sweets by his matron. He shrugged the sensation off.

'Do you know how to clean a fish?' she asked, sounding surprised.

Rather than give her a lecture on growing up on an estate with rivers and game, he simply nodded. 'I do indeed.'

Her expression lightened a fraction. 'Then I would indeed be grateful if you would do so. Thank you. You will find a sharp knife in the drawer. There is a pig bucket in the scullery for the innards and such.'

He equipped himself for the task and went outside into the sunshine. He and Simon had loved the outdoors; it was the one thing they had truly had in common. As boys they had cooked and eaten the fish they caught on the riverbank not far from their home. It was too bad Simon had changed so much once he entered Society.

The fish they caught in those days, grayling, had always tasted so much better eaten outdoors than it had when on a plate in the formal dining room. Indeed, he wished he could cook these fish himself, over a fire. But that really would not do. He'd be getting another one of those frowns of hers and that would put him off his dinner.

Everett sharpened the knife on a stone and lay the perch out on a flagstone. The skills of his boyhood returned quickly. Simon had shown him how to do this. Once he'd got the hang of it, Simon had always left Everett to the clearing, while he tended the fire.

He carried the cleaned fish back inside. She inspected them as he laid them on the end of the table.

'Excellent.' She nodded briskly and looked at him expectantly.

What? Was he supposed to produce something else?

A rabbit out of a hat, maybe? Or did she expect him to help with the cooking? 'Is there something else I can do?'

She smiled and for a moment he basked in the warmth from those upturned lips and the sparkle in her eye. 'I am almost out of wood. I should have asked John to chop some. Would you?'

'Of course.' After all, chopping wood and building a fire had been an integral part of his youthful fishing expeditions.

Her expression warmed even more. 'I am terribly grateful.'

He wasn't going to make the same stupid mistake of asking her why she didn't hire a cook or a maid or a footman. That conversation was due to happen later—in the library.

'The woodshed is beside the scullery,' she said, waving a knife towards the back door. 'You will find an axe inside.'

Off he went to chop wood for the first time in years. Didn't she realise there were all kinds of people who needed work and would be delirious with joy to find work in a house like this one?

Indeed, he would be most glad to teach her this basic duty of those in their position of wealth to hire those who needed to work to feed their families. This doing it all herself was utter nonsense.

And where was her friend who had been with her last night? Why wasn't she helping?

Not only did he chop the wood. He replenished the stove and delivered a bundle to the living room and dining room having been told firmly that John would look after the bedrooms on his return.

When he went back into the kitchen, wondering what

she would be having him do next, he was in time to admire the pie decorated with a Tudor rose and curling leaves sitting ready for the oven.

He started to brush the sawdust off his coat.

'Oh, no! Please. Do that outside.'

He made for the door.

'My lord, thank you for your help today.'

He turned and smiled at her. She stared at his face for a long moment. 'I will not be needing anything else,' she muttered and opened the oven door.

That was it. Dismissed.

'As you wish. I am very much looking forward to dinner if it tastes as good as it smells.' he said to her back. 'I am also looking forward to our conversation in the library. Shall we say, in one hour.'

He left swiftly, not giving her the chance to argue.

The hour passed quickly, and Venetia took a deep breath and removed her apron.

The marquess demanded her presence.

For all these years, her husband had ignored her very existence and now he thought to take charge of her life without so much as a by your leave.

And there was nothing she could do about it.

Although he had been exceedingly helpful today. And, oh Lord, when he had returned from fishing with his hair tousled and his skin ruddy from wind and sun, he had looked appealingly boyish. There had been a mischievous twinkle in his eye that had made her stomach flutter the way it had done on that day when he and his brother had called on her sister, and he had deigned to bid her good day.

An occasion he likely didn't recall.

Oh, yes, he had been polite, but in truth she did not think he really saw her. Like all the other young gentlemen at the time, he only had eyes for Florence. Her heart squeezed. He likely would have been less angry at being forced to the altar if Florence had been his bride. Unfortunately, Venetia had been so intent in saving her sister from the rakish Marquess of Gore, she had failed to notice that the man she was accosting was his brother. And then she had allowed her father to bully her into marrying him. Had she really believed her father's threats to punish Florence as well as herself? Or had she wanted to believe them?

Dreaming impossible dreams. Well, she certainly was too old and too sensible to be making a cake of herself over a nice smile and a handsome face. He might control the purse strings, but she had a mind of her own, something he would need to understand.

With firm steady steps, she made her way through the baize door to the main entrance hall. The carpeting in the corridor, although worn, muffled her slow footfalls. She certainly wasn't going to arrive out of breath and looking anxious.

When she walked into the oak-panelled room with its sparse collection of musty books, he was browsing through an atlas on the great reading table in the centre of the room. Light from the rose widow in the ceiling cast the room in warm hues and hid the decay and dust. She and the previous Mary had done their best with dusters, but each book really needed the attention of someone with skill.

It would cost a great deal of money.

He looked up at her entry and straightened.

Her heart skipped a beat, the way it had when she first saw him. Hearts were such foolish things.

No mischievousness lit his expression now. Instead, he looked grim.

He gestured to a chair. 'Please, sit down.'

The heavy old-fashioned chairs had mythical beasts carved into their wooden arms. She sank into the upholstery, which lacked stuffing and definitely needed new fabric. It had been brightly embroidered once, as could be seen in the crevasse at the back, but mostly was now varying shades of muddy brown.

He took the seat opposite.

'Here I am,' she said. 'As requested. Is your chamber to your satisfaction?'

'It is. Though the windows could use a good clean.'

She flinched. Blast. She had forgotten all about the windows. 'I apologise,' she said stiffly. 'I will ask John to see to them immediately.'

He didn't look happy. Did he expect her to climb a ladder and clean them herself?

'That is the problem,' he said as if making some wise pronouncement. 'You do not have sufficient staff. One man alone cannot be expected to maintain a house of this size.'

Heat rose up from her belly. She forced her temper down. 'I help as much as I can.' And so had both Marys.

His face darkened. 'Nonsense, you must know very well I am not asking you to do the work. You need to hire people. A footman, a butler, a couple of maids at a very minimum and a cook. Surely you know what is needed?'

Blankly, she stared at him. 'Of course I know. I simply do not know how to pay for them. My money won't stretch that far.'

His eyes widened. 'Madam, excuse me, but that is rubbish.'

She froze.

He stood up, paced to the window and looked out. 'Your allowance is more than adequate to run this household. I cannot imagine what you are spending it on.' He glanced over his shoulder with a disdainful expression. 'Certainly not garments.'

She forced herself not to shrink under that critical gaze. It was the same look of disdain she had received from her father when she failed to attract any suitors because of her 'lack of effort.' 'Adequate? I do not think it is adequate at all. It is barely enough to put food on the table.'

He turned to face her. 'I don't see how you can say my weekly allowance of twenty-five pounds is insufficient.'

A trickle of fear ran down her spine. 'I have never received more than five pounds a quarter. And that barely pays John's wages. I use the pin money I receive from my marriage settlement to pay for everything else.' Her temper slipped. Heat shot its way up from her chest to her face, where she could feel the fire blazing on her cheeks. 'So, don't you lecture me on how I should spend *my* money.'

Surprise filled his gaze. 'What are you doing with the rest of it? Investing in jewels?'

He seemed genuinely shocked.

'What are you talking about? There is no "rest of it."' She took a deep breath, trying to make sense of what he was saying. Was it possible he had actually sent funds for her keep? 'Perhaps you made a mistake when you sent your instructions. Or they were not clear.'

'I made no mistake. The money is certainly withdrawn from my account each month.' Offense coloured his tone. 'I don't know what the devil is going on here, but I intend to find out.'

'Are you saying you think I stole your money? How dare you?'

His expression of displeasure deepened. He lifted his hands from his sides in a gesture of confusion and returned to sit down.

He took a deep breath. 'Very well. Let us agree on this. I have been sending you a large allowance every month. You say you have not been receiving it—'

'You say you have been sending it,' she shot back. 'I have no proof that is so.' She wasn't going to buckle beneath the weight of his accusations.

His lips pursed. 'Put it this way, then. If I have been sending it and if you have not been receiving it, where has it gone?'

She shrugged. 'How would I know?'

His expression darkened. 'I see.'

'What do you see?'

'Look, our wedding was not what I wanted. My departure for India came at a very awkward moment, and after what you did...but had you been the least conciliatory—'

She drew herself up straight. 'Conciliatory? I have made the best of my situation here. I have left you in peace and I have survived. What more can you want of me?'

He grimaced. 'Not one word have I heard from you in five years.'

'Impossible. I wrote to you. Several times. Until...'

'Until?'

'Until Gore, I mean your brother, sent me a stiff little

note by way of his man of business telling me to stop troubling you with petty details.'

His expression went blank. 'Simon?'

'You only had one brother, did you not?' She winced. 'You are sure it came from Simon?'

She got up, went to the writing desk and riffled around in the desk. She handed him the note. 'His man of business handed it to me, the one time he came here.'

He stared at it, then raised his gaze to meet hers. 'It certainly looks like my brother's handwriting.'

'I hope you are not going to accuse me of forging it.'

'I— No. Of course not. But this has nothing to do with the question of what happened to the money I sent you.'

Everett felt all at sea. He had come here ready to demand answers and make his wife see sense, and now he had more questions than he had before.

And some of them could only be answered by a dead man.

The thing was, how could he believe anything she said after she and her sister had been so utterly deceptive? He wasn't a green youth with stars in his eyes any more. His forced wedding and his life in India had taught him not to accept anything at face value.

But this note was definitely from Simon.

The light from the skylight above cast her face into sharp planes and deep hollows. The bone structure of her features was remarkable in its purity. A sculptor would take great delight in such a face. Why had he not noticed the perfect symmetry of it the first time he saw her, or the luminosity of her green eyes? Eyes that right now blazed with anger.

Devil take it. He was the one who should be angry, surely? Indeed, he was angry, he had been for years, but right now he felt as if the ground had shifted beneath his feet.

Because she was acting all innocent and outraged. He knew that look of innocence of old. It hid lies. And in the way of all liars, she was trying to manipulate the situation to her own advantage.

'When I return to London, I will soon get to the bottom of where the money went, mark my words.'

To his surprise, she looked indifferent. 'I am sure you will.'

'And you will return with me.' He wanted her where he could keep an eye on her.

The indifference disappeared in a flash. Her breathing quickened. She looked at him aghast. 'Why do I need to go with you?'

'Why would you not go with me? You are my wife.'

'A recent realisation, I assume. You have taken little notice of the fact of our marriage prior to now. We have lived quite happily apart for years. Why spoil things?'

His expression darkened. 'You are housed, are you not? Fed? Clothed?'

'Barely,' she muttered.

He pretended not to hear. 'As my wife, it is your duty to me, to the title, to take up your responsibilities.' And he wanted her where he could keep her under his eye. He did not trust her for one moment.

She paled. 'What duties? What responsibilities?'

What was the matter with her? 'Good Lord, you surely do not need me to itemise the duties of a wife.'

She paced to the window and stared out. Her shoulders slumped, then straightened as if she had come to some sort of decision. 'If you insist. I will go to London. However, I cannot be ready to leave here for at least a month. It has taken you five years to return to England, surely a month is not too much to ask?'

He rubbed at his temple with one finger trying to dispel the onset of a headache. 'What must you do here that would take a month?'

She turned to face him, her hands gripped at her waist. 'I have commitments, social commitments. And a guest.' With a pained expression, she closed her eyes briefly. 'Besides, I have nothing to wear. I must have some gowns made up.'

Women and their gowns. He grimaced. But she certainly could not appear in town in what she was wearing. 'Two weeks should be ample time.'

'But Mrs Smith…' She must have seen the determination in his expression because she nodded, albeit reluctantly. 'I will manage. I will follow you to Town in two weeks.'

She had given in too easily. Had she asked for a month when she really wanted two weeks? It was the sort of thing Simon used to do. Manipulation. Lies. Half-truths.

When their father died, he and Simon had stood as a united front against the world. Or at least against their grandfather, who had been excessively strict with Simon, his heir. Everett had thought him unfair to his brother and had defended him through thick and thin, covering up for his misdeeds to save him from their grandfather's wrath.

Everett had seen it as his duty to keep his brother out of mischief. At first, Simon, charmer that he was, always apologised for putting his brother to so much trouble. Over time, Everett came to realise that by helping his brother, he was enabling behaviour that went far beyond foolish boyhood pranks.

Leaving for India was the only way he could see of making Simon take responsibility for his actions. Only to have Simon land Everett with a wife on the day of his departure. Simon's way of trying to stop him from leaving, he had assumed. A heinous deed after his years of devotion, for which he had refused to forgive him.

Devil take it. He wished he hadn't let the sun go down on his anger on that occasion. It was too late for them ever to make amends.

And he was stuck with a wife he hadn't chosen, who apparently baulked at the simplest of requests.

If he had to make the best of it, so did she. But he wasn't going to be manipulated or lied to. Not by her, or by anyone else.

'Two weeks, it is, then. I will write to my valet and have him bring additional clothes.'

Her eyes widened. 'There is no need for you to remain here. I am sure you have important business awaiting you in London.'

He smiled grimly. Oh, yes, she was definitely keeping secrets. Well, he wasn't having it. 'My business can wait. Come to think of it, where is Mrs Smith? I have not seen her all day. When does she go home?'

She looked ill at ease. She did not like him asking questions. Too bad. It was his right to know what was going on under his roof.

'We did not set a precise date.' She sounded breathless. And uncertain. More lies.

'Request that she cut her visit short and return home next week.'

'I...' She was clearly searching for more lies or excuses.

He glared at her.

'Yes,' she said. 'I will ask her. I am not sure anyone is at home to receive her, but I will ask her to make the necessary arrangements as quickly as possible.'

He nodded his satisfaction. 'Good. I shall look forward to meeting your friend, Mrs Smith, at dinner this evening.'

Unhappiness filled her gaze. She lowered her head. 'As you wish.'

Dammit, he liked her better when she was facing him down.

'If that is all,' she said quietly, too quietly, 'I hope you will excuse me,' she said. 'I need to look at my pie.' She swept out.

Leaving him feeling very ill at ease about the whole situation. Well, he had given her two weeks, and he would keep his word. In the meantime, he would use the time to learn about this property, since it was part of the estate. As well as get to the bottom of his wife's secrets.

Since there was nothing for him to do until dinnertime he would go for a walk and explore the neighbourhood. While fishing, he had noticed one or two small dwellings in the distance, and his map had shown a village not too far distant.

From there he would mail a letter to his valet. He certainly could not spend two weeks here without adding to his wardrobe.

He dashed off a note and returned to his room to collect his coat and hat. John was there, making up the fire. He rose upon Everett's entry. 'Can I help you, my lord?'

'No. I believe I have all I need. I thought I might stroll down to the local village.'

John touched his forelock and went back to his work.

Everett left the house, walked down the drive and set off in the direction of the nearest village, St Oswych. According to the signpost at the crossroads it was situated half a mile distant from the house. As he walked he became aware of a salty tang in the air and a stiffening of the breeze.

The sea must be a great deal closer than he had realised.

The village proved to be more of a hamlet. It boasted a tavern located on the ground floor of a mean-looking cottage, three or four fishermen's dwellings and a track through sand dunes to a small cove. Two or three boats lay on their sides on a patch of sand at what was obviously low tide alongside nets stretched out to dry above the high-water mark. Seagulls screeched and wheeled overhead. The waves, white topped and wind driven, charged towards land with a vicious-sounding hiss.

The clouds which had been white and fluffy when he left the house now had grey hearts, threatening rain. Dammit, he had not thought to bring an overcoat.

A fisherman with a set of grey bushy whiskers and a knitted cap crammed down over his ears sat on a boulder near the nets puffing on a clay pipe. He rose to his feet at Everett's approach.

'Good day to ye, sir.' He clamped his teeth down on his pipe with a frown. 'Do ye be lost?'

'Good day to you also. I am Gore. And you are?'

The old fellow touched his forelock. 'Jeb Caldicut, sir.'

'Caldicut, I hoped to find a post office in the village, but I believe I am out of luck.'

The man shook his head. 'You need to go to the next village over for that, sir, so you does. Five miles along the coast it be.'

Everett huffed his annoyance. 'Is there a lad about who could carry a letter for me?'

The fisherman removed his pipe and spat on the sand. 'Bert has a lad.' He looked up at the sky. 'He won't be a sending him today, though. He'll be getting a wet shirt if 'n he goes now. This morning would a' been all right. But now? No.'

Blast. But there was no denying that the clouds pushing in from the sea were getting thicker and darker and ever more threatening.

'Shall I pass it to him to deliver tomorrow?' Jeb asked. 'Or he can collect it from Walsea.'

So, Jeb had worked out where Everett had hailed from. He shook his head. 'Never mind. I may post it myself tomorrow.'

The old gentleman nodded his head and stuck his pipe back in his mouth.

'Is the fishing good here?' Everett asked, looking at the tiny fleet, if one could call three boats a fleet.

Jeb puffed out smoke. 'Low to middling, I would say.'

'Then why not go somewhere better?' He could not imagine living in such a desolate place if the fishing was 'low to middling.'

'Growed up here, we did,' the fisherman answered. A grin split his face and revealed rotting and brown-stained front teeth. 'An' besides, it ain't only fish that boats can carry.'

Everett recalled the very good brandy in his wife's keeping. The locals must be smuggling. Another rea-

son not to care for the place. Smugglers were a rough
and ready lot.

A raindrop landed on his arm. Another on his hat.
And then a gust of wind blew in off the sea and he
grabbed at his hat, just in time. A downpour began in
earnest.

'Best take shelter, sir,' the old man said, turning up
his collar. He emptied his pipe and started up the beach.
'I be going to the Seaman's Rest.'

And was no doubt hoping Everett would buy him a
pint or two. Aware of rain drumming on his hat and his
shoulders, Everett hurried along beside the old fisherman.

When Jeb pushed open the door of what served as
a tap room, a billow of choking smoke issued forth,
along with the unmistakable odors of unwashed men
and stale beer.

Everett hid a grimace. 'I think I will head home. I
don't want to be late for dinner.' He passed the man a
coin. 'Thank you for your information.'

'You'll be getting a right soaking, sir,' the fellow
warned.

'Then I best hurry.' Fortunately, the wind was behind
him. Unfortunately, Jeb had been right; it did not take
long to become soaked through to the skin.

Chapter Four

Rain pattering on vegetation… Brought alert by the sound, Venetia realised that while she had been weeding between the rows of peas and mulling over her separate conversations with Gore and Mary, the sky had darkened, the wind had picked up and she was about to get wet.

The weather changed in minutes in this part of England. She held her basket above her head and ran for the back door.

Brr… Even a few drops of rain were enough to cause a chill to run down her back.

John stuck his head out of the scullery where she had set him to peeling some potatoes. 'His Lordship with you, my lady?'

John seemed to have adapted very quickly to all this my lording and ladying nonsense.

'The last time I saw His Lordship, he was in the library.'

John frowned. 'He said he was a going for a walk.'

Rain splattered against the window and the wind boomed in the chimney. It looked like they were in for one of the wild storms that sometimes blew in from the sea.

'Oh, dear. I hope he has enough sense to find shelter somewhere.'

The front door slammed open with a bang. She closed her eyes. Apparently not.

She and John hurried to the front door. Gore was stripping off his coat. He had already discarded his hat. His hair was plastered to his forehead and his shoulders were soaked. He rubbed his hands together and shivered.

'John, please draw His Lordship a bath. Is the fire alight in his chamber?'

John shook his head. 'Needs a match to the spills, is all, my lady.'

Venetia glared at Gore. 'Don't you know to take cover in a rainstorm?'

He glared back. 'This was the closest shelter, on the way from the village.'

She huffed out a breath. 'Get along, then. Get out of those wet clothes and into a nice hot bath before you catch an ague.'

She shooed him up the stairs and followed behind, calling over her shoulder as she went. 'John, be as quick as you can with that hot water.'

She stopped off at the linen cupboard, collected an armful of towels and marched into Gore's chamber.

With his back towards her, Gore was naked except for his stockings.

She gasped at the sight of his strong wide back. It was a lovely back, the defined musculature rippling beneath his pale skin. The hard round globes of his buttocks drew her gaze. So disturbingly lovely…

He snatched up his shirt and turned, bunching the

bundle of white cloth against his lower torso. She stared at the triangle of dark curling hair adorning his wide chest. It trailed downwards and disappeared behind the crumpled shirt.

She forced her gaze up to his face, met eyes which had that beguiling gleam of mischief she had noticed before.

'Can I help you?' he asked.

She flushed all the way from her chest to the roots of her hair. She could not recall ever feeling quite so hot all over.

'I brought you some towels.'

He tilted his head. 'In the olden days it was expected that the mistress of the house would bathe her lord when he arrived home tired and weary.'

'This is not the olden days, my lord. You will find the tub in the dressing room. Perhaps you would like to place it in front of the fire.' She tossed the towels on the bed and scurried out.

She forced herself to slow to a walk and to catch her breath. Why on earth was she so flustered?

It certainly wasn't because she had been very tempted to take him up on his challenge. Certainly not.

She just had not expected to find him naked when she walked in. She pressed her hands to her hot cheeks. How would she ever look him in the face again?

She didn't have a choice. No choice at all.

Her next task was to find Mary and ask for help setting the dining room table before they went back to the kitchen to arrange the dishes on trays for John to carry in once they were seated.

Mary stared at the heavy epergne in the middle of the table. 'Do we have enough dishes to fill it?'

Venetia frowned at the monstrous thing. 'We do not.'

Mary attempted to lift it. Venetia brushed her aside. 'Let me. Your shoulder is nowhere near healed yet.' She carried it to the sideboard.

'I saw his brother from a distance once or twice. Your husband is very like him, is he not?'

In Venetia's eyes, Everett was nothing like his older brother. There had always been a bitter twist to Simon's mouth, even at his most jocular. Had no one but her seen it? Certainly her sister had not. It was why Venetia had intervened in what she thought was an assignation between her sister and the late marquess. She had feared his intentions were dishonourable.

And in a way, she had been right. It had not been Simon lurking in the garden, as the note had promised. It had been a very drunk Everett. In her haste to stop her sister from being ruined, she had fallen into Everett's arms and they had been forced to wed.

She suspected that Simon had intended to be rid of her sister Florence's determined pursuit of himself by foisting her off on his brother.

The end result had pleased no one. Not Simon, not Florence, not Everett and certainly not herself. But none of that was important right now. Getting Mary to safety was her first concern.

'You have nothing to fear from Gore. Remember your name is Smith and that your home is in Somerset and all will be well.' They had chosen Somerset because it was the next county over from Hampshire where Mary grew up and she was very familiar with the towns and villages of that county.

'Leave me to do most of the talking,' Venetia said. 'Earlier today, I sent a note to Lucy telling her that we need to get you away by next week at the latest. It is all in hand.'

She hoped.

She eyed the table. It would have to do. 'Come, help me in the kitchen. You can stir the soup, and then we will meet him in the drawing room.'

Mary giggled. 'If my husband could see me now, serving up dinner to the Marquess of Gore, he would be having conniptions.'

'Really? Why?'

The laughter died from her eyes. 'He would say, there you go, a typical chit with no idea how to go on. A lady doesn't do housework.' She sniffed. 'It seems to me a lady doesn't do much of anything.'

'Do you have no family who can help you with regard to your husband?'

She shook her head. 'My parents died when I was small. My uncle made the arrangements with the baron and got a goodly sum out of the settlement too.' She grimaced. 'It wasn't so bad at first, though he is terribly old. But after two years and no heir—' She shook her head. 'It was all my fault that he got so angry.' Her pretty blue eyes welled up. 'I should not have said it was likely he was the problem I hadn't caught. I don't know what he will do if he ever finds me.'

Men and their fragile egos. 'Hush,' Venetia said. 'Soon you will be safe, where he cannot reach you.'

If Lucy could not help them in time, then Venetia would think of something.

The hot bath had been exceedingly welcome, Everett thought on the way downstairs. Surprisingly, he had his wife to thank. He had not expected her to be so thoughtful.

Nor had he expected the surge of lust when he saw the way she was practically devouring his nigh-on nakedness with her gaze. All the hairs on his body had stood to attention. Along with another part of him.

But perhaps his desire was not so surprising, since it had been a long time since he'd been with a woman. Despite his very real anger at the trick she had played on him, all these many years he had remained true to his marriage vows.

Not that he hadn't been sorely tempted on occasion. In India there had been more than one widow on the prowl for a rich protector. But he had never been as rich as they initially hoped. Most of his funds had been tied up in maintaining his wife. Or so he had thought.

And for a second there, in that moment between them, with the air charged with the sort of electricity one feels before a storm, he had felt—hopeful.

Then she'd glared at him and fled.

As if what had happened was somehow wrong. As if she wasn't his wife. Perhaps she needed time to adjust to the idea of being a married woman.

A wave of nausea followed swiftly by a flash of heat stopped him short. He gripped the newel post, inhaling a deep breath. It was too soon, surely, for another bout of fever. He must be hot from his bath. Or perhaps he had caught a chill from his soaking. He would take some of the medicine provided by his doctor before he went to bed, just to be sure.

He took a deep breath. Now was not the time to be laid low by the ague. He had too much to accomplish and he certainly didn't want to show weakness in front of his wife.

He pulled himself together and strolled into the drawing room.

Both ladies rose upon his entry. Venetia wore a severe gown of dark blue with an unfashionably low waist and high neck. Mrs Smith, by comparison, looked like an angel in a rose-coloured dress decorated with silk roses at the hem and a fichu tucked into her bodice, instantly drawing one's eye to the generous décolletage on display.

Both ladies dipped a curtsey. Neither of them looked particularly pleased to see him.

Of John there was no sign, but a tray with an assortment of libations had been set on a low table against one wall. 'May I offer you ladies a glass of something?' Perhaps it would warm the chilly atmosphere.

Both ladies shook their heads.

'I hope you won't mind if I indulge?' If he had caught a chill, a drop of brandy might well ward it off.

'Not at all,' Venetia said. 'I hope you are none the worse for your drenching.'

It was almost as if she had read his thoughts. He opened the stopper on one of the decanters and sniffed. The same brandy as in his room if he was not mistaken. 'Not at all.'

He splashed a generous amount in one of the glasses and took an appreciative sip. He turned to face them.

'It was quite a storm,' he said.

'Most unexpected,' Venetia agreed.

'I hope you did not get caught out in it, Mrs Smith?' he asked. 'I gather you were out running errands today.'

The young woman cast a strangely fearful glance at Venetia, then took a deep breath. 'I needed some ribbons and thread. I arrived home before the rain started, so your hope was fulfilled, thank you for asking, my lord.'

'Home?'

'Mrs Smith thinks of this as a second home,' Venetia said swiftly. A little too swiftly, perhaps.

'You have visited Walsea before, then, Mrs Smith?'

The lady gulped. 'Once or twice, Your Lordship.'

A lie. Why on earth would she lie about such an innocent thing?

'How pleasant for my wife to have your company from time to time.' He could not keep the wryness from his tone and Venetia cast him a puzzled glance.

John entered and his gaze found Venetia. 'Dinner is served, my lady.'

She nodded. 'Shall we go in, my lord?'

'Indeed.' He offered an arm to each lady and they walked through to the dining room, where he seated first their guest and then his wife at the table covered in a pristine white cloth and set for three at one end.

John placed several platters on the table and left them to serve themselves. The pie she had baked earlier smelled delicious. The fish he had caught lay on a platter and was drizzled with parsley sauce. A ham hock carved into slices sat in pride of place surrounded by buttered parsnips and roasted potatoes. A dish of spring greens completed the meal.

'And where is your home, when you are not visiting my wife, Mrs Smith?' Everett said, picking up on their earlier conversation. He placed some of the meat on a plate and passed it to her.

She squirmed like an insect on a pin.

'Somerset,' Venetia said.

Did the woman not know where she came from? Or was she just terribly shy?

'A beautiful county,' Everett said. 'I have some good friends there. The Swansanbys. Do you know them?'

Mrs Smith shook her head. 'I can't say as I do,' she whispered.

He narrowed his gaze on her face. 'You must know the Rand-Fitzes from Wiltshire. Everyone knows them.'

'Mrs Smith does not move in those sorts of circles, Gore,' Venetia said calmly.

Really? 'Then where did you two meet and become friends?'

Colour stained his wife's cheeks. 'At school. Mrs Bennington's Academy.'

Now why would she lie about such a simple thing?

Mrs Smith gave a quick nod. 'Her Ladyship was ever so kind to me there.'

'I had no idea you went to school, Venetia.' He waited for her next bouncer.

'It was a fortunate choice,' she said. 'Mrs Bennington believed in education, so I learned a great deal more than how to embroider slippers and paint in watercolours.'

Finally, she was actually telling him the truth and her expression became animated, as if she was imagining a happy time in her life. Once more he was struck by her aesthetic beauty. He gave her an encouraging smile. 'What sort of things did they teach, then?'

'Latin, geography, mathematics, among other things, as well as the usual subjects such as penmanship and housewifery, of course.'

'You are a veritable bluestocking, then.'

She froze.

Dammit. He hadn't meant to sound critical.

Mrs Smith glanced from one to the other. 'I like doing sums,' she said, filling the awkward silence. 'Not much of a one for geography, though. I like a bit of history too. I can recite all the Kings and Queens of England, backwards and forwards, if you like.'

Venetia shook her head with a smile. 'How marvellous. Who is your favourite king or queen?'

Mrs Smith seemed puzzled by the question. As if she had learned the names by rote, but knew nothing about them.

'Personally, I like William the Conqueror,' Everett said.

His wife chuckled. 'Hardly surprising. Your family arrived in England from Normandy and did very well.'

'You have been checking up on us. And yes, William was very gracious in recognising the sacrifices made by my ancestors to help him gain his rightful crown. What about you, Venetia? Which of our past rulers do you admire?'

'I would have thought you would be able to guess. Elizabeth, of course.'

Yes, he should have guessed. 'Good Queen Bess. If she had married and had children, England might have fared better in subsequent years.'

She gave him a long considering look. 'Or worse. It would have been a very different reign. And a very different country. Who would she have married? Spain? France? Would England want to be ruled from Europe? Or would she have married one of her courtiers, the way Mary, her cousin, did? Look how well that ended. In my opinion, remaining single provided the stability the country needed at the time.'

Mrs Smith nodded agreement, although Everett doubted she fully understood what Venetia meant.

'There is much to be admired in Elizabeth,' he said.

Venetia stared at him in astonishment. Had she expected him to disagree? 'Well,' she said grudgingly. 'I do not disagree that William was also a fine king in his time.'

A wave of dizziness hit him. It did not dissipate as quickly as the first one. This was no chill. He recognised the symptoms. He was going to be in for a rough night.

The sooner he got dinner over with, the sooner he could take his medicine and go to bed.

Why was Gore questioning Mary so closely? Did he suspect wrongdoing? Or was he simply making conversation?

His bland expression gave nothing of his thoughts away. And yet his questions seemed quite pointed.

Venetia frowned. Beneath his slight tan, his skin had a sickly hue. And if Venetia wasn't mistaken he was sweating. Beads of moisture had formed around his hairline and on his upper lip. Could he possibly have caught a cold from getting caught in the rain?

'Ham for you?' he asked.

'Yes, please.'

His hand shook slightly as he passed her a plate. She was pleased with the way the pie had turned out. She cut it into quarters and offered a piece to each of them before serving herself.

They helped themselves to vegetables from the other dishes.

Gore raised his glass once they had said grace. 'My compliments to the cook.'

She blushed. She had received so few compliments in her life she was like a silly schoolgirl when someone said something nice. He would think her easily charmed. 'It seems a little premature. You haven't tasted anything yet.'

'It certainly looks and smells good enough to eat.'

She glared at him. Was he laughing at her?

Everett frowned at Mary, who was struggling to use her knife.

'Is something wrong with your arm, Mrs Smith?' he asked.

Mary coloured. 'I—'

'Mrs Smith took a tumble when we were out walking,' Venetia said swiftly. 'She wrenched her shoulder.'

Mary swallowed. 'Yes. I tripped. Very foolish.'

He gave her an odd look. 'I see. You must take care of yourself when walking, then.'

He ate a mouthful of pie, followed by some of the fish he had caught, with a generous coating of her parsley sauce.

His gaze met hers and she realised she had been watching him, waiting for his reaction. She looked away quickly and focused on cutting up her own ham now she had finished with Mary's.

'It really is delicious,' he said quietly.

Pleasure rippled through her.

'But...' he said.

But? She froze and looked at him.

'A marchioness should not be cooking her own dinner. Tomorrow, we will see about hiring a cook from the village and some extra help for John. You will assist me in this.'

She stared at him. Was he trying to make her feel inadequate? It was the sort of thing her father would do to her mother. It must be that, otherwise why would he interfere? 'I assume these extra employees will apply to you for their wages?'

'Naturally. Which reminds me, we should also go over the household accounts.'

She stiffened. What she did with her money was none of his business. And besides, he would see the expenses related to her previous guest. Her stomach dipped. Would he find it suspicious that she had laid out for clothes for that woman and bought none for herself?

She would have to pretend she bought them for herself. If she was lucky, he would not ask to see them. 'As you wish.' Hopefully she sounded a lot calmer than she felt.

His gaze narrowed. 'I do wish. This house looks as if it could do with a great deal of refurbishment.'

More criticism. It stung. She had done her best. What more did he want from her?

She put down her knife and fork, her appetite diminished. She sipped at her water. 'I find the house comfortable. However, if you wish to change it, that is your prerogative, I suppose.'

He turned to Mary. 'And what about you, Mrs Smith? Do you find it comfortable? You are not troubled by the draughts from ill-fitting doors, or the rattle of loose windowpanes?'

Mary stared at him, mouth agape. Clearly, she had not expected to be called upon to take sides. 'I— No. I mean…it is a very old house to be sure. But a good cleaning and some fresh paint… 'She glanced at Venetia and swallowed. 'It would help,' she finished weakly.

It seemed they had all lost their appetites. Gore had

put down his knife and fork and Mary was toying with the remaining food on her plate.

Venetia rang the bell and John arrived a few moments later. A broad grin lit his face when he saw the leftovers.

He began removing the dishes to a tray.

'John,' Gore said, 'do you know of a good cook in the neighbourhood?'

'Apart from Her Ladyship?' John said, clearly not realising how awful that sounded. 'My sister Sarah's a pretty good cook. She helps her mam out with meals and such, when she is not looking after the young'uns.'

'Do you think she would like to work here as a cook?' Venetia asked.

John stopped what he was doing and looked at her and then at Gore with wide eyes. 'Wouldn't she! I mean yes, my lady. My lord. Work around here about is scarce. Of course, she would need a bit of guidance, I should think, her not having cooked for a big house before, but—'

'Then ask her to come as soon as she can,' Gore said. 'Also, see if you can find a couple of maids and a footman or two.'

John looked crestfallen. 'Will you be letting me go, then, my lord?'

'Certainly not. You will be in charge here, John, and act for me in my absence. And I should like you to continue to serve as my valet while I am here.'

John looked amazed. He swallowed. 'Yes, my lord.'

He quickly cleared up the rest of the dishes and turned to Venetia. 'Will Your Ladyship be taking tea in the drawing room?'

That would mean that Gore was sure to join them, and Venetia wanted some time to get used to the idea of a house full of servants and, if the truth be told, get away from his piercing stares. She certainly didn't want him questioning Mary any more. 'No, thank you, John. I would prefer to retire.' She glanced at her husband, who showed no reaction. 'Perhaps you would bring a bottle of port from the cellar. His Lordship might enjoy a glass after dinner.'

His Lordship shook his head. 'I am feeling a little weary myself. Perhaps another time.'

'You are unwell, my lord?' she asked.

'You look a little peaky to me,' Mary said, peering at him.

'I am perfectly well,' Gore said. 'I too have had a busy day and I have no interest in sitting at the table alone with nothing but a bottle of port to keep me company.'

Was he hinting that it was her duty to join him? Or that he actually wanted her company? The longing to be wanted she had so often experienced as a girl squeezed her heart painfully. If he asked her to stay… She drew in a sharp breath at her foolishness. No doubt his idea of good company would be to swill port with other like-minded men.

She glanced at Mary, who was staring at him like a besotted schoolgirl.

She was pretty and dainty and everything Venetia never could be. All those years ago, at their wedding, he'd shown exactly what he thought of her. It still hurt, if she allowed herself to dwell on his obvious disappointment. She never wanted to feel that sort of pain again.

'Very well, my lord.' She stood and Mary followed suit, as did Gore.

Venetia dipped a curtsey. 'I bid you goodnight.'

As they left the room, Mary tucked her arm through

Venetia's and leaned close. 'Your husband is very handsome.'

Too handsome for her peace of mind. 'The way a person looks isn't necessarily important.'

She just wished others felt the same way.

Chapter Five

Disturbed by the heat, Everett threw back the bed covers. He opened his eyes and recalled he was in England, not India. Then why was he so hot?

Pain throbbed at his temples.

He was in for another bout of the ague. He groaned at the realisation. He staggered out of bed and took a swig of the medicine he'd been given before he left India. A shiver shook his body.

Damnation. He had hoped the change of air would rid him of this rotten illness. Likely getting a soaking yesterday had brought it on.

He crawled back into bed.

There wasn't much to be done except take the medicine and ride it out.

He must have slept because the next thing he was aware of was John pulling back the curtains and brightness streaming in.

'Good morning, my lord. Her Ladyship is wondering if you are coming down for breakfast or if she should send up a tray?'

Everett covered his eyes. The pounding in his head made him feel nauseous. 'What time is it?'

'It do be around ten of the clock, my lord.'

Ten? Everett rose up on his elbows, preparing to arise, but a wave of nausea hit him and he sank back down and closed his eyes.

He was aware of John drawing closer. 'Are you ill, my lord?'

He forced his eyes open and glared at the worried face staring at him from the foot of the bed. 'It is nothing. A touch of the ague. It will pass. Leave me be.' Despite his covers, a shiver ran through him.

John took him at his word and left.

Heat rolled through him and he pushed the covers off him and raised himself to sit with his back against the headboard. He drained the glass of water on the bedside table.

Curse it. This seemed to be as bad a bout as any he had had in India. Devil take it, he should have asked John to pass him his medicine.

He closed his eyes, gathering his strength for the trip across the room.

'John says you are unwell.'

His wife? He hadn't heard her enter.

A cool hand pressed against his forehead. 'Oh, my word, you have a fever. I will send for the doctor.'

He forced his eyes open and caught that cool hand in his hot one. 'What are you doing in here? It is nothing. Merely an ague. The medicine on the dressing table is all I need.'

The hand slipped out of his grasp.

A moment later she was back with the bottle. 'This is what you require?'

He took it and swilled it down with a shudder at the bitter taste.

Her eyes narrowed. 'What is wrong with you?'

She was judging his weakness, no doubt calculating how she could use it against him.

'Nothing to worry about.'

'It does not seem like nothing.'

'I assure you, I will be quite well in a couple days.'

She frowned. 'You look as if you are at death's door.'

'Thank you.'

His attempt at humour failed, because she shot him a sharp look. 'The medicine is a cure?'

'I will be fine by tomorrow.' According to the doctor there was no cure.

Her nose wrinkled. 'I'll send John up to change the bedlinen and help you wash.'

A polite way of saying he smelled none too sweet after sweating like a pig for most of the night. 'Do as you please.'

She grimaced and left.

Her hand on his brow had felt very nice. Cool and gentle. And the medicine was doing its work; he began to feel more at ease. By the time, John arrived he was able to get out of bed and wash himself while John changed the bedlinens.

'Her Ladyship said to get back into bed, my lord.' John rummaged around in his valise and produced a clean nightshirt. 'She will be along with some tea and toast directly.'

Tea and toast. How very English. How very comforting. And yes, with clean sheets and plumped-up pillows, his bed looked inviting.

For he was still as weak as a kitten.

Dammit.

He slid back beneath the covers.

John bundled up the laundry and was on his way out of the door when Venetia bustled in with a tray, her face set in stern lines.

She set the tray on the night table and gave him an assessing glance. 'Do you need my help with your breakfast?'

He sat up and she arranged the pillows against the headboard.

'I can manage.'

She placed the tray on his lap.

His hand shook as he lifted the cup of tea to his lips. She grabbed the cup and steadied it. 'You will spill it and then John will have to change the sheets again.'

Too weak to fight, he gave in. He sipped at the aromatic tea from the cup she put to his lips, and bit off the toast she held for him, which was slathered with butter and deliciously tangy marmalade.

'Now try to sleep,' she said.

He snuggled beneath the covers. He hadn't felt so coddled since he was a child in the nursery. Except his nurse had been a great deal fonder of him than his wife.

Unsmiling, she picked up the tray and left.

When next he awoke, he was shivering.

Someone was raking at the fire.

He pushed up on his elbows to see his wife crouched at the hearth. 'What the devil are you doing?' he croaked.

She glanced over her shoulder. 'Making up the fire. Lie still and I will bring you your medicine in a moment.'

With his teeth chattering and his body shaking, he sank back against the pillows. 'I am perfectly fine.'

The raking sound stopped. She loomed over him and

put a hand to his forehead. 'You still have a fever.' She frowned. 'And you are shivering again. I am sending for the doctor.'

'No. It will pass. It always does.'

Her eyes widened. 'Always?'

He nodded. 'It is a common complaint in India brought on by the bad air.'

She looked anxious. 'Bad air? We are beside the sea. The air here is fresh.'

Heat infused him. He flung back the blanket.

She backed away. 'I am sending for the doctor.'

'I do not need a doctor.' He grabbed the bottle of medicine and took a swig.

She glared at him for a moment. 'On your head be it, then.'

He shivered and closed his eyes. His wife was as prickly as a holly bush.

'Is he going to be all right, Doctor?' Venetia asked the bespectacled, portly, balding man who she met in the hall as he came downstairs from attending to Gore. With bushy white eyebrows and a flowing beard, he had more hair on his face than he had on his head.

Dr Ruggle rubbed at his hairy chin. 'Apart from being none too pleased to see me, I believe so.'

'You are not certain?'

His forehead wrinkled. 'One can never tell with swamp fever. What kills one can be merely a nuisance in another.'

'Swamp fever? He could die?' Her heart sped up.

'Not likely. He is young and healthy, but for this ague. I doubt it will kill him any time soon.'

But eventually? Was that what he was saying? 'Is there anything you can give him to aid his recovery?'

'The medicine he has brought from India will do the trick. I will arrange to have some more made up. Fortunately, the fellow he saw in Calcutta saw fit to give him the receipt. The apothecary in Colchester can make it up for you.'

She took the piece of paper he held out. 'Thank you. In the meantime?'

'Keep him warm. Eliminate all draughts. Make him rest. That will be your hardest task. Young men are always such impatient fellows.'

Indeed. One had the feeling that one could not make the Marquess of Gore do anything he did not wish. Though he had agreed to see the doctor, despite being annoyed at his arrival.

'How long must he rest?'

'A few days. It will depend on him.'

Days? Heaven help her.

After receiving his bill for one guinea, she showed the doctor out. One guinea to be told to keep on doing what you have been doing. How on earth was she going to pay such an enormous bill?

Dash it. She would have to ask Gore for the money.

Mary joined her in the drawing room. 'Is the marquess going to be all right?'

'I think so. We need to fill this prescription. Oh, bother.'

'What is the matter?'

'I sent John to the butcher to get a hambone to make soup. Now I will have to await his return before I can send him to the apothecary for Gore's medicine.'

'I can go.'

'It is a long walk.'

'I am quite used to walking. Indeed, I would like the exercise.'

The only other alternative was to go herself and she did not want to leave the marquess with only Mary to care for him in case he asked too many questions.

'Very well. I will also ask you to post a letter for me.' She had to make Lucy realise that it was urgent that Mary leave as soon as possible, if not sooner.

Everett threw back the covers. A blast of blessedly cool air hit him. What...

Oh, right! The hunting expedition in the heat of the jungle, so real only moments ago, was nothing but a dream along with lingering memories of long, lonely nights after hours of drinking with bachelor friends.

Not so very long ago, he had said goodbye to India and his bachelor chums and returned to England. The country he had missed so badly all these years.

Why had he ever left? Bitterness rose in his gorge. Because of Simon. He had been fed up with cleaning up behind his older brother. Paying off disgruntled women. Settling debts and smoothing ruffled feathers. Simon had been a nightmare once he reached his majority. The older brother was supposed to be the responsible one, not the younger.

Not to mention the way hopeful debutantes viewed Everett as nothing but a way to get closer to Simon. The first girl Everett had developed feelings for, Rose was her name, he recalled, dropped him like a hot potato the moment Simon smiled in her direction. It had been a bitter pill. Especially as Simon had no interest in her at all. From then on, Everett steered clear of young ladies interested in marriage and found himself a jolly young actress on whom to lavish his attention without fear of losing his heart.

His departure from England should have given Simon time to settle down and marry, leaving Everett able to choose his own bride when he was ready.

But no. In the hours before Everett was due to embark, Simon had thoughtlessly landed him with a wife as a parting gift. It was the wrong sister. Simon had explained with great regret afterward. He had wanted to be rid of the other sister, the pretty one who would not be put off. Simon had decided the only way to be free of her was to marry her off to Everett.

Everett hadn't wanted a wife at all. The freedom from the responsibility of Simon he had sought by leaving for India had been instantly curtailed by the need to support a woman he did not know and cared for even less. His anger had known no bounds. He'd told the both of them to go to hell.

The irony was not lost on him. Five years of loneliness had been a wasted effort. Instead of Simon becoming a better man, his wildness upon attaining the title had only increased. And then Simon had got himself killed in a freak accident and passed all his duties and responsibilities to Everett.

And now, here was Everett, back in England, trying to salvage a five-year-old marriage that had never been consummated and...

A loud bang brought him upright in bed.

A wave of dizziness hit him.

Damnation. He'd been ill, he remembered. The ague had overtaken him and laid him low for a couple of days, cared for by John and occasionally by Venetia, whose touch had been by far the gentlest of the two.

And he felt as weak as a kitten. He was always weak for days after a fever. A weakness he hated to show.

He took a deep breath. And another. Became aware of a hollow emptiness in his gut. No wonder he felt dizzy, he was starving.

But what was that noise he had heard. A gunshot? Surely not?

As the man of the house, did it not behove him to find out? And besides, he needed sustenance. The pantry, a hunk of bread and a helping of cheese beckoned like a siren.

He climbed out of bed, shrugged on his robe and lit a candle from the fire's glowing embers. Outside, a wind buffeted the windows and whistled in the chimney. A storm?

The clock on the mantle showed one in the morning. Under normal circumstances, a bit late for prowling around a house where he felt like little more than an unwanted guest.

Still, there was that loud bang that deserved investigation. It might be a door left open, or a shutter torn free.

It had definitely come from below.

He pushed his feet into his slippers and headed downstairs. Before he reached the bottom of the stairs he became aware of the mutter of voices. More people awoken by the noise?

At the drawing room door, he paused. His wife's voice, he recognised instantly, but the other deeper voice was not that of John. How...odd.

He entered.

Venetia, facing the door, paused mid-sentence, mouth

agape. The man facing her swung around to see what had caught her attention.

'My lord,' Venetia gasped.

She was fully clothed.

The young man wore a dark overcoat and held his hat and gloves. He bowed. 'Good evening, my lord. Harper, at your service.'

Everett smiled tightly. 'Good evening. I presume what I heard was the bang of a door.'

'It was,' Venetia said, still sounding breathless and looking very uncomfortable. 'I apologise for the disturbance. Mr Harper is just leaving.'

Which begged the question, why was he here at this time of night in the first place?

'I have brought Her Ladyship a message from my mother,' the young man said smoothly. Too smoothly by half. 'A mutual friend of Her Ladyship's is ill nigh unto death. Mother thought Her Ladyship ought to hear about it at once.'

The fellow offered a toothy smile Everett didn't like one bit. 'I see.'

'It was very kind of Mr Harper to travel so far and so late at night,' Venetia said. 'And to agree to take my good wishes to the family.'

The young man bowed. 'I will deliver them the moment I arrive in Town.'

'Then let us not keep you,' Everett said. He frowned. 'Unless you plan to stay the night?'

Venetia started, a shocked expression on her face.

'No, indeed,' Harper said swiftly. 'My post chaise awaits. But I thank you for your kind offer.'

Had he offered? He didn't think so. He inclined his

head. 'Then we should not keep your horses waiting any longer. Let me see you out.'

He escorted the young man to the door. A hired carriage, its postillion sheltering from the wind and puffing on a pipe beneath the coach lamp, stood waiting. At the sight of Harper, he knocked the pipe on the heel of his boot and leaped up onto his mount. In short order, Mr Harper was on his way.

Everett returned to the drawing room and his wife. 'What a pleasant fellow,' he said.

'You sound as if you do not mean that.'

No fool, this wife of his. 'The woman whose illness he came to report must have been a very close friend of yours?'

'She was.'

She didn't elaborate. And Everett didn't believe her. She had the look of someone caught in something illicit. He knew that expression only too well. He had seen it often enough on his brother's face. And then there was that telltale blush. Not something that ever happened to Simon, who had no conscience.

'You are feeling better?' she asked, pointedly changing the subject.

'I am. Thank you. I apologise for putting you to so much trouble. And now I am starving. I was on my way to the kitchen to see if I could raid the pantry.'

She chuckled. Genuine amusement lit her face and once more he was struck by how fine she looked when she was not glowering at him from beneath lowered brows.

'Come,' she said. 'Let me help you. I will make us both some tea and I am sure I have something in the pantry to tempt your appetite.'

His mouth watered. 'If it is not too much trouble.'

'No trouble at all.'

Perhaps she thought feeding him would distract him from her entertaining a gentleman in her drawing room in the small hours of the morning. Clearly, Harper had not planned for a lengthy visit.

On the other hand, they had both looked as guilty as sin when he walked through the door. Why?

Her mind whirling, Venetia left Everett putting a kettle of water on the stove and went to the pantry. What rotten luck that he had discovered her with Lucy's son. The last time she had checked on the marquess, he had been fast asleep in his bed.

She gathered up a loaf of bread and a pat of butter and cut a wedge from a wheel of cheese and put them on a tray.

The last thing she had wanted was for the marquess to meet her co-conspirators. Harper was a good young man with a good heart. She hated that he had been put in the position of having to lie to Everett.

But the news he had brought was good. Two days hence, a small boat would transport Mary out to a ship waiting offshore to take her to Italy. Not a day too soon, in Venetia's mind.

All they had to do was get through the next two days without giving anything away, then she could focus on how to deal with her husband.

Her husband. She still had trouble believing he was here, in her house.

At one time she would have loved the sound of the words *her husband*. Youthful dreams of love and happiness. How very foolish she had been. Husbands were nothing but tyrants.

She carried the tray back into the kitchen.

Everett was prowling around, looking in drawers and cupboards.

'What do you need?' she asked.

'The tea.'

She nodded. Like any good housewife, she kept her tea locked away. It was very expensive. Not that she thought John would take it into his head to steal it, but one simply did not leave valuables around to serve as temptation.

She unlocked the cupboard, took down the caddy and handed it to him.

He opened the lid and sniffed. 'You have excellent taste.'

It was one luxury she afforded herself. 'Thank you. I suppose you learned a great deal about tea in India?'

He grinned. 'Enough to fill an encyclopaedia.'

She could not help herself, she smiled back. He really could be quite charming, when he wasn't glaring at her as if he had lost a guinea and found a penny.

What a mistake it had been to marry him. She should have refused point-blank. What would it have mattered that her reputation would have been ruined? No one expected the ugly older sister to make a good match, or any kind of match for that matter. Her father had despaired of her looks and her penchant for reading the same books as her brother. And the fact that she offered her opinion on the rights of women to anyone she came across had pretty well sealed her fate.

Her younger sister was the pretty one, the one who danced like a gazelle and fluttered her eyelashes and had no thought in her head besides whose title took precedence. The only books she ever read were *Ackermann's Fashions* and *Debrett's*. She was the one with all the prospects.

No man wanted a wife with a brain, according to her father.

Venetia would have been quite happy as a spinster. Or so she had told herself over and over again after her disastrous Season.

But some madness had induced her to agree to the marriage to Everett, a marriage forced on them by Society's conventions, and now she had to live with the consequences.

If for one moment she had thought Flo was truly in love with the marquess, and he with her, she would never have interfered. But Flo, who was an absolute dear and very much like their mother, lived in terror of Father and his threats. He had insisted she bring herself to the marquess's attention at every opportunity. When Venetia had seen an opportunity to put an end to what she saw as a looming disaster, she hadn't hesitated. And the fate from which she planned to save her sister had become hers instead.

And for Venetia to now harbour any hopes that their marriage might be better than convenient was foolish in the extreme. After one glance on their wedding day, her husband's declaration that he never wanted to see her again had been the honest truth.

No matter what, she wasn't going to let him hurt her again. But she could not help but feel a little bit sorry for him. Not only was it his brother's fault that he had been forced to marry her in the first place, it was his fault that they were now being thrown together again after years of living quite happily apart.

Could they live happily together? As a child she had wanted what every girl wanted—a handsome prince to carry her off to his castle where she would live happily ever after with a loving husband and a pack of little ones. Until around the age of fifteen she realised that girls like her, the plain Jane sort with no fortune to make up for the lack of other attributes, were unlikely to find any sort of husband, let alone a handsome prince. The fact that this marriage had been forced on them made it, at best, an unpleasant duty.

Hoping for more would be foolish in the extreme.

He warmed the pot with a dash of boiling water from the kettle before spooning in the tea, then filled the teapot. 'There,' he said. 'A couple of minutes and it will be ready.' He eyed the tray of food. 'That looks good.'

Oh, right. She'd been so busy watching him make the tea with manly assurance, she had forgotten to slice the bread.

Flustered, she picked up the bread knife. Bother, she needed plates. Getting herself back under control somewhat, she put out plates and knives and sliced the bread.

By the time she set the plate of bread and cheese in front of him, steam rose from the teacups. 'Milk for you?' he asked.

'Yes, please.' She seated herself opposite him, tried not to gaze at how interesting his face looked with two days' worth of stubble on his jaw and chin. She curled her fingers into her palms to stop herself from reaching out to see if it would feel soft or rough.

She did not want to know. She really did not.

He poured milk from the jug and pushed a cup in her direction.

'I am not surprised you are hungry,' she said, hoping she sounded matter-of-fact, but aware of the unusually swift beating of her heart. 'You ate nothing at all yesterday. I am very glad you are feeling better.'

'I am sure you are.'

She stiffened at the dry note in his voice. 'I do not wish you any ill.'

He raised his gaze to her and the starburst of yellow around his pupils seemed more pronounced than usual. She swallowed. Had she angered him somehow?

'I must have caused you a great deal of trouble and work. I apologise.'

It was almost as if he did not expect to be cared for during his illness. Her heart ached strangely.

If she reached out and touched his hand, offered reassurance, how would he react? The pain of rejection loomed large.

'It was no trouble. John did most of the work.' She sipped at her tea.

His eyebrow flicked upwards as if in surprise, but he made no comment. 'I must say I was surprised to come downstairs and discover a gentleman calling on you in the middle of the night.'

The words were spoken casually, but his intent gaze demanded an answer.

She took another sip of tea. 'The sound of the front door banging shut because the wind caught it must have awoken you. It is quite a storm we are having.'

Chapter Six

How neatly she avoided his question.

And just as neatly the gentleman caller in question had lied through his teeth. He'd grown up with a consummate liar. He could sense a lie from the first word out of someone's mouth.

The trouble with liars was that they began to believe their own untruths. They lied to themselves.

'Yes, that must have been what awoke me. That and hunger.'

He slathered two slices of bread with butter and placed them each on a plate, then cut the cheese into hunks. He handed her a plate.

She cut her slice in half and nibbled at it.

He topped his bread with cheese and took a huge bite. His stomach roared its approval.

People often said they were starving, but he doubted they ever came close to this level of hunger.

There was another hunger lying low in his belly. One he had ignored for the past five years. One he no longer had to ignore. He had a wife.

A wife who clearly didn't like him. And who entertained gentlemen in the middle of the night. Although to be honest, there had been nothing clandestine going on when he entered the drawing room. They had been talking. Nothing else.

'The woman Harper came about must be a very close friend indeed to warrant such a long drive.'

'We were close at school.' The frost in her voice did not invite further questions.

'And how are you supposed to be of help with regard to her illness? I assume there is something needed from you, that he would travel here so hastily?'

Her shoulders stiffened. She really did not like to be questioned. 'Mrs Harper knew that I would want to know, that is all.'

'It sounds like a hum to me,' he said mildly and took another bite of bread and cheese. He savoured the creaminess of the butter and the tang of the cheese. It really was good.

'Would you like a pickle?' she asked.

More diversionary tactics.

'No, thank you. Do you plan to visit your sick friend?' Was that how she planned to escape him?

'No. I wrote a note. It will be enough for her to know that I am thinking of her.'

'I see.'

Something had changed, though. She seemed less anxious than she had since he arrived. As if this visit from this young man had resolved something.

She had eaten almost nothing from her plate. Whereas he had finished everything on his. 'Are you going to eat that?'

'I find I am not that hungry.' She shoved the plate towards him. 'Do you want it?'

He wolfed it down and began buttering another slice.

'By the way,' she said casually.

Too casually. His breath caught for a fraction of a second. How often had Simon spouted one of his lies with those very same words? Too often to count. He did not want his wife to lie to him, yet he did not trust her to tell him the truth.

He continued to spread the butter and made only a soft *mmm* sound to encourage her to continue.

'Mrs Smith will be leaving the day after tomorrow. And so I will be free to join you to London as soon as the dressmaker sends along my gowns.'

While he had not known what she would say, this was not what he had been expecting. After all, this was what he had wanted.

'If she leaves so soon, then you might as well come to London with me.'

He watched for her reaction.

She looked uncomfortable. 'A day or so ago you were anxious to leave for Town. My gowns will not be ready for at least another week. There is no need to delay your departure on my account. I shall see Mary off and join you at the first opportunity.'

Why was she so anxious to be rid of him? Because she was certainly not pleased at the idea of leaving with him.

'The roads are dangerous for a woman alone. I prefer to accompany you. Have the gowns sent by mail.'

Her body stiffened. She did not like it when he issued orders. And he did not like it when she argued about trivialities. 'Venetia, please, this is a reasonable solution. Surely you can see that.'

She gazed at him for a long moment. 'Very well. We will journey to London together.'

Finally. Complete submission to his wishes.

He didn't like it.

He preferred it when she baulked at his demands. Good God, had he lost his mind? He should be satisfied that finally she was behaving like a proper wife.

'Good,' he said. 'I am sure Mrs Smith's husband will be glad to see her home again.'

She winced as if he had said something that hit a nerve. 'Yes,' she answered. 'I expect he will.'

She looked unhappy. Was she thinking about her own husband and how unhappy she had been upon his return to her life? He cast the thought aside. It was too late for regrets.

'Does a carriage call for her?' he asked. 'Or do we send John to hire a post chaise?'

Her eyes widened. A furrow appeared between her eyebrows as if she was trying to invent a story he would find satisfactory, though why she would lie about something so ordinary he could not imagine.

He paused, the last bite of his bread hanging before his face as he watched the struggle of emotions on her face.

Her expression cleared. 'She is not going by road. She will take a ship.'

To his surprise, he knew that was the truth. 'A ship? How unusual.' He finished off the bread.

She nodded. 'Not really. It will be faster than by road and less expensive. A friend of her husband's has a yacht and it will stand offshore. One of the fishermen will row her out.'

She seemed so pleased with herself. Had she planned

to board this ship also? Was that the reason she wanted him out of the way? The thought made his heart sink in a way he did not understand.

'Since I will be here, I shall be more than happy to help Mrs Smith with her embarkation. I assume she has luggage?'

For a moment, she looked surprised, but only surprised. Not anxious. Not put out. Merely surprised.

'She has a valise. And—' She bit her lip as if stopping herself from saying something untoward.

'And?' he pressed.

'And no doubt the men on the beach will help, but yes, please, she would appreciate your assistance. That is, if you are well enough.'

Not what she had been about to say. But again, he had no sense that she was lying.

Now he was confused. He did not like the feeling.

'I feel a great deal better.' Well, he would in a few days.

'Excellent. We shall need to be at the water's edge no later than three in the afternoon. That is when the tide will be right, I understand. I will send John with a message to Mr Caldicut, to arrange for a boat to be ready for us.'

Was this what she had been plotting with Harper? Why, then, did she not out and say so? Why be so secretive? If he asked her point-blank, she would no doubt lie. He decided against it, for the moment.

'I know Mr Caldicut. I met him on my walk.'

She smiled and her face lit up with amusement. 'Did he convince you to go to that dreadful pub and buy him a drink?'

'He tried. I took one look inside and decided to take my chances in the storm.'

At that she laughed. 'Oh, dear. However, I am not sure that you would not have been worse off to have spent time in the Seaman's Rest. Now, if you are finished eating, I hope you do not mind, but I find that I am exceedingly tired and it is time to sleep.'

'I am done.'

She rose and he offered his arm and escorted her up the stairs. At the top she turned for his room, then caught herself. 'Silly me. I nearly forgot I had changed rooms.' She freed her arm and hurried down the other corridor to her bedroom.

He turned for his, all the while wondering what it would be like to have a wife in his bed.

His body hardened at the thought. Patience. Soon enough he would find out. But tonight was not the right time. That he could sense.

'I am scared.'

When Venetia had told Mary the previous day that her journey to Italy was about to begin, the young woman had trembled.

Now, as they ate their breakfast on the day of her departure, she again voiced her misgivings. The young woman reminded Venetia of her sister, Flo. Young and vulnerable and scared of her own shadow. Before Venetia would agree to marry Everett, she had insisted Father not force her sister to set her cap at anyone else. That she should be allowed to choose.

While Father had not kept his word, Flo had been pleased with his next choice of a bridegroom. She was now happily married to a Scottish earl who spoiled her to death while she kept him happy by providing him with a passel of children, which kept her close to home.

Venetia got up from her seat and put her arm around Mary's shoulders. 'I promise you, everything will be fine. The previous lady who left from here wrote to me afterwards to let me know she arrived safely and is happy and well.'

Gradually, the trembles ceased. Mary dabbed at her eyes with her napkin.

The door opened and the marquess strolled in looking particularly handsome in a navy-blue coat with a Belcher handkerchief in red and blue paisley tied at his throat. He had got up for only a short time yesterday, but now it appeared he was fully recovered.

Venetia withdrew her arm from around Mary and straightened.

His gaze sharpened. 'Is something wrong?' he asked casually as he wandered over to the sideboard and inspected this morning's offerings, which were more or less the same as yesterday and the day before.

He took a plate and a generous helping of scrambled eggs.

Oh, yes, he was definitely feeling better. 'Mary and I were commiserating about her departure. We will miss each other.'

Mary sniffled and nodded.

'But you must be looking forward to returning home.' He turned his head as he spoke, looking at Mary intently, albeit with a smile.

'Yes,' Mary said, sounding flustered. 'Yes, I am.'

She rose from the table, her breakfast barely touched. 'If you will excuse me, I need to pack.'

It was that sharp stare of his that was so unnerving.

No wonder Mary looked ready to run like a frightened rabbit.

'Yes,' Venetia said calmly, 'Run along do. We must make the tide.'

Gore bowed as she left the room. He brought his plate now full to the brim to the table and sat on Venetia's left. 'Is she having second thoughts?'

'Not at all.'

He frowned. 'She looked quite upset when I came in.'

'Saying goodbye can be difficult for some.' It had not been difficult for him to say goodbye to her five years past. He had done so very publicly and with a good deal of bitterness. She had been completely humiliated.

Even her father, who was particularly obtuse about female sensibilities, had seen that he had been harsh and had upset her.

Not that she gave a damn what her father thought. He was as ignorant as he was harsh. And she had been happy to leave his roof. Unfortunately, as she had quickly come to learn, she had stepped out of the frying pan into the fire.

No, that was not quite true. While life as Everett's wife had not been particularly easy these last years, she had been her own mistress. Free from the sort of cruelty she had witnessed her mother endure. And that she and Flo had experienced once they left the schoolroom.

She had thought her father a particularly unpleasant man, but her experience with two runaways now showed her that he was far from unique.

'Yes,' he said thoughtfully. 'Saying farewell can be a hard thing to bear. She is lucky to have you as a friend. I wondered if she might be worried about travelling by boat. I have to say my experience on the journey to and from India was enough to make one never again want to set foot on a ship.'

'Really? Did you encounter a storm?'

'More than one. Though I had every confidence in our captain, the perils of travel by sea were not lost on me when we spent several days battling a tempest. I have never been so ill in my life. I could only stand in awe and watch the men climb the ropes to haul in sails and such when the ship bucked and rolled like an unbroken horse.'

'It sounds dreadful.'

'It was exciting and dreadful at one and the same time. More exciting, once I found what they called my sea legs. But perhaps that is why Mrs Smith is so upset about leaving. Might it not be better for her to go by land?'

Her breath caught in her throat. How was she to explain… 'The arrangements are already made. As I understand it her…her husband will meet her on board.'

'Her husband comes to fetch her? And he does not send a lighter from the ship?'

Why did he care so much about Mary? Because she was so lovely and so fragile? So unlike Venetia? 'Perhaps because it is faster to send a boat out to the ship from shore. It will not wait long. Or so I understand.'

He nodded. 'Of course.' He finished up his breakfast. 'Let me know when you are ready to leave for the beach. I will be in the library. I found an interesting survey of the land around the house that I want to take a closer look at.'

The hairs on her nape prickled. Her heart began to pound. She had been hoping to return here, once he realised she would be of no value to him in Society. 'You are not thinking of selling this house, are you?'

'I am merely interested in learning more about it. The marquisate has a great many holdings, some of which I know well. I wasn't even aware that this one existed before I returned to England.'

Mouth agape, she stared at him. How was that even possible? Surely it was upon his orders that his brother had bundled her into a carriage along with the trunk she had brought with her to the wedding, expecting to move into his house?

'You must have forgotten about it,' she said. He had certainly seemed to forget about her.

But really, how could a man send his wife off to the wilds of St Oswych and then say he had never heard of the place? On the other hand, why would he lie?

'Perhaps I did forget. My brother, as heir, had more reason to learn about the estate details, though this place appears to have had little care these past several years.'

She bridled at the implied criticism. 'I have done the best I could.'

He gave her a sharp look. Perhaps she had sounded a little too resentful. 'It was not your place to do anything. It was my brother's responsibility.'

She glared. 'I would have thought it was a husband's responsibility to ensure that his wife was comfortably situated.'

He flushed and an expression of guilt crossed his face. 'I did. How could I have anticipated my brother would have made a mull of such a routine request.'

Routine? Mull? 'It seems to me that your brother followed your wishes to the letter.'

'Neither I nor my family wish to see your face ever again.' The words he had flung at her before he left the

church rang in her ears. He had made sure his wishes were carried out too.

From that day until he arrived unannounced, she had seen hide nor hair of a single member of the Lasalle family. And as far as she was concerned that had been perfectly fine.

She folded her napkin and rose.

Of course *he* pretended to be the perfect gentleman and stood also.

She gave him a tight smile. 'I will go and help Mary. I will send word to the library when we are ready to leave.'

She marched out, instead of giving in to her emotions and hitting him over the head with a plate.

She smiled as she made her way upstairs. Perhaps a bash on the head would make him want to once more forget he had a wife.

Everett heaved a sigh at his wife's militant departure. What a prickly creature she was. She acted like he was the one in the wrong. He was beginning to think he might be.

Trusting Simon to do something sensible might well have been a mistake.

He finished his toast and made his way to the library. She was right, though. He had been wondering if it might be possible to sell the place. It needed a great deal of money spent on it to bring it up to scratch.

He recovered the yellowed ancient maps he had discovered in a drawer and spread them out on the great table.

There was also an architectural drawing of the house.

Of more interest, though, were the lands surrounding the house, showing cottages here and there. Tenants?

Did his wife collect the rents? Or did a bailiff? Or the estate's man of business?

He began making a list of things he wanted to check on. His time in India was coming in useful. He had learned a great deal about organising and tracking assets.

John came to tell him lunch was ready, but he waved him off. This was one task he really wanted to finish. The man arrived with a plate of sandwiches, and it was only a half hour later when he looked up from the maps having completed his inventory that he realised he had eaten them.

He glanced at the clock. It was past two of the clock and surely the ladies must be ready to set out on their walk to the shore.

He folded the maps and put them back in the drawer, along with his list. He would review it again later.

In the vestibule, he discovered what he assumed must be Mrs Smith's valise, but no sign of the ladies. Nor were they in the drawing room.

About to find John to discover their whereabouts, he heard voices, the ladies', coming down the stairs. Mrs Smith looked very fetching with a ruffled shirt collar framing her face and a jaunty chip straw hat perched on her curls.

Venetia had slung a shawl over the gown she had been wearing this morning, and her bonnet had seen better days.

The contrast was marked.

It was like seeing a prancing poodle alongside an elegant and aloof Irish wolfhound. Both had their attributes, but the one with all the dignity also held all the allure. For him anyway.

'Oh,' Venetia said. 'Gore. You are here. I wasn't sure

we would be sufficiently important to drag you away from your dusty documents.'

He had the feeling that she had been hoping to escape his company. Too bad.

'My word is my bond, ladies.' He hefted the valise. 'Are you ready to set off?'

'John can carry that.'

'No need for two male escorts, when it is such a small valise.' Indeed, how had she managed for so long with so little luggage? It did not fit with anything he knew about women.

Which, to be honest, was not an awful lot.

Venetia pulled on a pair of York tan gloves. They were as shabby as the rest of her outfit. 'As you wish.'

He opened the front door and followed them down the front path and into the lane.

It was a fine clear day. Perfect for sailing. Mrs Smith, it seemed, had all the luck.

They walked briskly down the lane. He had a lady on each side of him, Mrs Smith beneath a parasol and his wife with only her bonnet to shield her complexion.

It was almost as if she wanted to make herself as unappealing as possible. Well, it wasn't working. The ugly bonnet merely served to show off the strong cheekbones and jaw.

'You are fortunate with your weather, Mrs Smith,' he observed as they neared the seaside village.

She gave him a frightened look. 'Do you think it will hold?' Another man's protective instincts might have leaped to the fore at this show of feminine weakness, but he much preferred his wife's take-charge, nononsense attitude.

Even if he hadn't yet figured out why she was lying

to him about her friend and her midnight visitor. He was beginning to believe her about the money not reaching her, however. That he would have to take up with his brother's man of business. Week. A fellow whose looks he had not liked.

They walked past the Seaman's Rest and the fishermen's cottages. Venetia acknowledged the greeting of a woman sweeping her front step, and then they manoeuvred the sandy slope onto the beach. Today, it was high tide and two or three fishing boats bobbed at anchor in the little bay.

Jeb Caldicut was chatting with a young man beside a rowboat. He hurried up the beach to greet them. 'Good day, my lord, my lady.' He executed a flourishing bow and beamed at Mrs Smith. 'And here is our passenger, be she? Your boat be waiting, mum.'

He must have seen the anxiety in Mrs Smith's face, because he leaned in. 'Don't you worry none, mum. My son Pete will have you all safe and shipshape. Nought to fear. No indeed. He's had lots of practice.'

He winked at Venetia, who blushed.

Everett frowned. What on earth was he talking about, lots of practice?

'So I have assured Mrs Smith, Mr Caldicut,' Venetia said. 'Come along, dear one, the ship will not wait for ever.'

Everett scanned the horizon and in the distance was a larger craft than he had expected. It looked more like an oceangoing yacht than an inshore tender of the sort that plied their trade around England's coast.

He wished he had thought to bring his spyglass. He would have liked to take a better look at her.

Venetia hugged her friend before Pete helped her over

the gunwale of what was little more than a cockle and steadied her as she sat on the wooden seat in the stern.

The yacht hove to a little way offshore and shortened her sails.

A couple of men who had been lounging against an upturned dinghy and puffing on their pipes strode over to assist Everett and old Mr Caldicut to push the boat into the gently lapping waves. Pete began pulling at the oars and in short order he was closing in on the vessel.

Mrs Smith turned to wave. Already she looked tiny and distant.

Venetia waved back furiously, as if giving encouragement. For a long while, they stood side by side, the waves pushing up the sand with a quiet hiss, seagulls screeching and whirling overhead, and watched as their guest was lifted on board by way of a basket lowered over the side.

How peaceful it was here to be sure. Today the wind was a gentle tease, without the strength to disturb a single strand of Venetia's hair confined in a tight bun at her nape.

The tang of salt in the air and the undefinable scent of the sea imbued Everett with a sense of belonging that he had never experienced during his stay in India. He was home.

And he had duties and responsibilities which included a wife he did not trust, but somehow it all seemed less of a burden than a worthwhile challenge.

It was not long before Pete was rowing back, and the yacht's sail was unfurled.

After a brief word to Jeb Caldicut, Venetia turned away and headed up the beach. Everett handed the old man a silver sixpence. 'Share it with your son,' he said.

The old man touched his forelock.

In two strides, Everett caught up with Venetia. 'You will miss your friend, I think.'

She smiled up at him and his heart seemed to skip a beat.

'I will,' she said. 'She has been good company these past few weeks.'

'You will not lack for company when we go to London,' he said, thinking to cheer her spirits.

The smile fled and she looked...miserable.

'Did you find what you were looking for in your documents?' she asked, clearly changing the subject.

Again her reaction took him aback. She ought to be in alt at the prospect of leaving the dreary house and returning to the delights of London. Would he ever understand her? And did it matter if he did not?

Strangely enough, he found that it did. But then it was his duty, was it not, to ensure the happiness of his wife?

Chapter Seven

Gore was right, Venetia would miss Mary. And she was going to miss Walsea when she went to London.

'Why don't we watch them go from up there,' Gore said, pointing to the closest of the pair of headlands that rose a few feet either side of the cove. He sounded… sympathetic. As if he actually cared.

The small hill had well-worn tracks across the rough ground, where a couple of goats grazed on salty grasses.

If they watched the ship leave, would it be obvious that it was not sailing along the coast but instead was headed for the Continent? 'I really should be getting home. I must prepare dinner.'

'Nonsense. A walk will do us both good.'

She thought about refusing but recalled her mother's advice. Pick your battles carefully. Sometimes she had prevailed against their father. But only sometimes. Father had been the sort of man who did not take *disobedience*, as he called any kind of discussion of his orders, lightly.

Yet Venetia still hoped to dissuade Everett from forcing her to go to Town with him. Perhaps a walk might be the perfect occasion to reinforce her preference.

'As you wish,' she said.

He held out his arm as if she was some sort of delicate flower that needed help standing on her own two feet.

What could she do but accept his offer of escort, despite the fact that she had been tramping around the countryside hereabouts with no difficulty for the past five years.

The climb to the top was steady, but not steep, and he carefully helped her over every tussock and pebble they encountered as if she was made of bone china. She gritted her teeth and reined in the urge to tell him to stop fussing.

When they reached the top, he held her arm as they looked out to sea. After a few moments of squinting, she finally picked out the sails of the ship carrying Mary.

She pointed. 'There.'

'I see it,' he said. 'She has perfect weather. I have no doubts that she will arrive at her destination safely. I have nothing but admiration for the British sailor after my return voyage.'

'I have never been on a punt, let alone a ship. Was your journey terrible?'

'To be honest, a lot of it was dreadfully boring. After two days of keeping company with fellow passengers with whom one has nothing in common, the only entertainment is figuring out a way to avoid them.'

She chuckled. Could not help it. She recalled her evenings at balls looking for nooks and crannies where she could hide from *the fashionables* as they liked to call themselves. Fribbles, she had called them, when not calling them brainless twits. To herself, naturally. She would not have dared to voice her opinions. Father would have meted out some sort of dire punishment.

Her amusement fled. Would Everett be like her father? Her poor mother had never expressed any opinions that were not in accord with those of her husband. His temper was legendary.

His hand hard and swift.

Even the servants crept around the house when he was not pleased.

Was that to be her future also?

'Why the sigh?' Everett asked. 'Missing your friend already? I promise you, you will have plenty to do in London.'

Venetia turned and raised a hand to shade her eyes against the glare. The sails were already little more than a white speck.

She would miss Mary. As she had missed the first one. And now, because of him, there would be no more.

She had come to that sad conclusion as they walked down to the shore. Gore, her husband, the marquess, missed nothing. Trying to hide her smuggling of wives would be impossible. She dreaded to think what he might do if he learned of her activities.

And discovery might well cause a scandal, not just for her, but for her dear friend Lucy Harper.

'I was thinking about London,' she said, bracing herself to brave the issue. 'I would really rather prefer to stay here.'

He frowned. 'This again? I thought we settled the matter.'

'Settled. Hardly. You rode roughshod over my wishes. You decided I would go to London. I simply do not believe my presence there will be of any more use to you than would my remaining here. Indeed, I think I can be of more use here. Not to mention I am happy here. Why should I uproot myself just to please you?'

'You know why. It is your duty—'

'And duty is more important than happiness, is it?'

The muscles in his jaw flexed. 'Doing one's duty should make one happy. And it is my duty as a husband to ensure you do not shirk your wifely responsibilities.'

Oh, heavens, she had let her temper get the better of her and made him angry, when she had wanted to convince him that taking her to London was a mistake. But it was his fault she had lost her temper in the first place. He was a bully, just like her father. There was no reasoning with him.

'I hope you do not come to regret your decision, my lord,' she snapped.

His lips tightened. 'As do I. And forget any plans you might have to make things difficult.'

Her heart stilled, then pounded hard. 'What do you mean?'

'No matter. Look, I know we did not wed under the most auspicious circumstances, but we have no choice but to make the best of it. Let us make a clean slate and start afresh.'

'Just forget the past five years as if they never happened, you mean?' She could not stop herself from sounding incredulous. Was she supposed to forget the way he had looked down his nose at her on their wedding day and the words he had spoken as well?

'What choice do we have? Really? Neither of us wanted this, but there is no option but to make the best of it.'

By this, she assumed he meant their marriage. Certainly no one could regret it more than she. The only person who could be said to be pleased by the turn of events was her father.

'I need a wife to attend to the details of my household. I think this is something you could manage.'

'A good housekeeper and butler would do as well.'

He sighed impatiently. 'Do not be obtuse. A housekeeper cannot serve as my hostess. That is the sole duty of a wife.'

Obtuse was she? 'Not necessarily.'

His eyes widened.

She winced. She probably shouldn't hint at the idea that she would prefer he took a mistress. But she wasn't stupid. It was what many noblemen did. Her father had definitely kept a mistress and would entertain his friends at her house. Sometimes he used to compare her to his wife, and the mistress clearly came off best.

Everett glared at her. 'Enough. I will not bicker about this further. We both go to London and that is final.'

'On your head be it.' The misery of months of never being asked to dance, of being snubbed, rose in a tide of dread. 'But just so you know, I hate London.'

He looked shocked. Perhaps she had been a little too vehement. 'We won't spend all our time there.' He grimaced. 'We have estates we will need to visit, much nicer ones than Walsea, I might add.'

Did he think that would make her feel better about it all? Did he think she would take pleasure in trailing in his wake from house to house, dealing with the complaints of housekeepers and cooks, looking over inventories of linens and playing hostess to whomsoever he chose as his guests? 'How lovely.'

A seagull swooped close to their heads with a loud screech. She jumped.

He waved an arm and it flew away.

'Like it or hate it, you are going. And you will make the best of it. The same as I will.'

Best or worst, it was likely all the same.

Well, he certainly knew where he stood, Everett mused.

His wife didn't want anything to do with him.

The very thing he had wished for from the day they wed. Not only wished for. Had announced to all in attendance.

Except that, for some reason he barely understood, he had never strayed from his marriage vows all these long years. Duty and honour were hard taskmasters sometimes.

Another reason he had resented being forced to wed.

'I never wanted this marriage,' he said, 'I make no bones about it. But we haven't given it a chance.'

She bristled. 'Whose fault is that?'

'Mine.' In part. It did not seem the right moment to remind her that it was her actions that had precipitated the whole mess.

She turned her head from gazing out to sea to look at him. Surprise filled her expression. Well, at least he had got her attention.

Since arriving in England, nothing with regard to his wife had turned out as he expected. He had presumed that she would be only too willing to don the mantle of marchioness. Clearly, he had been wrong. She cared nothing for it. In a way, he felt glad to discover she did not care a fig for his newly acquired title. In a way. But he was the title now. And with the honour came a great many responsibilities.

Duties that were not only about properties and maintaining the family lineage, but also about the people who relied on the Marquess of Gore for their livelihoods and well-being.

Simon hadn't given a damn about those people, nor had their father cared about anything but his pleasure. His grandfather had cared and had tried to drum the same caring into Simon.

Without success.

But Everett *had* somehow absorbed his grandfather's lessons. He had greatly admired the old man and empathised with his views on duty and honour. Which was why Everett had hoped his departure would help his brother see sense.

Apparently, it hadn't.

Now the task of putting things to rights had been dumped in Everett's lap. This was his chance to turn things around and to know that his grandfather's life's work would not be wasted.

'I have a proposition for you,' he said as a thought flashed into his mind. 'We haven't gone on too badly these past few days. If you really try to make the marriage work, then if it does not go well, you can return here to live and I will promise we need never see each other again.' And in the meantime, he would do his darnedest to show her the error of her ways.

She looked suspicious. 'And if I do not agree to your proposition?'

Good question. In the old days, a husband might have

sent a recalcitrant wife off to a nunnery. 'Then I will insist you accompany me to London and I will sell this house.'

'You do not give me much of a choice,' she snapped, turning away.

'I believe I am being more than fair.' She owed him this. If not for her, he would still be single. He would have choices. But would he actually force her to go with him, if she refused his offer? Likely not.

'Very well. I will try it your way for two weeks.'

'Three,' he said, almost instinctively. He had become adept at bargaining during his time in India.

She sighed. 'Very well. Three weeks.'

'Then let us not put off our departure any longer than necessary. Now Mrs Smith is on her way, I see no reason why you cannot finish up any loose ends here in a day or so.'

She stood up with a sigh. 'The seamstress needs more than a day or so to complete my wardrobe.'

Relieved that she had accepted his offer, even if grudgingly, he stood looking down at her. He was surprised how vulnerable she looked with an anxious expression on her face and her hands clasped tightly at her waist as if she was about to climb the steps to meet the executioner. 'I doubt a country seamstress can produce what is needed for a grand entrance into Society anyway. Arrange for a dressmaker in Town the moment we arrive. I will spare no expense to ensure that she has a wardrobe ready for you in short order.'

Horror replaced anxiety. 'But I have ordered several gowns—'

'Have her forward those she has begun and cancel

the rest. I doubt they will be up to snuff. You can send for them later if you really want them.'

'How very extravagant you are.'

'Not in the least. I am being practical, and the less we have to throw away, the better. Indeed, don't have her forward any of it to London. Have whatever she has begun or completed left here. Certainly, if what you are wearing is a sample of her work, none of what she is making will be suitable for Town.'

'I see.' She spun around and stomped down the hill.

Dammit. He probably should not have criticised her appearance, but surely she did not think that what she was wearing was anything like what was required. She should be delighted that he was prepared to spring for the latest fashions. There was no pleasing her at all.

Well, she did not have to be pleased, but she did have to behave like a proper wife.

He caught her up and offered his supporting arm.

She ignored it.

He insisted.

She gave him a look of impatience and grasped his arm. 'I have walked these cliffs by myself upon more than one occasion, you know.'

'I have no doubts about your ability to walk,' he said. 'However, walking arm in arm is far more companionable, don't you think?'

'I see you are determined to make this proposition of yours work.'

'Of course I am. Aren't you?'

She glanced at him and away. 'I suppose so.'

Hardly a ringing endorsement of his idea, but she did seem to relax a little and let him take a fraction of her weight on his arm.

* * *

What on earth had she agreed to? Venetia wondered as she filled her trunk for the journey to London three days after Mary's departure. What choice had he given? Be a good wife, or be a good wife under duress.

No. That was not an entirely fair summation. If she proved she had given her marriage every chance and it did not work, then he would let her return here.

Let her. How that galled. More importantly, did she trust him to keep his word?

She sighed. It all came back to what choice did she have? And yet, she had the feeling he was a man who would keep his word.

Unlike his brother, whom she had never trusted. And the whole reason she had ended up married to Everett.

She would do her best to do as he asked. She really would try. But she had no doubt that it would be a miserable experience.

And then there was her family. The thought of seeing her father left her cold, but she would like to see Paris again after all this time.

And Florence too, although she was unlikely to come to Town. Her rare letters were full of the doings of her children and talk of how busy and happy she was being lady of the manor.

Flo would certainly never have been happy married to Everett's brother, Venetia was sure, and nor had she been the slightest bit enamoured of Everett. But would her sister hold it against her now that Everett was the marquess? Flo's next letter might well answer that question.

John knocked at the door. 'Be your trunk ready for taking down, my lady?'

She closed the lid. 'It is.' She handed him the straps.

'Please make sure they are fastened properly.' She didn't have a lot, but she didn't want to lose anything.

'Do not you worry, my lady. All will be right as a trivet.'

She put on her bonnet and tied the ribbons. After a deep steadying breath, she walked firmly downstairs headed for a place she thought and hoped never to see again.

Outside, her husband was waiting beside the post chaise he had hired the day before in Colchester.

Her trunk was to follow by carter and her valise with a change of clothes was already loaded onto the chaise.

'Ready?' Everett asked, eyeing her closely.

Was he expecting her to have a fit of the megrims? She glanced back at the house. She would be back here soon enough, when he realised how inadequately she performed as wife for a nobleman.

'I am ready.'

He handed her in and followed right after.

He gave the signal to the post boy and they were off.

At first, they travelled quite slowly as the carriage negotiated the lanes, but once they reached the main road, they sped along. She pulled out a book she had tucked in her reticule to pass the time on the journey. Everett propped himself in the corner and gazed out of the window. Sometimes he appeared to be dozing.

'What are you reading?' he asked after a while.

She looked up. Lost in her book, she had almost forgotten he was there.

'A treatise on the causes of the Black Plague. It is rather out of date having been written some twenty years ago, but it is one of the few books in the Walsea's library I have not yet read. I hope you do not mind that I brought it along?'

'Of course not. You are interested in that sort of thing?'

'I am interested in many things, but I find the discourse fascinating.'

'I wish they would find a cure for this ague of mine. I never know when it will strike me down.'

'It seems most debilitating while it runs its course, and yet you seem perfectly well now. Does it occur often?'

He grimaced. 'More often than I would like. They did say that the fresher air in England should make symptoms appear less often, but now I am not so sure.'

'Perhaps if you had not been caught in the rain...'

He chuckled. 'Well, if that is the reason, then I expect it will reoccur more frequently. There is nowhere in the world that it rains more than it does in England.'

His sense of humour about what must be a horrible experience was to be admired. 'Let us hope they find a cure soon.' She meant that, sincerely.

'Indeed.'

At the next posting house, they got out and stretched their legs while the horses were changed. 'Are you hungry?' Everett asked.

'Not in the least. Are you?'

'No. I think I can survive for another hour or so.'

And so their journey continued. They were polite and considerate, and conversed at intervals, but did not touch on anything important. They ate luncheon, and when during the course of the afternoon it rained, he lit a small lamp, but she had given up trying to read many miles ago.

Dinner was also a primarily silent affair. An uncomfortably silent hour of politeness before they set off once more.

And the closer they came to London, the more anxious she felt. This would not be like the last time she was here, when she merely acted as companion to her sister and could remain happily unnoticed. This time, she would be the Marchioness of Gore. She would have to be presented to the Queen, something she had happily avoided during her Season, because her father had sent her home early in disgust.

She wrung her hands in her lap. She could not do this.

'Is something wrong?' Her husband was looking at her with that intensely curious way of his.

Now was the time to tell him. To throw herself on his mercy and ask him not to force her to face Society.

'This is not going to work,' she blurted.

'What is not going to work?'

'This trial marriage thing.'

Even in the gloom of the carriage she could see his frown deepen. 'I thought things were going famously.'

'Famously politely.'

'You wish me to be impolite?' Confusion filled his voice.

'It has nothing to do with you.'

'If we are talking about our marriage, I believe it has a great deal to do with me. You gave me your word you would give it a try. You will not find me unreasonable. I understand that we do not know each other very well, but I am prepared to give you some time to become accustomed to your change in circumstances.'

That was the source of the problem, wasn't it? He did not know her. He did not know how impossible she found mixing and mingling with members of the *ton*. Unlike him. He was perfectly at ease with his peers. She knew this because she had seen him from a distance at the same balls and routs she had attended. 'You cannot possibly understand.'

The wheels rattled over cobblestones and streetlights cast patches of light and shadow into the coach. Each time a glimmer of light fell on his face, she could see puzzlement in his expression. 'I cannot understand if you do not explain.'

'Very well. I do not enjoy dancing,' she said. 'I do not converse well with people I do not know. In short, I do not enjoy being in company.'

There, she had said it.

He sat up straight. 'I see.' There was an ominous note in his voice.

Perhaps now he would finally understand and send her home.

Chapter Eight

This, Everett had not expected. He had thought they had come to an understanding and now she was making excuses again. Devil take it, she was his wife, he wasn't asking for the moon. 'I think you have spent too much time alone in the country. I am sure once—'

The carriage began to slow. He glanced out of the window. They were turning into Cavendish Square. This was not the time to get into difficult discussions.

'It is late. It has been a long journey. We shall discuss this after a good night's sleep.' While he had been determined not to show it, the journey had left him tired to the bone. He could not deal with his wife in this state of exhaustion.

A footman opened the door. Everett climbed down and helped Venetia to alight.

Potter admitted them to the house with a brief word of welcome. Venetia looked about her and he realised with a start of shock that she had never entered this house before.

Guilt assailed him.

How could he possibly expect her to come with him

willingly when she had been treated like a *persona non grata* for all these years?

He tried to see the house through her eyes. It was so familiar to him, he realised he had not actually looked at it. Now what he saw was a house decorated in the very heavy and the now unfashionable style of the last century. Clearly, his brother had done nothing to change the place after Grandfather had died. It looked dowdy and tired.

Not much better than where she had been living at Walsea. No, Walsea was in a bad state of disrepair. This house simply needed a modern woman's touch.

'May I offer you tea in the drawing room, my lord, my lady?' Potter asked.

Venetia shook her head. 'I should like to retire, if you do not object, my lord?'

'Not in the least. Potter, have tea sent up to Her Ladyship's room, would you? And have Mrs Kraft assign one of the maids to attend her.' He turned to Venetia. 'Mrs Kraft is our housekeeper. You will find her most able.'

Venetia nodded.

'Certainly, my lord,' Potter said. 'Will Her Ladyship's maid arrive with the luggage? And am I to expect their arrival tonight?'

'The luggage will arrive in two days' time and Her Ladyship will employ a new dresser at the earliest opportunity.'

While Potter said nothing, Everett could sense his surprise, and no doubt Venetia must sense it also. He repressed the urge to explain.

Potter bowed and signalled one of two footmen standing at attention in the vestibule. 'Charles, please show

Her Ladyship to her room. I will speak with the kitchen staff and Mrs Kraft at once, my lord.'

'Thank you, Potter.'

He followed his wife and the footman up the stairs, trusting that Potter would send his valet to him as soon as he went down to the servants' quarters.

In his chamber, he sank into the easy chair and poured himself a glass of brandy from the decanter on the table beside it.

Devil take it, he must be the only peer alive who had a wife who wished to be anywhere but where she ought to be.

He had tried to make conversation with her on the journey, but her answers had been little more than monosyllabic.

He tossed off his drink.

They must come to a common understanding soon, or he might very well find himself turning to drink.

He shook his head at his impatience. He had five years to make up for and that wasn't going to happen in a few days.

First off, she had to stop lying to him. Before his patience ran out.

After a surprisingly good night's sleep, Venetia came downstairs the next morning grimly determined that she would not be bullied by her husband. You could not make a silk purse out of a sow's ear, as her father had not hesitated to say on many an occasion, but she had given her word to Everett that she would do her best. But then she had done her best at Walsea, hadn't she? And he had done nothing but criticise her efforts in that regard, the same way Father had criticised her appearance and her love of reading and everything else she did. No doubt her best would not be good enough for her husband.

She had married Everett Lasalle against her better judgement and, like it or not, she was his wife. The past five years had merely been a reprieve.

Her heart faltered. When she had agreed to be wed, she had not expected to become the wife of a titled peer. She winced as she recalled the shocked look on the maid's face when she opened her valise and lifted out the gown she had packed to wear today.

The maid was better dressed.

Venetia should have packed her Sunday best dress in the valise, instead of putting it in the trunk that would arrive by carter. It was too late for regrets. Hopefully, she would not be expected to receive callers before she had a few new gowns to her name.

The housekeeper, who had come at her request while Amy, her temporary maid, was brushing her hair, had recommended a dressmaker, a hairdresser and a cobbler. The woman had proved most helpful and knowledgeable.

She straightened her shoulders and entered the breakfast room.

The only occupant, the footman who had shown her to her room the previous evening, stood at the sideboard. He bowed. 'Tea, my lady?'

'If you please.'

He disappeared through a door covered in the same paper as the rest of the wall.

She had wanted to ask after her husband, but he might find it strange that she did not already know of his whereabouts. She did not want to embarrass herself or Everett before his servants.

She filled her plate and sat down. The footman returned a few minutes later with a pot of tea and placed it before her.

'Will there be anything else, my lady?'

'Nothing, thank you, Charles.'

'Thank you, my lady. His Lordship would be grateful if you will attend him in his study at ten of the clock.'

And if she said no? Oh, she really must stop having these rebellious thoughts. 'Very well.'

Charles left her to breakfast in peace. She glanced at the clock. It was past nine already. It had been years since she had been so late with her breakfast. But getting up and getting ready at Walsea had been a different proposition to the ritual of being pampered with hot chocolate before she arose and then getting bathed and dressed here.

And what would she do with herself until the appointed hour to meet her husband?

One thing she ought to do was familiarise herself with the house. She rang the bell beside her plate.

Charles appeared in a moment.

'If Mrs Kraft is available, please ask her to join me.'

He bowed and left.

Mrs Kraft, a grey-haired woman of about fifty with a calm demeanour and friendly eyes, appeared not long afterwards. 'You sent for me, my lady?'

'I did, Mrs Kraft. I would like to arrange for a tour of the house, say at eleven this morning.' An hour should be long enough to meet with her husband.

'I shall be delighted to do so, my lady. I sent word to Madam Louisa, as you requested last night, and she will come this afternoon. I took the liberty of asking her to bring any items she has on hand that she might consider suitable. To tide you over until your trunk arrives.'

A tactful way of saying nothing she currently owned would likely be suitable, having seen what she was wearing today. Amy must have said something to her. Ready-made dresses might be just the thing, particularly if her sojourn in London was as short as she anticipated.

'How thoughtful of you, thank you.'

Mrs Kraft looked relieved. She must have wondered if she was overstepping her bounds. 'Will there be anything else, my lady?'

'Not for today.' No doubt this dressmaker, like the famous woman employed by her father to make the gowns for her Season, would poke and prod, lament about her lack of a good figure and find her complexion too pale to wear with this year's most fashionable colour, whatever it was. Oh, that would be more than enough for one day.

'Shall I send Chef up with the menus now, or would you prefer to see him later?'

Menus. Well, she was certainly used to preparing menus for the day. She just would not have to cook the food once she had figured out what to eat. 'Now would be best, thank you.'

By the time ten o'clock rolled around she had organised the meals for the following week. The chef had looked pleased when he left, despite that she had told him she did not yet know if her husband planned to invite any guests for dinner so they had selected dishes that could be easily expanded should it be required.

She would have to ask Gore whether he would entertain his friends here or if he would prefer to meet them at his club, which was what her father had mostly preferred, to Mother's relief.

She braced herself for the coming interview with Gore, knocked and entered the study.

Like the rest of the house, the room seemed gloomy, with heavy drapery and dark wood furniture and shelves full of ledgers and scrolls. A large desk behind which sat her husband took up most of the floor space. He looked up from the ledger he was reviewing.

'Good morning, my lady.' He stood and placed a chair in front of the desk. 'Please be seated.' The clock on the mantle chimed ten o'clock.

'You wished to see me?'

'I apologise for cutting short our conversation last night. I felt that we might both be too tired to discuss things with any degree of rationality.'

'Yes,' she admitted. 'One does not realise it, but travelling is wearing, although it involves little more than sitting for hours on end.'

His expression lightened. 'Exactly.'

He picked up a quill and toyed with it for a moment. He looked…concerned.

Perhaps he had come to the conclusion that bringing her to London was a mistake, after all.

She inwardly chuckled at the very idea. What man would ever admit he was wrong about anything?

She waited.

Everett had awoken in a better frame of mind. He had mulled over her declaration last night of not being comfortable in Society. Her excuse for wishing to return to Walsea.

Her words had been truthful enough.

He just didn't understand the reason behind it. He cast the pen aside. 'I have been thinking about what you said last night.'

Curiosity filled her face.

He plunged on. 'Neither of us wanted the responsibility that comes with the title. I would much prefer it if my brother had lived to fulfil his duty. However, no matter how much we may dislike it, we have no choice.'

She looked disappointed but resigned.

Resignation was a whole lot better than out-and-out rebellion. Wasn't it?

'And your offer of a three-week trial?' she asked. 'I hope it still stands?'

She certainly was not making things easy for him. 'I do not go back on my word, madam. But I must insist you give it a fair chance.'

She took a deep breath and shrugged. 'I promise I will try my best.'

It was all he could ask for, begrudging though her acceptance was.

'Good. I do not want there to be any misunderstandings. In order for me to meet the requirements of my position, you must meet your obligations also.'

Dammit, he sounded more like a father than a husband. Or like his grandfather talking to Simon. He'd heard that sort of lecture time and again growing up. Hopefully it would be the last time with her.

He shoved a pile of notes and cards towards her. 'These invitations arrived in my absence. It is extraordinary how quickly word got around that the new marquess has arrived home, I would like us to attend the Lawson ball and Almack's. Please look at the rest and pick out any you think suitable.'

She looked surprised and anxious. 'How would I know which ones are suitable? I haven't attended a social function in years.'

'Nor me. I will leave the matter in your capable hands. I have a meeting with my man of business shortly.'

She was staring at the pile of invitations in her hand with an expression of distaste. 'I will not be able to attend any sort of function or receive any calls until I have a new wardrobe.'

'A couple of days should be long enough to resolve that problem, according to Mrs Kraft.'

She made a face.

'You disagree?' he asked.

She glared. 'You must trust my judgement on this matter.'

'Very well. Provided there are no unnecessary delays.'

She straightened her shoulders. 'Was there anything else?'

He had a strong urge to offer her some comfort as she looked so unhappy, but if he did that she would likely see it as weakness and try to delay further, or ask to be excused her duties altogether.

Instead, he gave her an encouraging smile. 'Nothing that I can think of at the moment.' Devil take it. Yes, there was something else. 'Do you like to ride?'

She looked startled. 'Ride?'

'The stable master spoke to me this morning, asking if you would like him to find you a suitable mount while you are in Town. Also, he asked if you preferred to drive yourself or would like him to obtain a barouche for your morning calls and such.'

Her eyes widened. 'I do ride, but I see no point in riding in Town.'

Disappointing. He had been thinking they might ride out together. 'And the carriage?'

She seemed puzzled by the questions. 'I do not need anything special. Whatever is available will do for me.'

'It will not do. There is only one equipage in the stables. My brother's curricle and a pair of high steppers. If you do not wish to drive yourself, then I shall inform Butts that a barouche will be just the thing for now.'

She nodded.

'And another thing, please invite your family to dinner here at the earliest opportunity. Those that are in Town anyway.'

'My family?' She looked shocked. 'You want them to come for dinner?'

'Of course. I have little more than a nodding acquaintance with your brother and had only the briefest introduction to your father at our wedding. It is time we paid our respects, as is proper. They will be our first guests. I hope you do not have a problem with this request?'

She straightened her shoulders. 'Not at all.'

It was said in the tone of voice that said, *On your head be it.*

He decided not to inquire further. He had no wish to delve into her relationship with her father. Whatever it was, he was her husband and her father had no say in anything.

'That concludes *my* business. Was there anything you wished to discuss with me?'

She looked hesitant.

'Come, madam, say what is on your mind.'

'The chef asked me if there were any particular items of food you preferred or disliked. I was unable to answer him.' A little smile curved her lips and he was enchanted by the change in her expression. There was a teasing quality to it. 'I told him that as far as I knew you ate anything put on your plate. However, if there is anything special you would like him to prepare or anything to which you are averse…'

He had eaten everything she put on his plate so far, and she had cooked it too. That was the reason for that mischievous smile.

'There is one thing,' he said. 'I would love a Yorkshire pudding one evening. It is something that is never served in India, and I often thought about it when I was there.'

Her eyes twinkled. 'How interesting. I will certainly pass along your request.'

He rose to his feet as she left.

He would like to see her smile like that more often. But he wasn't sure either of them would ever let go of their past history enough to have more than an uneasy relationship.

Perhaps his upcoming meeting with his man of business would help. Or it might make things worse.

Chapter Nine

'Will there be anything else, my lady?' Miss Green, Venetia's new dresser, an amiable middle-aged woman, asked, putting away the last of the hairpins.

The dressmaker had, over the past weeks, fitted Venetia with several morning gowns and one evening gown altered from items she had on hand. Venetia had insisted that the styles be plain without being dowdy. If Green was disappointed that Venetia was not interested in being a leader of fashion, she had not shown it.

Satisfied that she looked as well as it was possible for her to look, Venetia turned away from the mirror. 'No, thank you.'

The woman nodded and left.

It was time to go down. Tonight would be her first public appearance as the Marchioness of Gore. Thank goodness it was only family.

While she was not looking forward to seeing her father, it would be lovely to see Paris after all this time. Paris had visited her at Walsea when she first went there. He had visited her against their father's wishes and she had begged him not to do so again in light of their father's threat to reduce his already meagre allowance. Poor Paris never had a feather to fly unless Father approved an expenditure.

A knock at the door broke her reverie. Surprised, she opened it to reveal her husband standing on the threshold, looking more handsome than usual in a navy-blue superfine coat that hugged his broad shoulders. His waistcoat was a soft grey and his neckcloth a froth of lace. A barber had cut his hair à la Brutus, which suited him admirably. He gazed at her, his hands behind his back.

'Are you ready for the ordeal?' he asked.

At breakfast this morning, she had told him she was rather dreading this family dinner, even if it was only her father and brother. Her sister, Florence, had regretfully declined, saying she and her husband did not expect to be in Town this season given they were expecting another happy event.

'I am ready,' she said.

'You look most elegant,' he said.

Elegant. Was that his way of expressing disappointment that she was not festooned with flowers or laden down with lace? She decided to treat it as a compliment. 'Thank you.'

He produced a small intricately carved casket. 'I wondered if you might like to wear these.' He opened the lid and held it out. Inside was a beautiful parure of yellow stones set in silver. The necklace, earrings and bejewelled hair comb were displayed on green velvet.

'Oh, how beautiful!' she gasped. 'Surely too fine—?'

'Not at all. How fortunate that you chose to wear green this evening.'

She liked forest green. It always had a calming effect

on her nerves. It had been one of the gowns the dress-maker had brought for her to try on and she had instantly fallen in love with it.

He set the casket on the dressing table and lifted out the necklace. 'Allow me.'

Cold metal and stone chilled her skin. Even as he fastened the clasp at the back, the sensation dissipated. She turned to face him, and he nodded. 'Perfect.'

She glanced in the mirror. They complemented the plain neck of her gown beautifully.

'Can you manage the rest?' he asked. 'Or shall I ring for your dresser?'

She looked at the other pieces doubtfully. 'You want me to wear all of them?'

A shadow passed through his gaze. Disappointment. 'You do not like them?'

She winced. Why did people not understand that fine feathers did not make fine birds? The jewellery would not turn her into a beauty. They would simply emphasise her lack thereof, as Father had pointed out when Mother had suggested she ought to have more than one ball gown for a Season in London. No one but a blind man was likely to make an offer for her, he had declared, so what was the point of wasting money on dressing her up? 'Yes, I like them. But it all seems a bit fine for dinner at home with family, but if you wish me to wear them, I can manage them myself.' She attached the earrings and tucked the comb into her hair above her left ear. Her hair was thick and should be able to support its weight, given the tightly pinned bun at her nape.

She did not look at her reflection. 'How is that?'

'Excellent.' He held out his arm. 'Shall we go down? Our guests should be arriving at any moment.'

Excellent. He meant the jewels, of course, not her.

They arrived in the drawing room not a moment too soon, as the sounds of men's voices floated up from the ground floor. The guests had arrived.

The drawing room, like all the others in the house, was old-fashioned and gloomy, not so much because of a lack of windows, but because of the decor with dark wood trim and fabrics. *Oppressive* was the word it brought to mind.

She seated herself on the sofa, while Everett stationed himself beside the hearth.

Her heart picked up speed, like a schoolgirl called to her father's study for some misdemeanour, instead of a married lady with a house of her own.

Father entered, followed by Paris. Father's gaze immediately sought out her husband, who took his outstretched hand. Meanwhile, Paris glanced around for her. She rose and made her curtesy.

'Welcome to our home,' Everett was saying to her father.

'You look well,' Paris said, sounding relieved. 'I have been worried about you,' he added quietly as he took her hand and bowed.

'I am well,' she said.

'And pleased with the return of your husband, no doubt.'

His sharp look said it was a question. She and Paris had used to communicate this way in the presence of their father.

'Indeed,' she murmured.

He frowned at the less than ringing endorsement. He turned to greet her husband, while her father approached. He eyed her up and down.

He had aged in the five years since she had seen him at her wedding and was more portly than ever, his eyes seeming to have grown smaller and meaner.

'Daughter,' he said. 'A marchioness now, is it? I hope you are behaving yourself. Not giving your husband cause for complaint.'

The fact that he had been forced to marry her was cause for complaint enough. 'No, Papa.'

He rubbed his hands together. 'A marquess. Never would have thought it. Your mother would have been surprised.'

Her mother, who had died a year before her come out, would have been utterly shocked. No one in the family had expected she would make a good match, if she made one at all. Not when Florence had been endowed with all the beauty. After her own disastrous Season, she had resigned herself to being a spinster aunt. But he was right, in her own quiet way, her mother might well have been happy for her ugly duckling, as she had once called Venetia. They had all expected Flo to be the saviour of the family fortunes.

And she had been, according to what Paris had told her on that one visit to Walsea. By all accounts, not only was Flo's husband, a confirmed bachelor before he became utterly smitten with her sister, titled, he was also rich.

During his visit, Paris had suggested she write to Flo for financial help should she need it, but Venetia had decided against it. She didn't want to embroil Flo in her difficulties in case Father should hear of it. She had told Paris she was managing very well on what her husband provided and had no need of anyone's help.

'May I offer you a drink?' Everett asked.

'Brandy,' Father said.

'I will take a sherry, please,' Paris replied.

An awkward silence fell as Everett poured and handed out the requested libations. He handed her a glass of sherry and gave himself a splash of brandy.

'Good health,' Everett toasted.

'To the happy couple,' Father said. 'I never did get to toast you at your wedding.'

'No one did,' Paris said.

Venetia winced. Were they really going to drag up the unpleasantness of that day? 'Then it is good you have your opportunity now.'

'Yes,' Paris said. 'To the happy couple.'

They sipped from their glasses.

'Let us hope we will soon be toasting the arrival of an heir,' Father said in jocular tones, but with a severe glance in her direction.

Venetia's face blazed heat.

Everett smiled calmly. 'That, dear sir, is in hands other than ours.'

'Well, it ought to be in your hands, or some other part of you,' Father said with a rather unpleasant laugh.

Everett stiffened.

Paris made a sound as if his drink had caught in the back of his throat. 'I think you have brought good weather with you from the country,' he said after an awkward pause. 'It has rained every day since the beginning of May, until now.'

'A blessing,' Venetia said. 'I was able to visit the shops yesterday without my umbrella.'

Father tossed off his brandy and held out his glass for a refill. 'What did you buy?' He turned to Everett.

'Watch your purse strings, young man. A wife will have you in the poor house in the blink of an eye.'

Father had never let Mother spend a penny without his approval. He turned his mean gaze on her. 'I don't think I have ever seen you looking so fine. Dipping deep, is she, Gore?'

Fine? She lowered her gaze. Father had never called her anything but skinny and horse-faced. Mother had tried to comfort her, and tell her she had good bones, but they had both known that she was no beauty like her sister. So why...? Oh, it must be the jewels he was looking at.

She touched the necklace. 'Everett gave them to me.'

'Part of the family jewels, then,' Father said. 'Take care not to lose them. Or give them to some beggar in the street. You always were too soft that way.'

Only once had she given the few coins of her allowance to a poor woman with a baby. Father had been indignant and stopped her allowance because she had no sense and had frittered it away.

Everett looked grim. He must think her most irresponsible.

Everett disliked his father-in-law. Samuel Blade, Viscount Townley, had the air of a bully. He wasn't sure of his opinion of his brother-in-law either. He had seen the glances that passed between him and Venetia. Like some sort of secret code.

Was he a co-conspirator with his wife? In the last few days, he had learned some things about his wife's family. The estate's need for an infusion of funds that had been apparently resolved once the daughters had wed. Was that where Venetia had directed his funds?

Judging from the way she seemed to shrink in her father's presence, he could imagine her being badgered to fork over money to support her family.

The meeting with his man of business had not solved the mystery of where his money had gone, except that they had been diverted to his brother's personal man of business, Week, on the grounds that it was a family matter and had nothing to do with the estate.

Everett intended to visit the man at his place of business, a seedy address in Covent Garden, at the earliest opportunity.

He poured Townley another brandy.

'Dinner is served, my lord,' Potter said from the doorway.

'This way, gentlemen.' Everett held out his arm to Venetia. She placed her hand on his sleeve. He was surprised to feel her tremble as he led his guests into the dining room.

Did she think he could not or indeed would not protect his own wife? The idea chilled him.

While the servants placed dishes before them, the conversation kept to the mundane topics of the weather, the state of farming and the price of corn.

Once they were alone, Townley turned to Venetia. 'You will find things much changed since you were last in Town, daughter. And I am not talking about fashion, my girl. Not that you need ever care much about that.' He chuckled nastily.

The hairs on the back of Everett's neck rose at the unpleasant sound. Venetia kept her gaze fixed on her plate. Either she was embarrassed or hurt. Everett could not tell which from her expression.

Before he could come to her defence, Townley turned to him.

'Gore, since you have been absent from Town for a several years, there are a great many pitfalls you would wish to avoid. You would do well to be guided by me, if you wish to make a go of it. I can do you a great deal of good, if you follow my advice. First off, you will avoid the stench of any sort of Whiggery.' He swallowed his wine in one gulp.

Everett could not see being in the company of his father-in-law for very long without the urge to plant the man a facer overcoming his good manners and respect for his wife's family. And from what he had learned, while Townley might try to ingratiate himself into the halls of power, he was generally thought to be self-serving and not terribly astute. In other words, the last man to whom he would want as a political ally.

'I appreciate the offer, Townley. I shall certainly consult with you should the need arise.'

Paris gave a cynical smirk. Because he thought Everett a fool?

'While it was a considerable surprise to the Whigs that Prince George did not avail himself of their members to form a government after he became regent,' Venetia said, 'not all of their ideas were bad.'

Her father glared at her, his eyes almost disappearing into the rolls of fat in his cheeks. 'There you go again, Venetia. Putting your oar in where it is not wanted. Women have no understanding of politics and should be seen and not heard. If Fox had been a little less besotted by that courtesan he married, he might have been a whole lot more rational, it is my belief.'

Instead of standing up for her views, Venetia bit her lip and said nothing.

She was a different woman around her father. Repressed. His gaze shot to Paris, and he thought he saw sympathy in the man's eyes as he gazed at his sister.

'I, for one,' Paris said, 'think Fox should have known Prinny would remember all that revolutionary stuff he spouted. The idea that the Whigs might have turned Britain into a republic overnight likely terrified him. In losing George's support we lost an opportunity to make some changes for the better.'

'Changes,' Townley spluttered. 'What was good enough for my father is good enough for me and should be good enough for you too. Besides, there is no point dragging up ancient history. The Whigs lost their chance in eleven, when the Prince Regent finally came to his senses.'

'The Prince showed his true colours, more like,' Paris said. 'A man who gives up his principles for the chance at a crown.'

His brother-in-law seemed like a decent fellow, after all. 'Perhaps the opportunity for change is not lost,' Everett said. 'Simply postponed. Sometimes improvements are like medicine, better taken in small doses.'

Townley turned deep red. 'Do not tell me you are a Whig,' he spluttered. 'Think of your title, man. Your position.'

'I seem to think of very little else,' Everett said mildly. He poured his father-in-law yet another glass of wine. 'So, tell me, are you investing in corn on the exchange or manufacturing these days?'

The conversation moved onto less vitriolic subjects

and Everett sensed Venetia relax a little, but the glance of complicity she sent to her brother gave Everett pause.

Had the pair been trying to show him the true nature of their father's character? He certainly had the feeling it was something of the sort.

At the end of dinner as the dishes were being cleared away, Venetia rose from the table.

They rose with her.

'Don't expect me to take tea with you in the drawing room,' her father grumbled. 'I'm for bed as soon as I've had m'glass of port. Paris, you can see me home.'

If Venetia was pleased or disappointed, she did not show it.

'I will join you, my dear,' Everett said.

Her eyes widened, but she inclined her head in acceptance. 'Then I bid you goodnight, Father. And you too, Paris.'

Everett could not help watching the gentle sway of her skirts as she left the room.

Father was such a boor, Venetia thought, sipping her tea. No one was supposed to have any opinions of their own. He had been a little more circumspect with Everett than he had with her and Paris. Indeed, she had been surprised at the way Paris had actually voiced an opinion.

He seemed a lot less fearful of Father than when she lived at home.

She inspected the tray of cakes she had ordered in case her brother decided to gainsay her father's wishes and join them for tea in the drawing room. She selected a strawberry tart.

Delicious.

The door opened to admit her husband. He sat down beside her on the sofa, and she poured him a cup of tea.

'Paris does not join us, then,' she said, disappointed. She had always had a soft spot for her younger brother. They had often joined forces to circumnavigate their father's unfair edicts when they were children.

'He expressed his regrets. Your father was not feeling quite well and needed to be seen safe home.'

'Father has aged a great deal since I saw him last.'

'But is still a force to be reckoned with.'

She nodded. 'He has always been that.' She passed Everett the cake plate. He selected a strawberry tart.

'Those are really good,' she said.

He finished it in two bites. 'You are right. My brother didn't take much interest in improving the house, but he certainly hired a superlative chef. Dinner tonight was excellent.'

'I am glad it was to your satisfaction.'

'I was interested to hear your opinion of the Whigs.'

She froze. Had she said too much? Father had thought so. 'I had a great admiration of Fox's ideas at one time. So did Paris. I suppose we were young and idealistic. Father found our views most objectionable.' She could recall one family dinner when Father had pounded on the dinner table and both she and Paris had been sent to their rooms before they had eaten a mouthful.

Mother had begged them not to annoy their father like that again. Knowing he had likely taken out his temper on their mother, they had both agreed to keep their opinions to themselves. It had not been easy, but at least they had each other to talk to. They had not included Florence in their discussions. She had been likely to say something damning in front of Father.

'Which of the things they wanted to accomplish did you find admirable?' Everett asked.

She frowned. Was this some sort of trap? Would he lead her on, only to show her the error of her thinking? Ought she to be like her mother and refuse to have any opinions of her own?

She recalled the way her mother tiptoed around her father. She could not do it. She lifted her chin and looked him in the eye. 'The changes the Whigs supported seemed to me to be of the noblest sort—abolition of slavery, the independence of America and other colonies, the dissolution of pocket boroughs. Fox was misguided about France, however. He should have admitted his mistake on that front, I believe.'

He nodded slowly. 'You show a great interest in political matters. Where do you come by your knowledge?'

'I realise that men do not believe in a woman's intellect, but I can read. When I lived at home, Paris always passed Father's newspaper on to me when he was done with it.' She bit her lip at the sharpness of her reply. 'But I have not kept up with politics since I was married.'

'Then these are your own opinions, not those dictated by another?'

'By Paris, you mean.' She frowned. 'Paris and I discussed these things, naturally. I also heard conversations at the dinner table, between my father and his guests, though I was not expected to participate.' She chuckled softly. 'After all, the duty of a daughter is to add beauty to the dinner table, and wit, but not wisdom. Sadly, I was unable to do either.'

Surprise filled his face. 'Your presence adds a great deal of beauty and wit.'

Her jaw dropped. Was this some sort of cruel jest on

his part? She saw nothing cruel in his gaze, only warmth. Or was it pity?

Heat raced up from her chest and stung her cheeks. 'I… You…' She stared down into her cup to hide her embarrassment. 'It is most kind of you to say so.'

He took the cup from her hands and with the curve of his forefinger under her chin guided her to face him.

The touch of his hand was warm on her skin. His breath, scented with strawberry jam, grazed her cheek and sent a shiver sliding down her back.

She lifted her chin and gazed up. His gaze heated. His breathing quickened to match the speed of her own. Her heart seemed to stumble, before picking up speed.

'I speak only the truth,' he murmured.

A surge of emotion welled in her chest. Hope. Longing. Desire.

Terrified by the strengths of those emotions, she jerked back. This was the kind of thing the women she had rescued had talked about. The charm that made them let down their guard only to have their trust destroyed.

She forced herself to remember the way he had looked at her on their wedding day. The dismay. The disdain. She recalled her hurt at the curl of his lip as he gazed down into her unveiled face and the speed of his departure.

It was not a moment she wanted to relive.

She picked up the plate of cakes and thrust it between them. 'Would you like another?'

He glanced down at the pastries, hesitated, then shook his head. 'No, thank you.'

The moment was lost. The formality in his voice chased the very idea of intimacy into the shadows of the far corner of the room.

'Then I shall retire,' she said, wishing she sounded more relaxed, more sure of herself. She forced a calm smile.

'Goodnight.' He sat back against the cushions. He looked tired. Perhaps even irritated.

This was his true feeling was it not? Annoyance at not getting his own way. The kindly looks and gentle touch were merely ploys to break down her defences.

How easily she had nearly succumbed.

On legs that seemed weak, she rose.

He pushed to his feet with a sigh. 'I will be tied up with business matters most of tomorrow.'

'And dinner?'

'I am not sure. May I let you know tomorrow?'

'Of course.' What else could she say? Men came and went as they pleased. She dipped a curtsey and left.

Outside the door, she lingered, feeling strangely as if she had missed an opportunity that might not present itself again.

But she had watched her mother try time and again to please her father, only to have her overtures rejected. She was not going to turn herself into that sort of doormat.

As a wife, she had duties and responsibilities and she would fulfil them to the best of her ability, though she was sure he would soon find her lacking. There was no rule that said she had to wear her heart on her sleeve. Indeed, if she recalled the ways of Society correctly, the *ton* frowned on couples who had the least hint of April and May about them.

Chapter Ten

'Where is Her Ladyship?' Everett asked, handing over his wet coat. He had decided to walk to his appointment. His very interesting appointment.

'Her Ladyship has a caller, my lord,' Potter said. 'A Mrs Harper. They are in the drawing room taking tea.'

A caller? At this hour of the day? And after his wife had made it plain she planned to accept no callers until her wardrobe was complete? An occurrence she had indicated would take at least another week. Perhaps she had underestimated. And why did the name Harper sound so familiar?

He dredged through his memories.

Ah, yes, the young man who had visited Walsea. This must be the mother. Venetia's friend. 'I will join them as soon as I have changed.'

'I shall send along another cup, my lord.'

'A cup of tea would be most welcome.' He bounded up the stairs and changed out of his pantaloons. The puddles in the City had been so bad in some places he was wet to the knees. Fortunately, his top half had remained dry thanks to his umbrella.

When he entered the drawing room, the two ladies were perched on the edge of their seats, clearly anticipating his arrival with some nervousness.

'Gore,' Venetia said. 'Allow me to present my good friend Mrs Harper. You met her son last week.'

Everett bowed over the matronly lady's hand. Her greying hair, topped by a widow's cap, curled around an attractive but lined face.

'Delighted to make your acquaintance,' Everett said. 'How is your mutual friend? The one your son came to tell us was ill.'

Mrs Harper smiled serenely. 'Sadly, she has departed for a better place.' She seemed almost pleased.

'My condolences,' he said.

'It is hard for those who remain behind,' the lady said, 'but I believe it to be a blessing for the lady in question.'

His wife nodded agreement.

Everett could not put his finger on it, but he felt a strange undercurrent to the conversation. As if it held hidden meaning. 'It was good of you to call and bring my wife the news.'

'It was the least I could do. Now I really must be on my way. Goodbye, my dear Lady Gore. I am not sure when I shall have the pleasure of meeting you again but you may always rely upon my friendship.'

What the devil did that mean? Whatever it was, it made his wife blush furiously.

She looked adorably flustered.

'Let me see you out, Mrs Harper.'

Her eyebrows rose, but she accepted his arm and he accompanied her down the stairs.

'I am sorry you are not staying in London, Mrs Harper,' he said as they reached the vestibule.

She glanced up at him with an expression of surprise. 'Why is that, my lord?'

'I think my wife would like to know she had one friend in Town as she re-enters Society after a long absence.'

She frowned. 'I hardly think I could be of assistance in that regard. I do not travel in such high company.'

'Harper,' he mused. 'My grandfather introduced me to a chap named Harper. A navy man if I recall. A vice-admiral.'

She missed putting her arm in the sleeve of her coat being held out for her by the butler. The second attempt proved successful.

'That would have been my husband,' she said calmly. 'He died four years ago.'

The wife of a vice-admiral who was high enough in Society to be acquainted with his grandfather could not be considered a member of the lower orders, despite her claim. Interesting.

The butler opened the front door. Rain blew in.

'Let me send you home in my carriage,' Everett said. 'You will be soaked.'

The woman looked at him closely, as if seeking assurance of something. Her expression seemed to lighten. 'You are most kind, my lord, but my coachman is waiting around the corner.' She glanced at the butler.

'I sent word, madam. And here he is now.'

A coach pulled up at the curb.

She inclined her head. 'Good day, Lord Gore. And thank you.'

Her voice seemed much warmer than it had when she first greeted him.

And not, he thought, because he had offered her transportation on a wet day.

He climbed the stairs and in the drawing room found his wife looking down into the street.

She turned and smiled, but there was sadness in her expression.

'You are sorry to see her go,' he remarked.

'I am. Would you like a cup of tea? The footman brought a cup for you and some hot water.'

'Yes, please. Did you have a pleasant visit?'

'I did, thank you. How was your morning?'

'Interesting.'

She pulled a piece of embroidery from the bag at the side of her chair and began stitching. 'Really?'

'Yes. I think you would find it interesting also.'

She looked up. 'How so?'

'I met with my brother's so-called man of business. A rather disreputable sort of fellow.' He hesitated. 'He tells me that Simon used the money I sent for your keep to pay off debts he accumulated while my grandfather was alive.'

She gasped. The needlework fell onto her lap. 'He... what?' Fury filled her face. 'Why would he do such a thing?'

He grimaced. 'First of all, because my grandfather set things up so he could not squander money from the estate. I presume the easy access to the funds I forwarded proved too much of a temptation.'

'Why did you trust him?'

He bridled at her accusatory tone. 'Why would I not? I handed Simon enough money for your keep for a year before I left. After that, I sent the money to my grandfather's man of business. I admit that I did not check that all was proceeding as planned, but I had no reason to think otherwise.'

She glared at him from beneath lowered brows, her eyes flashing fire. If looks could kill, he would be ashes. 'You talk about my duty as your wife, but what about your duty as a husband?'

He had never seen her so angry. Shame filled him. Because she was right. He should have checked. He should have come home when his grandfather died and checked on his wife. But his anger at her underhandedness had held him back.

'I knew he had debts, but I never imagined he would do anything so underhanded. Week said he intended to pay it back when he was dibs in tune.' Even to his own ears it sounded like a feeble excuse.

She raised her voice. 'Dibs in tune?'

'When he had sufficient funds.'

'Your brother was a marquess. He had all the money he needed once he inherited. And you knew exactly what he was like when you left England. You simply didn't care. And now you expect me to trust you to make the right decisions about my future. Well, I don't.'

His temper got the better of him. 'Week told me my brother said it would do you good to suffer after you poked your nose where it wasn't wanted just to steal a march on your sister. What do you think he meant by that little gem of information?'

She stared down at her sewing as if she had never seen it before and pursed her lips. 'I did interfere. And rightly so.'

A nasty sensation swirled in the pit of his stomach. A sense of impending disaster. 'Do you intend to enlighten me or not?'

She took a deep breath and shifted in her seat so as to face him full on. 'The evening of the ball, a lackey put a note in my hand addressed to Miss Blade. Even before I opened it, I knew it was intended for my sister, Florence, because it came from your brother. It asked her to meet him privately. It was most inappropriate. If she had gone, I knew it was quite possible she would be ruined. Despite her hopes, I was sure he did not have marriage on his mind. But had she asked my father if she should go, he would have said yes. He was adamant that she make a good match to restore the family fortunes.'

She pressed her lips together. 'I believed that your brother wouldn't give a fig for anything my father might have to say on the matter of his daughter's reputation.'

Everett frowned. It sounded almost plausible. Almost. 'So, since your sister did not know about the meeting and was therefore in no danger at all, why go yourself— if it was not to steal a march on your sister and catch a marquess for yourself?' He narrowed his eyes. 'Strange coincidence that all those people arrived at that spot in the garden at that very moment.'

Her eyes blazed anger. She shot to her feet. 'How dare you?' Her voice shook with fury. 'If that is what you think of me, then—' She turned away. 'Then there really is no more to be said.'

The ring of truth in her voice gave him pause. He was beginning to think that he could not be sure of his instincts in regard to his wife. That he could not be sure he knew a truth from a lie, she was so good an actress.

And yet...

He glared at her rigid back. 'Then if not that, then why?'

For a moment, he thought she would refuse to answer.

She drew in a deep breath, her narrow shoulders rising and falling as if she was under some great strain. She turned to face him, and the shadows in her eyes harboured pain. He found himself wanting to comfort her, no doubt as she intended. He stared at her coldly, waiting for her explanation, hoping for the truth, but expecting more prevarication.

'I wanted to have words with your brother,' she said in a low voice. 'To ask him—'

'So why the devil did you throw yourself at me?'

Her eyes widened. 'There you go again, assuming the worst. I did not throw myself at you. You were sleeping. It was dark. And I thought you were your brother.'

None of it made any sense. 'Then you *were* throwing yourself at my brother?'

'Will you never listen? I was trying to awaken you. Or rather awaken Simon. To tell him to leave Flo alone. By the time I realised you were not him, you leaped up and knocked me into a bush. You were so drunk, instead of helping me up, you fell on top of me.'

'And my brother and a group of busybodies conveniently arrived to find us rolling around in a very compromising position.'

'That is how you came to marry the wrong sister,' she said bitterly.

The wrong…? 'I did not wish to marry anyone.'

Clearly, she did not take comfort in his assertion.

She returned to her chair and busied herself putting her needlework away, not looking at him. 'I am so glad you have resolved the matter of your missing money, but I do not see that it changes anything. I already knew I was innocent of any wrongdoing.'

Devil take it.

He had come with good news and had become embroiled in an argument. A cold feeling swirled in the pit of his stomach. If she was actually speaking the truth and had not planned to trap Simon, then...was it possible someone else had been behind that farcical scene? He could still recall the humiliation of that moment. Who, then? Simon? But why?

The defiant look in his wife's face gave him pause. Was this a way of distracting him from something she wanted to keep hidden? He recalled how guarded she'd been about her friendship with Mrs Harper. The pair had reeked of secrets when he first entered the drawing room. Was that what this was about?

The grim look on Everet's face made Venetia want to run away. The way she had run from her father as a child, when he had that sort of look in his eye.

She was not a child any more to be intimidated by an angry man. Nor was she a mouse to bear his temper in silence. She lifted her chin and held her ground.

'Where did you meet Mrs Harper?' he asked. 'She is quite a bit older than you.'

Oh, so now he was going to question what friends she had, was he? 'She was a friend of my mother's. They were at school together.' Venetia had not known it when she lived at home, but Mrs Harper had tried, on more than one occasion, to convince her mother to leave her father.

'Strange the way she denied being a member of Society.'

Her heart gave a panicky thump. He was suspicious. And perhaps this was how he intended to exert his power. To separate her from friend and allies. She would not allow it. She looked down her nose. 'Not everyone enjoys being in Society. Certainly, I do not.'

His gaze narrowed. 'That is as may be, but why lie?'

'How was it a lie? She merely said she did not move in such circles. She does not. She lives quietly in the country. It was merely an unfortunate choice of words.'

He sighed as if tired. 'Perhaps.' He did not seem convinced, but she was glad he did not wish to pursue the matter further.

He frowned and leaned back in the chair. 'Speaking of Society, I assume you are prepared for our first outing this evening?'

The ball she had been trying not to think about it. 'I am ready.'

'Good. It is about time we set about making ourselves known.'

The thought made her feel ill. Tonight, he would come to realise all of her shortcomings. 'Have you decided if you will dine at home before we go?'

'I am afraid not. I am meeting a fellow at White's with regard to a business venture. I would have put him off, but he leaves London in the morning. I shall be back in time to escort you to Lawsons'. In the meantime, I need to prepare for my appointment.'

She breathed a sigh of relief at being spared any more of his probing questions today. 'Then I will see you later.'

He bowed and left.

As the rest of the afternoon passed, the ball loomed large in her mind. It was just as well Everett did not join her for dinner; she found it almost impossible to eat and getting dressed was torture.

As Green was placing the last of the pins in her hair,

she heard Everett's arrival. Heard him climb the stairs and pass her room on the way to his chamber. She was dreading his expression when he saw her in the gown the dressmaker had produced with such pride.

When she had tried the primrose-coloured gown on for size and before the alterations, she had not realised the neckline would be quite so low, or that the woman would have added so many silk flowers around the hem.

The gown was far too lovely for her to do it justice. She touched the diamond necklace where it lay on her collarbone, still not quite believing he had given her such a beautiful piece of jewellery. It looked stunning with this gown.

Once she heard him moving about in his room, she quietly slipped downstairs to the drawing room to await their departure.

Agitated at the thought of the evening to come, she picked up her embroidery. Plying her needle always soothed her nerves. She had decided to embroider Everett's initials on a set of handkerchiefs. It wasn't as fine as the parure he had given her, but since her funds were limited it was the best she could do.

A half hour later, he walked in looking so handsome her heart did that silly skipping thing. Pride warmed her at the thought that this gorgeous man was her husband.

No wonder he had been so disappointed at the sight of her on their wedding day. The warm feeling fled, leaving a cold empty space in her chest. She was as she was. There was nothing either of them could do about it.

She rose to her feet and tugged on her gloves. 'I am ready.'

He eyed her up and down.

She braced herself for some disparaging remark. She knew she looked ridiculous.

'Are you sure you will be warm enough with only that shawl? You know, the wind is quite cool this evening. I'll ring for Potter. He can have a cloak brought down.'

Mouth agape, she stared at him. Why was he being so nice to her? So thoughtful? She felt strangely feminine.

No doubt it was all a ploy to get on her good side. To bend her to his will. And once she came to rely on his kindness, on his smiles of approvals, then he would show his true feelings. Mother had warned her about that. She had said if she had known what Father was truly like, she might never have married him.

Venetia would not make those errors. She would do her duty, but she would not make the mistake of looking for… Her heart gave a little pang. Of looking for anything, she told herself firmly.

He rang the bell and her cloak arrived in short order.

'The carriage is waiting at the door, my lord,' Potter said, helping Venetia into her cloak. As they stepped outside, Venetia knew the truth of Everett's words. The wind had a chilly edge to it. She was very glad of her outer wrap.

Everett followed her into the carriage and sat beside her, rather than opposite. He took her hand in his. 'Ready for the fray?'

Had he sensed her nervousness? Was he worried that she would make a fool of them both? 'I am ready,' she said grimly.

'Will your brother be in attendance?'

Unable to read his expression, she chose her words carefully. 'I do not know, actually. Did you wish to speak with him about something?'

'Not really. I enjoyed his company the other evening and I thought you did also.'

Startled, she gazed at him. She plucked up her courage. 'Why did you forbid Paris to communicate with me during your absence in India?'

His hand tightened around hers briefly. 'What? Nonsense. I did no such thing.'

She pressed her lips together. That was what her mother had always done when corrected by her husband. But Venetia was not her mother.

'Why would I fabricate such a tale? When Paris voiced an objection to my being sent off to Walsea, he was told to mind his own business by my father, on instruction from the marquess. I assumed it was your decision.'

'It was not.' His voice was chilly in the extreme. 'I apologise on behalf of my brother. He overstepped his authority. I will certainly rectify the matter.'

Her heart lifted. She and Paris had been close when they were younger. Seeing him at dinner the other evening had only made their estrangement seem worse, because Paris had matured in the intervening years. 'Thank you. I should like that.'

This time the squeeze on her hand was deliberate and gentle. Affectionate?

Her heart repeated its odd little sweetly painful thump. An urge to trust her husband welled up.

With difficulty, she bit down on the words which would have left her completely vulnerable. If he knew she and Mrs Harper had spirited two wives away from their husbands, his reaction might not be so kindly. Indeed, what husband would be pleased to know his wife had been engaging in what could be construed as criminal activity?

He was looking at her expectantly. As if he knew she had been going to say something. 'I cannot recall the last time I went to a ball. I hope you do not expect me to dance.'

The atmosphere chilled. 'You do not wish to dance with me?'

'Not if I can help it.'

He released her hand. The loss of his touch hurt. 'It seems we have arrived,' he said, glancing out of the window.

It seemed he had nothing in common with this wife of his. Everett had always enjoyed dancing. He had assumed his elegant wife would be an excellent partner.

Still, she had been able to hold her own when conversing about politics with her father and brother the other evening, so she did have other talents, including a bright and lively mind.

It would have to be enough.

Belmane House was as crowded as one would expect for one of the most fashionable events of the season. After they changed into their dancing slippers and rid themselves of their coats, it was at least thirty minutes before they could make their way through the throng to the ballroom.

The closer they got to the footman making the announcements, the more Venetia tensed up. Inwardly, he sighed; she had said she did not enjoy being out in Society. He should have taken her at her word.

Not all men brought their wives with them to London. But if one wanted to be taken seriously, to become involved, to have influence on advances in the laws of the country, a wife acting as a hostess was invaluable.

In his opinion, husbands who came to town merely to enjoy the entertainments offered were fribbles and feckless ne'er-do-wells.

Like his brother and his father.

Venetia would become accustomed to her role in due time.

The butler announced them and he was aware of a good few glances sent their way. Beside him, Venetia seemed to shrink. Against his better judgement, he patted her hand in encouragement.

The look she cast him seemed to contain genuine fear. What the devil?

A man stepped away from a nearby group with his hand out. 'Lasalle.' He caught himself with an embarrassed start. 'Gore, I mean. Devil take it, but it's been years. My condolences on the loss of your brother.'

The warmth in the other man's voice made Everett grin from ear to ear. 'Grant Thank you. How are you? The last time we met, you were crying in your tankard over the vagaries of a horse named Beetle.' Grant had been his brother's friend at school.

'Good gad, you remember that?' Grant chuckled. 'What did you think of India?'

'A great deal more than I expected. My dear, may I introduce Colonel Grant, late of the Forty-Fifth and an old school chum of my brother's.'

Venetia's smile was positively frosty. 'Colonel Grant,' she murmured and inclined her head.

'Delighted to meet you again, my lady,' Grant said. He turned to Everett. 'Have dinner with me at White's tomorrow. I want to hear all about your adventures.'

He winked in Venetia's general direction. 'I expect you have a few stories not fit for the ladies' ears, what?' The sly note in Grant's voice had him wincing. He was long past that sort of schoolboy innuendo. Some men never seemed to leave it behind.

'Hardly. Are you also wed?' Everett asked.

'Footloose and fancy free, my boy. I can't afford a wife.'

'It is a wise man who recognises his limitations,' Venetia remarked.

Everett frowned at her chilly tone. No doubt the remark about adventures had not pleased her. 'I have to be honest, India was more work than play. However, there were a couple of hunting trips when I thought of your shooting prowess.'

'Hunting, eh? I shall be interested to hear all about it.'

'I hope I have an opportunity to regale you with them sometime soon.'

He bowed and he and Venetia moved on.

The chilly expression on Venetia's face was enough to freeze a pond. Did she think her consequence so high she need not be friendly to his acquaintances? A man who had served his country?

He was going to have to speak to Venetia about displaying such an unfriendly manner.

She pulled her hand from his arm.

For a moment, her expression changed from distant to delighted. She looked radiant.

'What is it?' he asked.

She stilled. 'Nothing. Why do you ask?'

'You looked as if you lost a penny and found a sovereign.'

'Oh. I have seen an old acquaintance. Someone I have not seen for a long time and did not expect to meet here.'

He would be interested to meet an acquaintance who made his wife look so radiant. 'Shall I take—'

'Gore!' The familiar deep timbre of the voice had him swinging around.

This time, a good friend of his own beamed at him.

'Alex!' Everett said. 'I had no idea you were in Town or I would have sent a note round to your lodgings.'

Alex Paxton chuckled. 'Not lodgings, old chap. Like you I inherited a year or so ago.'

'I should probably get your advice, then. I am pretty well all at sea at the moment. Let me—' He turned to introduce Venetia, but discovered her gone.

It seemed she had waltzed off to meet her friend. He finally spotted a flash of yellow in the corner farthest from the musicians and apparently skulking behind a large decorative fern.

The friend was a woman. And Venetia looked exceedingly happy. It seemed she was never happier than with her female friends. He was not sure whether to be pleased or...worried.

He turned back to Alex. 'I will introduce you to my wife a little later. It seems she has run across an acquaintance.'

Chapter Eleven

Venetia had spotted the distinctive sandy-haired, freckled face of a friend she had not expected to see, lurking behind a potted plant. They had occupied many a dark corner together five years ago. She stretched out her hands in greeting. 'Augusta Wells, such a pleasure to see you again.'

Augusta's eyes widened. 'My word. Venetia! Is it really you? You look…wonderful.'

Venetia stared at her in amazement. She wasn't sure what to say. They had always commiserated on their lack of the feminine attributes, particularly her own lack of curves and the size of Augusta's proboscis, the largest nose ever to grace a woman's face. 'Thank you. I did not expect to find you in London.'

Augusta drooped. 'This will be my last Season.' She tossed her head. 'And I am glad of it. Finally, I will not have to endure any more of this matchmaking nonsense.'

'The last time we met you were about to be married. What happened?'

'The old fellow died a week before the ceremony.'

'Oh, goodness me. I am sorry.'

'I was sorry about it too. At least for a while. I had decided that it was better to be married, even if he was ancient, than be companion to some elderly relative. Had we married before he died, I would have had far more freedom than I do now. No such luck. If I do not make a match this Season, it is off to Great-aunt Madge and her pesky parrot, Percy.'

'Augusta. How will you bear it?'

'I will have more time for my studies, hopefully.' At school, Augusta had been fascinated with medicine. She had wanted to become a doctor, which of course was impossible.

'Enough about me. How did you like India? Must have been fascinating.'

'I didn't go to India. I have been living in the country for the past five years.'

'Really? I was sure someone told me you married a man who went to India.'

'My husband went to India. He's back now.'

'Are you happy?'

Venetia shrugged. 'I am not unhappy. One does not expect happiness in a marriage of convenience.'

She did not want to discuss the state of her marriage; it seemed somehow disloyal. 'I suppose it is too early to tell as yet.'

'Do you have children?' They had talked of their desire to have children, back in those days when they had no expectations of ever having husbands.

She and Everett hadn't even ever... Heat rushed to her cheeks. 'No,' she mumbled. 'Not so far.'

'Well, naturally, you wouldn't since he has been away all this time.' Augusta glanced across the room. 'Is that him, heading our way? If so, he is very handsome.'

He was indeed heading in their direction, with a very purposeful stride. He looked so strikingly handsome in his evening wear, his short hair gilded by the light from the candles in the enormous chandeliers. The bronze tinge to his skin from his years abroad had faded somewhat.

Augusta groaned. 'I have to go. Mama is beckoning for me to meet some poor fellow.'

'May I call on you? I need to seek some advice about a medical matter.'

'Of course you may. Though I do not have any of my books here in Town. Oh, dear, now I am getting the eyebrow. I have to go.'

She shot off.

The last view Venetia had of her before Everett arrived was of her dipping a curtsey to an old gentleman with a walking stick and an ear trumpet. Another suitor? Venetia shuddered.

'Why are you hiding over here?' Everett asked when he reached her side.

'I wasn't. I met an old friend,' she said.

'So did I. I would have introduced you, but you disappeared.' He sounded disgruntled.

'I am sorry. I haven't seen my friend Augusta for five years and—'

He frowned. 'She left when she saw me coming.'

There was a slightly accusing note to his tone.

'Her mother required her presence.'

'I see. And who is she, may I ask?'

He sounded more like a father than a husband. She bit back her irritation. 'Miss Augusta Wells. We had our first Season the same year. I plan to call on her next week. She is very good *ton*.' Even if she was a bluestocking. 'Would you care to meet her? She and her mother are over there, near the orchestra.'

He glanced in the direction she indicated with her fan and shook his head. 'I came with quite a different purpose in mind.'

His eyes danced with mischief. His expression became boyishly naughty and thoroughly endearing. Her heart raced a little. She felt...breathless. 'What purpose?'

'To persuade you to dance.'

He was teasing her. And yet there was no slyness in his tone, no cruelty.

'Oh,' she said. 'I—I told you, I do not like to dance.'

'This is our first ball as a married couple. I really would like to dance with my wife.' He was smiling at her, but his gaze held determination.

Her heart gave a stupid little flutter. 'And if I refuse?'

'It is your prerogative, of course.'

In other words, he wouldn't force the issue, but he looked surprisingly disappointed. How could she refuse?

'If you wish it, I will dance with you,' she said, feeling flustered.

The band struck up, of all things, a waltz. She knew how to waltz. After all, she and Flo had received their training from one of the best teachers in London, but she had never felt comfortable in the dance. Most of the time when she was learning, she had played the male part for Flo, because she was taller and, no doubt, her lack of femininity.

She preferred the more energetic English country dances, though she did tend to look a bit like a flea on a hot plate, according to her father.

'You want me to waltz?'

'Of course. Why not?'

Why not? What excuse could she possibly have that he would not see as some sort of slight. 'I was never granted permission, you know. One is supposed to have permission.' Flo had been introduced to the patronesses of Almack's, but no one had thought to bring Venetia to their attention.

'Unless things have changed drastically since I was last in Town, married women do not need permission to dance with their husbands.'

Oh, right. She was married. She winced. 'No, I do not think things have changed. I will waltz with you if that is what you wish.'

Her stomach sank. Once he saw how badly she performed, perhaps he would be happy to send her back to Walsea and things could go back to the way they were. A small pang of sadness tightened her chest.

She braced for what would be fifteen minutes of torture.

He led her onto the dance floor, bowed and held out his hands.

Around them, other couples were doing the same.

She had the overwhelming urge to flee.

Everett caught Venetia's hands. The terrified expression on her face had him thinking she was about to run and leave him standing there like a fool.

She had done it once this evening. He wasn't about to let her do it again.

The music started and he led off. He almost tripped over her feet.

'Sorry,' she mumbled, her face flushing bright pink.

Devil take it, she had told him she didn't like to dance,

not that she could not. This was like trying to steer a ship with a broken rudder.

'Easy,' he said softly, much as one might speak to a skittish horse. 'Relax. Just follow my lead.'

Some of the stiffness went out of her, and they glided down the length of the dance floor without difficulty. He smiled down at her. 'There we go.'

He swept her into a turn at the end. For a second, she resisted his guidance, then she visibly relaxed and they sailed into a lovely twirl followed by the side-by-side steps that took them in the other direction.

And she was smiling.

She glanced up at him shyly. 'I never danced the waltz with anyone but my sister before, and I usually took the man's part.'

The admission stunned him. How could this be? She'd been a debutante.

He recalled the dash she had made for the far corner of the room. Had she been one of those perennial wall-flowers that all the young men ignored? He certainly did not recall seeing her at any of the events he had attended. He did recall her sister.

Her younger sister.

He frowned.

She tensed. 'Is something wrong?'

'Not at all.' They executed a few of the more difficult steps, and she handled them beautifully, her steps completely in tune with his. 'I was simply thinking that London's young gentlemen were a bunch of idiots for not asking you to dance. Me included.'

She gasped. And a blush coloured her cheeks. For a moment, he thought she might stumble. 'Perhaps none of them had your fortitude.'

'I do not mean to embarrass you, Venetia, but I really do mean it.'

She gave him a look askance as if she suspected him of a falsehood. 'You are being kind,' she murmured.

'I forgot to mention how beautiful you look tonight.'

A throaty chuckle sent blood racing through his veins. It was the most sensual laugh he had ever heard. 'Enough, sir. Or I shall suspect you of flattery.'

He laughed. There was something he liked about her prickly responses. She was no simpering miss, throwing out artful lures. At least not to him. But beneath the dismissive response, he sensed vulnerability. Was this inability to accept any sort of compliment a sign she was not as resilient as she appeared at first sight? Had her sojourn at Walsea these past many years left her to expect the worst from him? Clearly, he had made a bad mistake leaving her in Simon's care. But how could he have known Simon would take it upon himself to punish Venetia for her 'interference'? Marriage to him, to the untitled brother with little or no fortune, was punishment enough, surely.

Clearly, not in Simon's view.

It had not been Simon's place to exact retribution should it be needed. That was the responsibility for her husband. And if her story was true and she was simply trying to protect her sister from Simon, then she had been badly served indeed.

The thing was, did *he* believe her story? If he did, he owed her an apology and more. And he would see that she got it.

On the other hand, if she wasn't lying about that, she was definitely lying about something. And until she revealed exactly what she was keeping secret from him, he had every reason to mistrust her word.

He would not rest until he discovered the truth. But for now, he would enjoy the closeness of the waltz and the bright smile on her face. She moved with such ease and such grace he was proud to be her partner. When he gazed into her eyes, he became lost in their forest-green depths. How had he missed such inner beauty on their wedding day?

He slowly became aware of changes around him, the thinning of other dancers around them, the quieting of chatter. Good Lord, he and Venetia were alone on the dance floor, and an audience around the edge was watching them as the dance came to its conclusion.

He saw the moment Venetia became aware of it too. He gripped her hand, offering support as well as restraint as he realised the reason for the interruption.

The Prince of Wales had arrived. He was watching them with a benign smile on his face. An equerry whispered something in the Prince's ear and gestured to them to approach.

'Gore,' Wales said as they made their courtesies. 'Our newly minted marquess. My condolences on the loss of your brother.' He leered at Venetia. 'And who might this lovely lady be?'

'My wife, Your Highness,' Everett said coolly. He did not like the look in the Prince's eye. 'Lady Gore.' Venetia rose from her curtsey and gazed boldly back at the portly royal.

The Prince's eyes glinted. 'I don't believe we have met.'

Everett ignored the fact that the Prince was clearly

addressing Venetia. 'We have not, sir. I have been in India for the past five years.'

'So that is where you have been hiding all this loveliness, is it?'

'No, Your Highness,' Venetia said calmly. 'I have been living in Essex.'

The regret on the Prince's face indicated he believed he had missed some sort of opportunity. Everett repressed the urge to call him out. Prinny always had been a bit of a spoiled brat. He had not improved with age.

'They make a fine couple on the dance floor, do they not, Your Highness?' the equerry said in jovial tones, knowing full well the Prince was far too fat to cut much of a figure in the ballroom. 'An excellent addition to court, wouldn't you say, sir? Ah, I see our host is waiting to offer you some refreshment.'

Distracted by the offer of a libation, the Prince moved on.

At Everett's side, Venetia relaxed. It was only then that he realised she had been holding her breath. 'You don't have to worry about Prinny,' he said quietly. 'Not with me by your side.'

'He's a beast,' she said under her breath.

'Shall we get some air?' He certainly did not want a conversation of that sort to be overheard.

She took his arm, and they strolled out onto the terrace overlooking a small formal garden. It reminded him of the garden where they had... He grimaced... Where they had fallen, literally, into their marriage.

'Thank you for forgiving me my outburst,' she said. 'I will try to exercise more restraint in future.'

'Oh, you are welcome to express all of your opinions to me. And I do not disagree. I just did not want us to be overheard by some toady. The Prince is very sensitive, you know.'

They both laughed.

She glanced around, but he had already ascertained no one was close enough to overhear their conversation.

'I almost fainted when I realised everyone had stopped dancing and was watching us, waiting to see what the Prince would do when we finally realised why. I half expected him to give us a set down.'

'He was too interested in learning your name to do so.'

Her expression became strained. 'Did you know he would attend this evening? I really do not like him.'

Everett had accomplished what he had set out to do this evening. Make his first foray into Society. Dance with his wife. Meet the Prince of Wales, though he had not quite planned the latter to occur precisely in that way.

'Shall we leave?' he asked.

'Can we?'

'As I understand it, we can do more or less anything we like.'

'Except annoy the Prince of Wales.' She sent him a sly little grin.

'Except that,' he said gravely, though it was hard not to laugh.

Venetia could not quite believe how much she had enjoyed the evening. The dance with her husband had been utterly enchanting.

He had been so sweet, so gentle, and yet commanding. Once she handed over control, the dance had seemed effortless. At least on her part. She couldn't wait to do it again.

Had he, like her, really not realised the Prince of Wales was watching them dance alone with every eye in the room upon them?

She certainly had not. She had been too engaged in gazing at the handsome face of her husband and melting at the way he guided her around the dance floor. Not to mention the way he had smiled at her as if he was actually enjoying her company.

She glanced down to where her hand rested in his. He had helped her into the carriage and had not released his hold. It felt so natural resting on his thigh. A sort of promise of an evening not yet concluded.

She shivered. Fear or excitement. Or a little of both.

No, it was definitely fear. Was he going to insist on his rights as a husband? After five years?

Up to now he hadn't seemed the slightest bit interested.

But, as she was learning, he was a man who took his duties very seriously.

And she was, after all, a duty.

Once indoors, he helped her remove her shawl, and they climbed the stairs to the second floor. Her heart pounded in her chest. Her mouth dried. She couldn't swallow.

'Let me offer you a nightcap before we retire,' he said softly. 'I have some very old brandy my grandfather laid down. I should value your opinion.'

She recalled the brandy she had offered him at Walsea. Smugglers' brew.

She drew in a quick breath. Why not? 'That would be lovely.'

Instead of stopping at her door they continued on. His

chamber door was ajar. His valet glanced up, saw them both and left the sitting room without a word.

Had Everett planned this? Or was his valet used to him bringing ladies to his chamber at the end of the evening?

The flutters in her stomach increased.

He gestured for her to sit on a love seat set in the bay window. The curtains were closed, but in daylight it would afford a view of the mews behind the house. The same view as from her chamber window.

The flickering candlelight from the wall sconces and one candelabra on a table gleamed off the heavy wood furniture upholstered in purple and embroidered with the family coat of arms in gilt thread.

She perched on the edge of the seat, trying to look elegant and self-assured. A lady did not slouch. A lady did not wipe her sweaty palms on her skirts or speak her mind. A lady did not swoon when a man smiled at her in just that way. Did she?

On the dressing table a silver tray contained a half-full decanter and two crystal snifters, into which he splashed the golden liquid.

The glass, when he gave it to her, had a pleasant heft to it, and she cupped her hands around the bowl. The aroma, delicate yet rich, floated into her nostrils. She cradled the glass until it felt warm against her skin.

Mellow notes of candied orange and chocolate enticed her palate as she sipped.

'It is very good,' she said and eased back in the chair.

'I thought you would like it.'

He took the seat beside her and leaned back, a picture of masculine elegance. He had been attractive five years ago, but maturity made him beyond handsome. He had an air of confidence, a presence that commanded admiration.

It left her breathless and feeling awkward, ungainly.

The way she had always felt when in the presence of beauty. And given the great good looks of Paris and Florence, it was a feeling she had known for most of her life.

While she needed both hands to hold her glass, he easily held his in one, his long well-formed fingers curling around the bowl. The other arm he rested along the back of the sofa, half turning him towards her, his gaze resting on her face.

She tried to hold her gaze steady with his, but seconds later focused on her drink. She took an unsteady sip, almost choking on the warmth that hit the back of her throat.

A coughing fit would be the perfect way to end the evening.

'What makes you smile?' he asked, his voice a darkly quiet murmur.

She swallowed. It was hopeless. She could never match his *savoir-faire*. She should just be the person she had always been.

'I almost choked on my drink. I was imagining what a mess that would have been.'

He chuckled. 'Those sorts of things always happen at the worst of moments, don't they?'

She relaxed and sank back against the cushions. 'They do to me.' She sipped at her drink and savoured the lovely warmth and flavours and inhaled the floral scents that wafted beneath her nose. 'This is indeed a very fine brandy.' She set it on the small table at her side; she did not want to spill it.

'It improves as it warms, does it not? I like it immensely. My grandfather laid down a good deal of it in his day, but my brother made quite a dint in it. Potter tells me he liked to serve it at the parties he held here.'

'Your brother enjoyed his bachelor life.'

His mouth tightened. 'He did. To the point of recklessness.'

They sat silent for a while. 'Do you miss him?'

He huffed out a breath. 'I loved the brother I grew up with. I do not miss the man he became. Reckless. Self-indulgent, I think you would call it. I did my best to make him see sense, as did my grandfather. The old man rubbed him the wrong way most of the time. I think I was wrong to leave as I did.'

'You surely do not blame yourself for his accident?'

She met his gaze and found it intense and searching. This time she did not look away.

'Your perception always takes me by surprise,' he said. 'I think if I had not left, I believe he might well still be alive.'

What would her life have been like had he not left for India? Life with a man who took one look at her and left her standing at the altar, like a fool? 'I see.'

He sighed. 'Or perhaps not. I hoped, without me to pick up the pieces of his escapades, he might see the harm he was doing, that he might finally learn to live up to his responsibilities.'

She nodded. 'I heard he was quite reckless at times.'

'Reckless and feckless and an all-round ne'er-do-well. Grandfather always said he was just like our father, a compliment my brother revelled in. And yet he could be kind and generous and understanding when the mood struck him. That was the brother I loved. The one I wanted to save.'

The pain in his voice struck a chord in her heart. Had she not always tried to protect Flo from their father? Perhaps he was not like her father and his brother. Not all men were bullies. She put her hand on his, where it held the glass. Felt the warmth of his skin and the roughness of the crisply curling fair hair. 'I doubt anyone could have predicted he would fall out of a hot air balloon.'

He dropped the arm from the back of the chair to curl around her shoulders. She relaxed into his gentle hold as a way of offering comfort. Not to mention the very pleasurable sensation of being held.

'I tell myself that.' He sounded a little wry. 'If you only knew some of the scrapes I got him out of over the years... But there is no sense dwelling on it. What is done is done.'

'And we have to make the best of a bad job.'

His grip around her shoulders tightened briefly. 'I am hoping we can do better than that, to be honest.'

She glanced down at where her hand lay over his and back up to his face. There was nothing in his face except kindness and hope. No anger. No demand for obedience. She should not judge every man as if he was her father.

She wanted to trust in him.

To take him at face value.

And she had promised to try to make their marriage work.

Even as she looked at him, trying to form an answer, his gaze seemed to heat. Her heart picked up speed. Her hand trembled.

He leaned forward. Closer. Her heart pounded as if it would jump right of her chest. Then his lips touched hers. A brief little brush. She gasped and a dart of wicked pleasure tightened her breasts.

He put aside his glass and cradled her cheek in his palm.

He was going to do it again!

She couldn't breathe.

Chapter Twelve

Everett felt his wife tremble. She was as skittish as a colt let out to pasture for the first time. All the ladies to whom he'd made love in the past, and it had been a long time ago, had been widows or courtesans. Experienced women, happy to show a young chap the way of it. That had been years ago.

And now here he was, a man married five years, with a wife who looked like she might bolt for the door if he took one wrong step.

His suspicion that she might have been giving her money to a lover had been unfounded, but it was hard to imagine that a woman as beautiful as she had not found solace in his absence.

Perhaps that was why she was so nervous.

The only one thing he could be sure of was that she had not fallen into the arms of his brother. She was not his type, in so many ways. Simon had always preferred older women. Motherly types was the way Everett had thought of them. Comfortable, easy-going and often quite stupid. Seemingly unconcerned by his brother's antics, they rarely remained in favour long.

Venetia was nothing like them. Outwardly cool and collected. Exceedingly intelligent. But there was fire beneath the sharp tongue she used as a weapon to such great effect.

Her lips parted and his body tightened at the sign of this unconscious welcome. Slowly, so as not to startle, he pressed his lips to hers, using little flicks of his tongue to encourage her to kiss him back.

She made a tiny sound in the back of her throat. A protest? He began to withdraw, but her hand went around the back of his neck, pulling him closer.

Thank God.

He stroked her cheek with his thumb. Such delicate soft skin. He increased the pressure against her mouth. She imitated his movements and when her lips parted, he touched her tongue with his own.

She stilled.

Then, as if realising what had happened, and that she liked it, she reciprocated. His heart sang with the idea that this was all new to her, that she was the pupil and he the teacher.

And guilt assailed him. How lonely she must have been all these years. What a fool he had been to abandon his wife.

With great care, he eased her onto his lap and kissed her deeply, supporting her with one hand and pulling the pins from her bun with the other. He had been wanting to see her hair free of its confines from the first day they met. It spilled around her shoulders in heavy silken waves. She gave her head a little shake as if it felt good to have it set free.

He combed his fingers through the thick tresses. It reminded him of cool silken sheets and hot passion.

Returning his kisses with fever, she angled her body towards him, pressing her breasts against his chest. Her hands moved over his shoulders and back as if she would learn the contours of his body. He wanted her hands on his naked skin.

When they were both breathless, they broke apart as if by unspoken agreement and he gazed at her rosy lips and her hazy eyes. And...

He had intended to move slowly this evening. Had intended this tryst to serve as a gentle introduction to passion.

To the devil with that. 'Hold on,' he growled and rose to his feet, with her in his arms.

She stared up at him.

'My, how strong you are.' There was a note of teasing in her voice, and a touch of bravado.

She wasn't truly sure of him, or of herself, he guessed. But she wasn't yelling blue bloody murder.

A good sign. He carried her from his sitting room into his bedroom. Blood pounded in his veins. His body hummed with desire.

With great effort, instead of racing to the bed and the bliss he hoped awaited him, he paused on the threshold, giving her one last chance to call a halt.

She was breathing fast. Her hands now around his neck were gripping unbearably tight. And not because she feared he would drop her. No, this was all about what he would do.

Her shaky breathing indicated she feared for her safety.

He reined in his desire. This was, to all intents and purposes, the start of their five-year-old marriage. A very shaky long-postponed start.

'Let us take this slowly,' he said, cursing himself for a soft-hearted idiot. 'Take our time to learn to please each other, in the ways of a husband and wife. Any time you say stop, I will call a halt to the proceedings. This I promise.'

If she said stop right now, he was going to regret his offer, and badly. But he would do it. He had given his word.

The pause, as she stared at his face, was unbearably long. The haze caused by their kisses had begun to fade from her eyes. Doubt filled her expression. He almost groaned out loud.

She nodded.

Relief weakened his knees. That she was giving him her trust in the light of her doubts was doubling daunting.

It might not be so bad, if it had not been years since he had made love, apart from in his dreams. He had set himself a task of huge proportions. And yet perhaps his years of celibacy in the face of many temptations would stand him in good stead.

Firmly, but without hurry, he strode to the bed. An enormous wooden four-poster thing. On one side, the heavy drapes had been drawn back ready. A candelabra on the bedside table gave the cave-like interior an inviting warmth. He hoped.

He kissed her briefly, sat her on the edge of the bed and knelt before her.

'Oh,' she said, looking down on him with a surprised expression. The fear on her face had been replaced by curiosity.

'Allow me to be of service,' he said, drawing on

some instinct that she would feel more comfortable if he handed her control.

He lifted her foot and with a glance asked for permission. Her small white teeth caught at her bottom lip, but she nodded.

He removed first one shoe, then the other, and pressed a little kiss to the bridge of each foot while massaging her arch with his thumb.

She made a sound of approval.

A smile curved his lips. That was the sound he wanted from her when he entered her body.

Everett continued to massage her feet, until her hands, at first clenched nervously in her lap, moved to the bed to support her weight. Her head dropped back. Her hair pooled on the counterpane.

Her expression became dreamy.

A stab of desire sent a pulse of pleasure to his cock. Blood on fire and his shaft as hard as steel, he fought to retain control over his urges.

A deep breath helped hold him in check. Slowly, he caressed her ankles and upward beneath her skirt, stroking her shapely calves. He glanced upward and discovered her watching his progress with her full lower lip trapped by small white teeth. Nervous but game.

His heart welled with a feeling of pride in this brave wife of his. He kissed the bridge of each foot and flipped up the hem of her gown, carefully folding it up, stopping occasionally to stroke the stocking-clad limbs he gradually uncovered. Finally, he revealed her knees and the dainty garters restraining her silk stockings. Such delicate items for a woman who seemed to prefer plain dresses to ruffles and lace.

'Very pretty,' he said, untying the first one.

'I made them.' Pride coloured her voice.

He kissed her knee. 'They are beautiful. Just like you.'

She made a scoffing sound.

Puzzled, he looked up and saw she was pleased, despite her reaction. He removed the second garter and carefully placed them on the bedside table. If they were precious to her, then they were also precious to him.

He rolled down her stockings and slipped them over her feet, baring her slender toes and delicately arched foot. He massaged the balls of her feet and she sighed.

A lovely encouraging sound indeed.

He stood up and she parted her legs to allow him to stand between them. Clever girl. She had sensed exactly what he wanted.

He wanted her so badly his vision had blurred.

She gave him a mischievous smile. 'Would you like help with your cravat?'

God save him. He managed to nod. 'If you please.' His voice was hoarse with passion, but he managed to hold still while her fingers undid the knot and pulled the cravat free. He stripped off his coat, and she ran her hands over his shoulders.

'Allow me to help you with your gown.' He reached around behind her neck, burrowed his hand beneath her hair, seeking the bow tucked beneath the neckline of her gown.

She leaned backwards. Obstructing his efforts. Dammit! Had she changed her mind?

'It will be easier if I stand up, don't you think?' she whispered.

Thank You, God. He grinned at her. 'It would indeed.'

He helped her off the bed, and sweeping her hair aside, she offered her back. Elegantly sloped shoulders. Pale skin. And tightly tied criss-crossed tapes that once freed from their guides revealed the stays and chemise beneath.

'No ties?' he said, surprised.

She turned to face him. 'They open at the front. Much easier when you do not have the assistance of a maid.' She tugged the bow between her breasts undone.

Guilt assailed him, and anger at his brother. But now was not the time for recriminations. 'A practical solution.'

She looked pleased. He liked the way she solved her own problems.

He pulled the cords free, and her breasts, free of their confines, stood pert and high, her nipples tightly furled buds pushing at the fine lawn of her chemise.

They were gorgeous.

He kissed each pointed peak and was rewarded by her moan of approval.

He slid her gown down over her arms to her waist, then eased it over her hips. It puddled on the floor at her feet. She stepped out of it. Pale long limbs warmed by candlelight met his gaze.

A shadow at the apex of her thighs beneath her chemise, the promise of pleasure, had his blood pounding in his veins. He stared like a moon calf at the vision before him.

She rose on her toes, gave him a quick buss on the lips and scrambled up the step onto the bed, presenting the most erotic view he had ever seen, of her bottom and quim, before she reclined against the pillows.

'Your turn,' she said with a rather imperious expression that he found enchanting.

He did not need a second invitation. He slipped out of his waistcoat, toed off his shoes and peeled of his pantaloons and stockings. Clad only in his shirt, he climbed up beside her on the bed.

'That was quick.'

He hoped the rest of it did not happen too quick. The thought cooled his ardour, just enough to stop him from leaping on her like a lust-maddened fool. Even if he was one. 'I did not want you to feel lonely in this great big bed.'

'I have never watched a man undress before. It was interesting, but not very illuminating. Your shirt is not terribly revealing.'

Her cheeky smile made his bollocks tighten. Good Lord, where was his cool distant wife? This woman was practically seducing him.

Her honest curiosity was incredibly dear and amazingly arousing.

'Then we must rectify the omission.' He kissed the tip of her nose. 'Perhaps you wouldn't mind helping me.'

He rose up on his knees and lifted his chin. She made short work of the buttons and ran a finger down the open V, a soft scrape that sent shivers down his spine.

Was he wrong about her lack of experience, after all? Disappointment rode him hard.

If so, it was his fault. He was the one who had left her to her own devices and, as he was discovering, she was a woman of passion.

He had no right to complain.

Truth was a bitter pill.

He pushed the thoughts aside. The here and now was what was important. And the future.

He pulled his shirt off over his head. Her gaze slid from his face, down his chest and lower, taking in his arousal. 'Oh, my,' she murmured. Her gaze darted back to his face and to his surprise he saw genuine concern.

He had been wrong to doubt her.

He stroked her hair back from her face. 'Do not worry. We will take it slowly. I will do nothing that you do not like. You only have to say stop, and I will do so.' He hoped.

He kissed her deeply, waiting until he felt her return his kisses, waiting for her body to relax. He let his weight press her back against the pillows, their tongues dancing and playing. Her hands roved over his back, pulled him closer, her soft breasts tantalising, brushing his skin, his erection trapped between his belly and her hip. An agonisingly sweet pleasure.

He pressed one knee between hers and he cupped her sweet quim, feeling her heat. She stilled.

He stroked her tongue with his and she parted her thighs and arched her hips into his hand. He pressed down.

A small moan issued from her throat.

He eased the tip of one finger into her hot wet passage; this time her hesitation was brief, and he pressed deeper.

He came over her and pressed her knees apart with his. Carefully, he lined up his shaft and eased himself into her. She tensed up.

He inched forward, giving her time to become accustomed to the feel of him inside her before he moved again.

Her legs came up and around his hips, and he could wait no longer.

'Hold on, darling,' he said and buried himself in her hot wet sheath.

Venetia knew the mechanics of making love—her mother had made sure of that—but she hadn't expected it to be quite so exciting.

The pinch of pain she had experienced had been minor, and instead of lying there waiting for it to be over as her mother had suggested, her body was humming with sensations, urges and desires where lying still was not an option.

The feel of Everett's naked back against her palms, the rise of his buttocks, the roughness of the hair on his legs against her inner thigh, the feeling of his body inside hers, so much—

And then he moved.

Her body tightened.

Thought became impossible. There were no words, only sensations, wonderful indescribable shivering sensations

A feeling of something just out of reach.

He raised up on one hand and looked down into her face. His expression was strained. As if he too was stretched beyond endurance.

His hips moved in a steady but urgent rhythm, pushing deeper inside her with every stroke, the sensation of pleasure building until all she could do was hold on to his shoulders and... Whatever was holding her fast seemed to fly apart, and she with it.

Pleasure rippled outward from her core, followed by overwhelming heat and exhaustion. He made a sound deep in his throat and collapsed on top of her. She couldn't move. Could not think. She felt utterly lax. Contented.

Wonder filled her.

She felt womanly.

Finally, she felt like a wife.

As her body cooled, she became aware of his weight pressing her down into the mattress, making it difficult to breathe.

She pushed at his shoulder, and he shifted away with a groan as if in pain. She felt stickiness against her thigh and was chilled by the loss of his warmth.

She shivered.

'Sorry,' he mumbled, sounding genuinely concerned. 'Got a bit carried away.' He reached down and pulled the covers up over them and snuggled up against her. 'Give me a minute or two.'

She curled into him, enjoying the intimacy, the closeness, the feel of his soft breathing tickling her shoulder.

Was this how it would be between them?

Was it possible?

If so, it was most unexpected. And quite delightful.

Did she dare trust it would last?

Not according to what she had seen over the years, with her own parents and the tales she had heard from the wives she had helped.

Both of those wives had been beautiful creatures. If they could not hold the affections of their husbands, why would she do any better? She crushed the hope that had begun to blossom.

Perhaps she should enjoy it while it lasted. It was awfully tempting.

A lassitude fell over her and she drifted off to sleep.

* * *

Sounds of movement in the room brought her to consciousness. A heavy weight was pressed down on her legs and across her chest.

His leg. His arm. Her husband was pinning her down to the mattress. It wasn't unpleasant. Not in the least.

She shifted and he rolled on his back.

Bright light flooded the bed, along with the sound of curtains being drawn back.

'Good morning, my— Oh, I beg your pardon.' His valet beat a hasty retreat and stood out of sight. 'I am sorry, my lord.'

Everett pushed up on one elbow. 'No matter, Godfrey. Have them send up tea for me, would you, and—' He raised an eyebrow and looked at her.

'Chocolate,' she said.

'And chocolate for my lady. Thank you.' He planted a kiss on her lips, sank back against the pillows and put one arm behind his head. 'Good morning, Venetia.'

He sounded very pleased with himself.

'Good morning, my lord.'

'I hope you will consider calling me Everett.'

'Good morning, Everett.'

He grinned. 'That's the ticket. Last night wasn't so bad, was it?'

Did he mean what they had done in this bed? She had thought it was amazing. Had it not been so for him?

'I met an old friend. I would have liked to introduce you. Next time.'

Oh, he was talking about the ball. She realised she had tensed up and forced herself to relax. 'It wasn't as bad as I expected.' Because of him. And not just because she was the wife of a marquess and therefore outranked almost every lady present. Dancing with him had been one of the nicest experiences of her life. She'd felt cared for. A novel sensation. But was it real or simply him using his charm to get his own way? She wished she could be sure of his motives.

The aroma of chocolate wafted into the room.

'Would you like the tray on the bed, my lord?' his valet asked. 'Or on the table?'

'The bed,' Everett said.

Aware of her nakedness, Venetia pulled the covers up to her chin, while Everett sat up and made a flat spot between them.

Gaze averted, the valet handed him the tray, deftly picked up the clothes scattered beside the bed and retreated. 'I have left your dressing gowns on the chest at the end of the bed, my lady, my lord.'

The soft click of the chamber door indicated he had departed.

The tray held everything they needed, little biscuits dusted with icing sugar, a pot of tea, a pot of chocolate and two cups.

Feeling rather shy, she sat up, making sure to keep herself covered by the sheet. Her husband was not troubled by modesty, apparently, and sitting cross-legged as he poured her chocolate exposed every inch of his naked self to her view.

No matter how hard she tried not to stare, she could not help but sneak little looks at him from the width of his shoulders, down the wide expanse of chest to the ridges of muscles at his belly and the intriguing shapes nestled amid their nest of hair at his groin.

That part of him looked a whole lot more like the

statues she had seen here and there than the enormous phallus he had presented to her view last night.

He passed over her cup. 'Careful. It is hot.'

He dipped one of the little biscuits in his tea. 'Mmm, shortbread. My favourite.'

She nibbled at the one he gave her.

'So good,' she said.

'Dip it,' he said. 'But do not leave it in the chocolate too long or it will melt.'

He dipped one in his tea and grinned with obvious enjoyment.

He was like a little boy with a treat. She could not help smiling at him. She followed suit. He was right. The biscuit melted on her tongue, sweet, buttery and chocolatey.

'Delicious.'

'I wonder what time it is,' he said when they had finished their drinks and he had put the tray on the bedside table. 'I arranged to meet a friend on Rotten Row this morning. If I had known...'

And here she was thinking he had planned this whole thing. 'Go,' she said. 'Meet your friend. I have a fitting with the dressmaker this morning. The last one, thank goodness. I need to be ready for her.'

Everett leaned across and briefly kissed her lips. 'Very well. I will be lunching at White's today, so likely I will not see you again until dinner. Do we go to Almack's this evening?'

'No. The gown I plan to wear will not be ready in time. Next week we will go. Tonight we have no engagements.'

He grinned. 'For once I am glad your dressmaker is behindhand.'

Surprised, she laughed. 'You do not care for Al-mack's? Then let us not go at all.'

'We must, I am afraid. You need to meet the patron-esses and it will not do to slight them by not attending at the first opportunity.'

She sighed. This was what she had always hated about Society. The power these so-called leaders held over outsiders like her.

He leaped out of bed, brought her robe and held it out for her to put on.

Hot all over, she slid out of bed, no doubt giving him a good look at her from head to toe. Unwilling to see his disappointment, she turned her back and quickly slipped her arms into the sleeves.

From behind, he wrapped the silk around her and tied the belt. He nuzzled her neck, holding her fast in his arms. 'You smell delicious—chocolate and lavender.'

The soft brush of his lips beneath her ear, along with the warm note in his voice, sent shivers down her spine.

She felt special. Treasured. Her heart felt too full for words.

He was a whole lot more considerate than she ever would have expected. Perhaps being married would not be so bad, after all.

She turned to face him. 'Thank you,' she said.

Puzzlement filled his gaze.

She rose up on her toes and dropped a little kiss on his lips. 'For a wonderful night.'

He looked...pleased. 'If I may make a suggestion,' he said, picking up a lock of her hair and rubbing it be-tween his finger and thumb, 'a nice warm bath will ease any aches and pains you may experience.'

Heat rose to her face. She had felt a little discomfort

down there. And, of course, he must be very experienced at this sort of thing. He probably even had a mistress somewhere.

Of course he did. Her father had.

Why did the idea make her stomach dip? She was being nonsensical. Theirs was a marriage of convenience. The only difference between them and so many others was the delay in consummating their vows.

'Thank you for the advice, no doubt based on your vast experience,' she mumbled.

Shocked at her rudeness, she fled back to her room.

Yesterday, two days after the Lawsons' ball, the last of Venetia's wardrobe had arrived. Among the gowns and pelisses had been a burgundy riding habit trimmed with black velvet. Venetia no longer had an excuse not to ride out with Everett when he had once more teased her about her lack of exercise when they had taken tea together the previous afternoon. It was the only time she had talked to him since the morning after the ball. His business affairs seemed to keep him busy morning, noon and night. She was beginning to feel sorry for him. Which was likely why she had agreed that today would be the day she would join him on his morning ride.

In her youth, she had always loved the sense of freedom going at full tilt across a meadow with Paris in hot pursuit. Those were times when she had been free of father's repressive eye. Free to enjoy herself. Not that one could gallop along Rotten Row. It wasn't done.

Everett was waiting for her in the entrance hall when she came down. He looked exceedingly handsome in a dark green riding coat and also very pleased with himself.

No doubt he was congratulating himself on his powers of persuasion.

'Good morning to you,' she replied.

She filled her plate with scrambled eggs, two slices of ham and some toast and took her place at the other end of the table. The footman poured her a cup of tea and left them to it.

'I hope you don't mind,' Everett said, 'but I have taken the liberty of organising a picnic for us.'

'A picnic in Hyde Park?' Startled, she stared at him open-mouthed.

He grinned and there was a touch of boyish mischief about that smile. 'We are not going to Hyde Park. We are going to Falmount. I thought it would be more fun if we had a day in the country. It is only a short drive, and my stable master says there is a mare there that would be perfect for you. The park is ideal for a long ride and the folly just right for a picnic.'

Of course she had heard of Falmount. It was one of Gore's estates an hour's drive from Mayfair. It was said that the previous Marquesses of Gore had not liked to be far from the centre of power and made sure of it by having houses in almost every county in England. But that Everett had organised a visit without letting her know—that was a puzzle.

'Falmount is where I spent most of my childhood,' he said. 'I would like you to see it. Unless you do not like the idea.'

There was a wistfulness in his voice. Clearly, this was something he had been looking forward to. To disappoint him would be mean. And he was giving her a choice. 'It sounds like a fine idea. I will enjoy getting out of the city.'

Everett beamed. 'We will take my curricle. It will be faster than a carriage.'

The morning was bright when they stepped out into the street to board the curricle waiting at the door. It was a very smart new vehicle, pulled by two matched chestnuts.

It seemed the new Marquess of Gore intended London to take notice of his arrival.

He helped her in and climbed up beside her and glanced up at the clear sky. 'Let us hope the weather holds for us today.' He set his horses in motion and expertly joined the traffic.

'I quite like riding in the rain,' she said. 'Though the going is slower, of course.'

He briefly glanced her way, then returned his gaze to the road. 'I do not mind if I have the proper gear. I expect there are oilskins at Falmount that would do for us, if needed. There always used to be.'

'Is it a large park?'

'Large enough. A good portion of it is forested. The riding trails provide some excellent views of the surrounding countryside.'

She gazed at him for a long moment. Was he trying to show her what she would be missing if she decided their marriage would not work? First the town house, then the ball, now the country estate. Was it some sort of bribery?

'Why?'

'Why am I taking you there?'

She nodded. 'You have gone to a lot of trouble for a morning ride.'

He stared off into the distance for a moment. 'I have fond memories of the place. It is an opportunity to visit it again. We left there after my mother died. Grandfather wanted my father and us under his eye.'

London gave way to rolling green countryside and the curricle made good speed along a road with very little traffic.

'England is lovely at this time of year, isn't it?' she said.

'It is. I missed the changing seasons during my time in India.'

'It must be very exotic,' she said, recalling the articles she had read and the pictures she had seen in books.

He chuckled. 'Very. They use elephants the way we use horses, cows are considered sacred and monkeys dance in the street for money. It is also exceedingly hot after midday.'

'What about the ladies?'

'Ah, the ladies. The colours of their saris, the patterns they draw on their skin, it takes some getting used to.'

Had he got used to it? 'Do they have balls as such, like we do? Do they dance?'

'To be honest, I was too busy making my way to go much into Society. But I attended a few dinners and balls put on by the governor. The British tend to stick together, which I thought was a shame. I was made most welcome at a party given by the local maharajah.' He glanced at her with a frown. 'I went to India to work. To make my fortune. I now wish I had spent more time learning about the people. But some of the men I knew who immersed themselves in the culture were drawn into smoking opium and hashish, a pitfall I wanted to avoid.'

'Did you make your fortune?'

He grinned. 'I did very well. And all for no reason as it turns out. But I learned a great deal that will prove useful to me now. Becoming Gore is a huge responsibility and I mean to do the best I can for the title and the estate.'

He seemed sincere about living up to his duty as marquess. It was hard to align this side of him with the man who had so carelessly walked away from his husbandly duty.

Everett could not have been more pleased that she had agreed to go with him to Falmount. He had been wanting to go ever since he arrived in England. It was where his happiest memories resided. When they had been a real family.

But it wasn't only the thought of visiting Falmount that had lifted his spirits. For the first time since he and Venetia had reunited, he felt as if they were actually talking like civilised people. Her interest in India made conversation easy.

They passed through a village on the edge of the estate. 'Not much further now,' he said.

'When did you first catch the ague that affects you so badly?' she asked.

He stiffened.

She turned her face away. 'I have no wish to pry,' she said, her voice chilly.

That experience was not something he particularly liked to discuss with anyone. He hated the way the bouts of fever left him feeling weak and as helpless as a child. And yet it was part of him now. Something over which he had no control. And if he wanted her to share her secrets with him, would it not help if he told her about this?

'Three years ago or so, I let myself be talked into a hunting expedition. There was a tiger attacking a village—actually, the villagers' children. It had taken two of them. They asked for the maharajah's help to be rid of it. We weren't friends, exactly, but we'd had a good conversation when I went to his party. I suppose that is why he invited me to go along.'

'Did you catch the tiger?'

'We killed it. He was huge, but old and apparently having trouble hunting, which was why he saw the village children as easy prey. He now occupies pride of place as a rug in the maharajah's bedroom, I was told.'

He turned off the road. Falmount's gates stood open. They were expected.

'And that is when you caught the ague.'

'I believe so. The area was marshy and the air bad. Shortly after that I had my first bout of fever. I thought I was going to die.'

She made a small sound of distress. 'To be ill so far from home and family. It must have been awful.'

'I would not wish it on my worst enemy.'

The drive was lined with trees. Any moment now the old house would come into view. 'Luckily for me my employer knew of an excellent doctor. He said it was a good thing when I told him I was returning to England.'

'Why did you not leave right away?'

'I was close to a partnership. I wanted my position secured.' He closed his eyes briefly. 'I was determined not to end up as Simon's lackey because of a dearth of funds. There it is. Falmount.'

To his relief, nothing about the old place had changed. Surrounded by wide lawns, the Queen Anne house with its warm stone and brickwork quoins on each corner offered comfort. A sweep of steps leading up to the carved stone door beneath a triangular pediment seemed welcoming. Everett followed the drive around to the back of the house where the stable block lay.

'I imagined a much larger house,' Venetia said.

Was she disappointed?

'It is one of several smaller estates the marquisate owns, much like Walsea. Traditionally, the heir resides here if he marries before he inherits.'

Samuel, the stable master, greeted them as a lad ran to the horses' heads. Two saddled horses waited nearby, a small mare and large-boned gelding.

'Everything is ready, my lord,' Samuel said. 'Mrs Moss sent word that lunch awaits you at the folly.'

'It is good to see you again, Samuel.'

Samuel touched his cap. 'Yes, my lord. It has been a while.'

Everett lifted Venetia down and her warm smile of thanks gladdened his heart, the feel of her lithe body beneath his hands another sort of pleasure. Visceral.

They walked hand in hand to meet their mounts with Samuel, leaving the lad to lead his team into the stable.

'You'll have no trouble with them, my lord,' Samuel said. 'I walked them out myself a half hour ago.'

'Thank you, Samuel.'

Everett turned to Venetia. 'Samuel was here when I lived here. He was a stable hand then. I suppose old Joshua retired?'

'That he did, my lord. He has a cottage in the village if you care to drop by.'

Everett made a face. 'We won't be staying that long, I am afraid. Perhaps next time I come. When you see him, please give him my regards.'

Venetia stroked the mare's nose and she tossed her head playfully. 'What is her name?'

'Coquette, my lady,' Samuel said. 'And the big fellow here is Major.'

Venetia smiled. 'Very fitting, I should say.'

They mounted up and rode out. Venetia looked elegant in her deep red habit. Her low-crowned hat was perfect for riding. And she sat a horse with grace and confidence.

Any man would be proud to call her wife.

The little mare had a nice gait for a lady's saddle and once they cleared the house and the outbuildings they set off in an easy canter towards the path through the woods that led to the lake and the folly on the hillside.

When they reached the open again, he urged his horse into a gallop and heard her laugh. He looked back to see she too was putting the little mare through her paces. At the top of the hill, he slowed and pulled up.

Venetia's cheeks were pink from the wind and her eyes sparkled with happiness. 'It is years since I went for a good gallop.'

He winced as he thought about what that meant. 'I am sorry you did not have a horse of your own at Walsea.'

She shook her head. 'No matter. I had no time to ride and no money for feed.'

Her words offered him no comfort. Nor should they. She should have had all those things and more besides. That she hadn't was his fault.

They walked the horses to the folly, an octagonal Grecian-columned, dome-roofed structure set on the side of the hill overlooking the lake. They tied the animals to a tree and removed their saddles. They each fetched a bucket of water up from the stream.

'They will be fine here for a while,' he said. He took

Venetia's hand and led her up the steps and into the building.

'Oh, my,' she said, looking around. 'It looks so inviting.'

A picnic had been laid out on a table against the back wall; the front and sides of the structure were open, to take in the view, and cushions had been arranged on several sofas and chairs.

'My parents used to picnic here, so I was told. Simon and I used to ride up here and use it as a fort. Many a battle were fought on those steps.'

'It is lovely. And yes, I can see it would make a great fort for a pair of boys with good imaginations.'

'I am sure you must be hungry and thirsty. Let me make you up a plate.'

He took her over to the table and poured her a glass of champagne, then filled a plate with smoked salmon, cold chicken, miniature savoury tarts and cheese. He added a slice of bread and a pat of butter. 'More?' he asked.

'Goodness me, no. I will be lucky if I can eat half of that.'

He grinned at her. 'Then why don't we share.' He poured a glass of champagne for himself and gestured for her to sit on the sofa with the best view of the house and the park.

She sat down and sipped on her champagne. 'I should not drink too much of this or I won't be fit for the ride back.'

He chuckled. 'That's all right. I'll carry you if I have to.'

'You will not.' She laughed. 'I am far too heavy.'

'Do you fear I will drop you?' He flexed his biceps. 'I assure you I have carried far greater weights than you.'

She tested his muscle with a fingertip. 'Hmm. Maybe so.'

He picked up a fork and fed her a bite of smoked salmon.

'Oh, that is delicious,' she said.

'Try this.' He held a tart up to her lips. 'Asparagus, I think.'

She tasted it and closed her eyes. 'Your cook certainly has a light hand with pastry.'

'I will let her know you are pleased.'

He popped one in his mouth. It really was good. All the food was good. The cook had clearly put a great deal of effort into the meal.

Venetia picked up a tiny pasty and bit into it. 'Mmm, that is so good.' She held one up to his lips and popped it in his mouth.

'Oh, yes,' he said. When he could speak.

They fed themselves and each other until finally Venetia put up a hand. 'No more. I could not eat another bite.'

'More champagne?' he asked.

She shook her head. 'I enjoyed what I had.'

'Sensible woman.' He kissed her cheek.

Or at least, he meant to kiss her cheek; she turned her head at the last moment and his lips touched hers.

She stilled.

And then she kissed him back. And what had started out as an affectionate peck became a kiss that made his head spin and his body demand more.

But this was not the time nor the place.

He broke away and angled himself so she could lean against his shoulder. He was not going to behave like some sort of lust-mad youth. He wanted her to enjoy today. He wanted her to feel comfortable and at ease.

She snuggled against him, as if fully understanding his purpose. For once they seemed to be in perfect accord.

'How splendid the view is,' she said quietly.

'My family was happy here while Mother was alive. Everything changed after she died.'

'I lost my mother when I was young also. It was very hard.'

'Simon took it very badly. He changed. He had always been a bit wild and a terrible tease, but he became increasingly difficult. I was always having to save him from Grandfather's wrath. Our father didn't help. He drank too much and gambled more. Grandfather was determined Simon would not follow his lead. But I think by being so strict with him he just made it worse.'

'Are you making excuses for your brother's behaviour?' she asked.

'I did then. I loved my brother. We had been close as children. He protected me from bullies at school. So I tried to protect him. But I did come to realise that by covering up for him, I was relieving him of his responsibility. It was why I chose India. I thought it was far enough away that he wouldn't call on me for help. He was not pleased at my decision, I realise now.'

'It seems he was a vindictive man.'

He huffed out a breath. 'Yes. I can see that in hindsight. Back then all I could see was the brother who taught me to fish, the friend who fought anyone who hurt me and my companion in mischief. I can't help wondering if things would have turned out differently had I stayed.'

'You will never know,' she said softly.

His gut twisted at the pain in her voice.

'Becoming the marquess must have been quite a shock.'

'I never realised just how much there is to do. I cannot believe how many people think they have a call on my time, simply because I am Gore.'

'Well, you certainly have a good spot here where you can get away from it all.'

He smoothed a tendril back from her cheek and bent to press a little kiss in its place. 'A spot where *we* can get away, I hope. A place where we can talk about any problems we are facing...'

Her breathing hitched a little.

As if there was something she wanted to tell him, but wasn't quite ready. What more did he have to do to prove himself? He bit back his words of impatience. There was time to get to the bottom of what troubled her.

Today had been a first step in his attempt to break down the barriers between them. Barriers that were his fault. But some of them were hers and until he understood them fully, they seemed insurmountable.

'It is time to head back,' he murmured, much as he hated to end their time here.

She sighed. 'Yes. Thank you for today. It was a lovely surprise.'

He took her hand and kissed it. 'Thank you for indulging me.'

He helped her to her feet.

'What about all this?' she said, looking around at the table and the cushions.

'Samuel will bring the pony cart and collect everything up. Do not worry. Nothing will go to waste.'

He walked her back to the horses and they saddled up and took a gentle ride back to Falmount.

She was quiet on the drive back to town. Thoughtful. He was happy to have it so. He liked the quiet comfortable feeling between them

Today had been a step in the right direction. They had got through a whole day without an argument.

Chapter Thirteen

Two days after the picnic the little mare Venetia had ridden at Falmount had arrived at the mews behind the town house as promised.

Since, as usual, Everett was not at home that afternoon, Venetia went down to the stables to ensure she was properly cared for. She found Samuel there making Coquette comfortable.

'You had no trouble on the journey?' Venetia asked him.

'No, my lady. None at all.' He continued with his brushing.

'You will be sorry to lose her, I suppose.'

'Major more than me, my lady.'

'Oh, dear. I did not think of that.'

'Perhaps you will come to Falmount again soon.'

'Perhaps.' She offered the little mare a carrot she had purloined from the kitchen on the way out. The mare made a soft sound of appreciation. She rubbed her neck while the mare munched happily.

'What are you giving her?'

Venetia spun around at the sound of her husband's

voice. 'I thought she deserved a treat after such a long journey.'

'There's nothing worse than an overindulged equine,' Everett said. 'Old Joshua taught us that, didn't he, Samuel?'

'He did, my lord, but—'

'No buts, Samuel. No one gives sugar to my horses.' He glared at Venetia.

She glared back. 'I thought she was my horse.'

'She is yours to ride. But I am the one responsible for her health. I am the one who must pay the veterinarian. Therefore I make the rules.'

'How dictatorial.' She gathered her skirts and pushed past him. 'All I gave her was a piece of carrot. I suggest if you intend to join me for dinner you arrive in a better frame of mind. I do not know what has you in a temper, but please do not vent your anger on me.'

Men. He must think her completely stupid if he found it necessary to berate her like a child over a small thing like a treat for a horse.

It was exactly the sort of thing her father would have done.

An evening at Almack's. Everett eyed the silk knee breeches Godfrey had set out for him to wear tonight with distaste. He hadn't been to Almack's since his first Season. He hadn't needed to go there. He wasn't the heir and he wasn't seeking a wife.

He had thought he had plenty of time before he needed to settle down. Indeed, he had decided that he would not be a leech on the marquisate and would make his own way in the world.

Godfrey handed him a starched and pristine white

neckcloth. He wrapped it around his neck and tied it in his usual barrel knot. His valet nodded his approval. 'It is not many gentlemen who can tie a cravat correctly the first time,' he commented.

Everett made a face. 'That is because they try too hard. I don't care what it looks like, so it always turns out fine.'

Godfrey made a huffing sound. His version of a polite laugh, Everett had come to understand. At least he could entertain his valet, even if he could not quite seem to get on an easy footing with his wife.

Women. He would never understand them. Take the way his wife had responded to his perfectly reasonable edict that no one feed sugar to his horses. Yes, he had guessed wrong about what she had been giving the mare when he arrived in the stables, but he would bet his best boots that she would have given the horse sugar if that was all she had to hand. Too many people did not understand that a horse was not a pet, like a lap dog. He'd seen an overindulged pony as a lad. It hadn't survived.

He did wish he had not spoken quite so harshly, however. His meeting with his banker this morning had been a bit worrisome and he had let his annoyance at Simon's misuse of funds affect his mood. And if his wife had not stomped off, he would have apologised for his hastiness.

He pulled on his britches, over his stockings, and slipped on his shoes. Godfrey eased him into his tight-fitting coats. He picked up the velvet pouch from the dressing table and tucked it in the pocket in his coat. It made a little bulge in the snug fit, but it would not be there long.

Hopefully, she would accept his peace offering and put a good face on for the evening. If they were to take their proper place in good Society and if he was to achieve success as the twelfth Marquess of Gore, he needed to observe all the political niceties, including being in the good graces of the patronesses of Almack's.

Surely Venetia would understand and make a good showing.

He went along to the corridor to his wife's room. Her maid was there tidying up. 'Her Ladyship has gone down already,' the young woman said, dipping a curtsey.

Damn. He had wanted to see her before she went down.

It was his experience that women liked to keep a man waiting and make a grand entrance. Not his wife, apparently. She preferred to sneak downstairs ahead of him.

He took the stairs two at a time and entered the drawing room where she was seated with her head bent over her embroidery.

As usual her hair was dressed plainly and confined tightly in a bun at her nape. The more he thought about it, the more he had the idea that it was the sort of hairstyle worn by a widow rather than a young wife or matron even.

She must have felt like a widow all these years. Guilt was a hollow feeling in his gut. He did not like feeling guilty all the time. The past was the past. Why could they not let it go and move on to a better future?

She rose to her feet. 'I am ready,' she said. She sounded as if she was ready for the guillotine.

'Buck up,' he said. 'It will not be that bad.'

She gave him a wan smile.

Her dress was a dark blue silk, cut modestly high at the neck and long at the sleeves with the only ornamentation a scallop at the hem. The colour suited her, despite its plainness. On her, it looked coolly elegant.

And he had known the colour of the gown she had planned to wear. Obviously, she had chosen not to wear the yellow diamonds because they would not suit.

He had known that too, having set his valet to acquire the information from her maid. He drew the little pouch from his pocket.

Her eyes widened. 'Please,' she said. 'You really do not have to—'

'Most of the jewellery that belongs to the marchioness are in the safe at Sansfaut. As marchioness, they now belong to you. You must decide which pieces you will keep and use, which should be modernised and which should be put away. These I sent for, because they were particular favourites of my grandmother. You will see them in several of her portraits.'

He tipped the pearls onto the table beside her chair and picked up the triple-string necklace. 'I think they would strike exactly the right note with that gown.'

The pearls glowed in the candlelight.

'They are beautiful,' she murmured. She put a hand to her throat. 'Far too fine—'

'Nonsense. Pearls are pearls. Let me help you put them on.'

He recalled the intimate way he had helped her into her dressing gown the morning after they made love and felt a surge of desire. He quelled it with barely a thought. He was used to keeping his ardour under control. He'd had more experience in that regard than what she had accused him of.

He fastened the bracelet, also a triple row of pearls

interspersed with tiny white diamonds, around her wrist over her glove.

He stood back to admire the result. 'Now you are ready. You look lovely, my dear.'

She blinked and looked away.

It was as if she did not like him to compliment her looks. Once more he felt left-footed. 'Shall we go?'

He held out his arm and escorted her to the waiting carriage.

Of all the events Venetia had attended in the years during and after her come out, Almack's had been the worst.

She had always been grateful that she had never been presented at the Queen's Drawing Room. After listening to Flo talk about it, she could only imagine how horrible it would have been to have been stared at and found lacking by the upper echelons of the *ton*. Flo, of course, had thoroughly enjoyed the whole thing. But then she was the reigning beauty at the time. Everyone adored Florence.

No, Almack's was definitely Venetia's worst nightmare. She had been steeling herself for this moment of entry all day until she could scarcely think.

She touched the pearls around her neck, felt the stones warm against her fingertips. Never had she seen such beautiful pearls.

Why was he being so nice to her? Was he trying to make up for his temper in the stables this morning? Father had often given her mother small surprises after he had been particularly unpleasant, as if a gift was all that was required to make amends. Her stomach pitched.

By accepting such tokens, was she consenting to his behaviour?

Perhaps she should have refused to wear the pearls.

It was too late to do anything about it now, not without causing a scene. Already the lackey at the door had glanced at their tickets and waved them on.

She took a deep breath.

Everett glanced down at her. 'Almack's never gets any easier, does it?' he said.

She stared at him in astonishment. Did he also feel a sense of dread entering these hallowed portals? Hallowed to the *ton*, that was. Before she could answer, he was leading her into the assembly room, his hand over hers where it lay on his sleeve.

Overcome by the sense of many eyes gazing their way, she had the urge to run. His hand pressed down on hers, whether to offer support or as a warning she wasn't sure. He wasn't looking at her. He was watching a beautiful lady who was clearly headed their way.

'Everett!' she said with obvious delight.

'Gloriana.' He bowed over her outstretched hand.

'I heard you had returned from India. My condolences, my dear, but it is a pleasure to see you after all this time.'

Venetia cringed. Clearly, they were old friends. Perhaps more than friends.

Everett subtly brought her forward. 'My wife, Gloriana. Venetia, this is Mrs Best, who used to be Miss Overstreet. We were neighbours growing up.'

Venetia curtseyed. 'Mrs Best.'

The lady curtsied deeper. Of course she would. Venetia was a marchioness, no longer the daughter of a lesser nobleman. She really must remember that when she was introduced to anyone.

'Lady Gore,' Mrs Best said. 'I am delighted to meet you. I have wondered about you all these years. How did you like India?'

Venetia stared at her blankly. 'I did not go to India.'

'Venetia remained here, at our estate in Essex.'

Mrs Best frowned. 'Oh, I could have sworn Gore—' She shook her head. 'Well, I am very pleased to meet you. I hope we shall be dear friends. You will call me Gloriana, will you not?'

Venetia nodded, a little numbed by the speed of this speech.

'How is Charles?' Everett asked. 'Is he here?'

Then there was a Mr Best? Perhaps she and Everett were simply friends. A feeling of relief rushed through Venetia Again, she pulled at her hand, but found Everett's grip quite firm. If she tugged free it would be far too obvious.

Gloriana grimaced slightly. 'You know Charles. Always more interested in beetles and caterpillars than parties and balls. He is off to South America next week on an expedition. I keep telling him he is getting too old for such adventures, but he does not listen.

'The boys need their father. They are becoming far more than I can manage. but if I tell him that, he would just as likely take them with him.' She laughed. 'Bless the man. Perhaps we will all go with him next time.'

'You should.' Everett glanced around. 'I need to pay my addresses to the denizens of this place. I was introduced to Sally Jersey many years ago, but I do not see her here.'

'Only Mrs Drummond-Burrell is here this evening, so far, at least. Would you like me to introduce you?'

'I would be for ever in your debt,' Everett said.

'Very well. But do not expect me to stay. I cannot abide the woman.'

Chill stole down Venetia's spine. She had met Mrs Drummond-Burrell once. The woman had looked her up and down and said, *How unfortunate*, when her chaperone had presented her for approval.

She shivered. Likely the lady would not recall their brief introduction. She lifted her chin and squared her shoulders.

Gloriana's eyes widened. She leaned in towards Venetia with a little chuckle. 'Don't let her scare you.'

The chill became worse.

Everett followed in Gloriana's wake and Venetia could do nothing but go along, when she would sooner get a tooth drawn.

The imposing figure of one of Almack's lady patrons stood surrounded by her acolytes. When she saw them approach, to Venetia's surprise she offered a cool smile of welcome. No doubt she knew who Everett was and expected to meet him as was her due.

'Mrs Drummond-Burrell,' said Gloriana. 'May I introduce you to my good friend Gore, recently returned from India, and his wife.' Having done her part, Gloriana walked away.

The imperious lady held out her hand. 'Gore. My condolences on the loss of your brother.' She turned to Venetia and dipped a curtsey.

Venetia inclined her head and waited for whatever would come out of the woman's mouth.

'It is a pleasure to meet you,' Mrs Drummond-Burrell

said. 'It is good of you to join us this evening. I hope I shall have the pleasure of calling on you.'

Venetia blinked.

The lady turned to Everett. 'You are indeed fortunate in your wife. Such elegance is rarely seen these days. Most of the young women who are introduced to me are nothing but hoydens out of the schoolroom who one cannot trust to behave with decorum.'

Venetia's jaw dropped. This sort of praise she had not expected.

Mrs Drummond-Burrell frowned at her, and Venetia braced herself. 'I have the sense that we have met before. Have we?'

Everett looked surprised.

Venetia lifted her chin. 'We have indeed. My come out was six years ago now, but we met upon the occasion of my sister's come out. Miss Florence Blade as she was then. Now Lady Hatworth.'

'You are—' Mrs Drummond-Burrell shook her head. 'You are very different from your sister. She was the Season's incomparable, if I recall correctly. I apologise for not remembering you, my lady.'

No one ever noticed Venetia when she was in Flo's presence. Why would the patroness of Almack's be any different? At least she hadn't recalled her initial reaction.

A little of the old resentment rose in her. 'You didn't give me permission to waltz, if *I* recall correctly.'

The woman tittered. The plumes in her headdresses shivered and swayed. 'Goodness me. You are a married lady. You do not need my permission.'

Everett gave her hand a squeeze. A warning to mind her tongue? When she briefly glanced up at him, she could not see any annoyance in his expression, but perhaps there was a little anxiety. Was he worried that she might be the subject of gossip?

She gave Mrs Drummond-Burrell the cool condescending smile she reserved for the village gossips at Walsea. 'It has been a pleasure to renew your acquaintance, Mrs Drummond-Burrell. I shall look forward to your call. Shall we say Thursday?'

The woman nodded eagerly. 'Thursday. Very well, my lady. I shall bring Lady Jersey with me also. I shall look forward to it.'

Everett led her away, and in spite of her very real desire to run and hide in the nearest darkest corner, she walked steadily beside him.

'I say,' he said when they had walked a dozen or more steps around the edge of the dance floor. 'Capital set down.'

Mortified, she stared at him. 'Oh, dear, was I rude?'

'Not a bit of it. You were magnificent.'

Everett's admiration knew no bounds. Venetia had very cleverly established her place in the *ton* in those few words with Mrs Drummond-Burrell. Those sorts of people would pounce on any sign of weakness. And his wife had shown her mettle.

He relaxed his hold on her hand. For a while there, he had thought she would bolt the way she had at the Lawsons' ball.

'Oh,' Venetia said. 'Paris is here. I had not expected to see him this evening, had you?'

She sounded thrilled. A pang of guilt hit him once more at what his brother had done. Clearly, his wife was really fond of her younger brother.

'I have not heard from him since we had dinner the other evening,' he said. 'Why don't we say hello?'

He walked her over to greet the young man, who gave them a pleased grin.

'My, you look very elegant, Paris,' Venetia said. She lowered her voice. 'The last time we spoke about it, you said you despised Almack's and all its arcane rules.'

Paris was, of course, dressed in satin knee breeches, as Everett was. No man who wasn't properly attired was permitted to enter, whether he had a ticket or not. It was worse than attending the Queen's Drawing Room, in Everett's opinion. Paris's waistcoat caught his eye. Fashioned of pink silk and embroidered with forget-me-nots instead of a subtle shade of grey or beige, it dazzled. Perhaps the regulations had relaxed somewhat since Everett last made an appearance.

Paris's gaze wandered across the room and stopped at a group of debutantes. 'I occasionally drop in.'

'Like that, is it?' Everett said.

'Like what?' Venetia asked.

'Your brother has his eye on a young lady.' Everett gave Paris a little jab with his elbow.

Paris rubbed at his ribs. 'Steady on, old chap.'

Venetia's eyes rounded. She looked thoroughly intrigued. 'Who is it?'

'No one you know,' Paris said. 'And besides, it is hopeless.'

'Why?' Venetia asked.

'She is the most beautiful woman in London. And her parents are hoping to snare a duke.'

In Everett's opinion none of the ladies present were more beautiful than his wife, and in the group Paris had pointed out on the other side of the room, he certainly did not see her equal.

'In fact,' Paris said, anger filling his expression as two of those debutantes were escorted onto the dance floor. 'Coming here tonight was a mistake.' He turned around and left.

'Oh, dear,' Venetia said. 'I wonder if there is anything we can do?'

The last thing Everett wanted to do was to become embroiled in his brother-in-law's love-life. Or lack thereof. But if it would please his wife...

'I will invite him to lunch with me at White's and see if I can be of assistance.' He tried not to heave a sigh, but was gratified when her expression brightened.

'Would you? How kind of you. Thank you.'

Something in his chest felt warm when he saw the happiness in her face. Perhaps this could be the beginning of a new understanding between them. Perhaps when she realised he meant for the best, she would finally trust him.

'Would you like some refreshment?' he asked.

'I would. Thank you.'

He signalled to a waiter, but the fellow sailed past them with his nose in the air, curse it. 'I will be back in a moment.'

He headed for the refreshment table and acquired the usual watery ratafia they served for his wife and some very bad sherry for himself. Some things never changed.

On his return, he discovered Venetia was not where he had left her. Devil take it, where had she got off to?

'Hello again, old chap.'

Grant. Again.

'You are the last person I expected to see here,' Everett said.

Like his brother, Grant had been absolutely scathing about attending the marriage mart.

Indeed, Everett had occasionally thought that Grant encouraged his brother to indulge in some of his worst excesses. Nonsense. Simon needed no help on his path to ruin. He'd been pushing the boundaries of good taste and good *ton* from the day he went to university.

Where he had met Grant.

Grant grimaced. 'It certainly isn't the bad sherry or the stale sandwiches that bring me.' He nodded to the dance floor. 'My niece is in town for her first Season. My brother had to return home on some estate business, so I offered to accompany his wife this evening. The one in white sprigged with forget-me-nots dancing with Cargrew. She has taken London by storm.'

It was one of the young ladies from the group Paris had been covertly watching. Were the forget-me-nots on his waistcoat some sort of message? Poor Paris. The Grants were notoriously poor. No doubt the girl was expected to reverse the family fortunes by way of a good marriage.

'Lovely,' he said. Though the girl was not to his taste.

'Would you care for an introduction?' Grant asked. There was an odd note in the fellow's voice. A strange sensation trickled down Everett's back. He glanced down at the two glasses in his hand. 'Perhaps another time. Right now, I need to give this to my wife. If I can find her in the crush.'

'Over there. With that awful bluestocking Augusta Wells.' Grant nodded to the far corner. Venetia with her willowy beauty was easy to spot. If one knew where to look. So why the devil had Grant got his eye on her?

Augusta Wells was the woman she had been talking to at the ball and who had strangely scurried off at his approach. Now they had their heads together again. Even as he watched, he saw the red-haired Wells woman hand Venetia a note, which she quickly tucked in her reticule.

'Ah, yes, I see her now,' he said. 'Thank you.'

'You are welcome. My sister is having an at-home next week. She would be thrilled to have a marquess and his wife grace her little affair. I will have her send you and your wife an invitation.'

Irritated by the man's assumption that he would accept the invitation, Everett gritted his teeth. Grant had been a good friend of his brother's; he likely felt Everett owed him such an act of kindness. For Simon's sake.

'I shall look forward to it.'

Grant beamed. 'Join me in a game of cards later, if you are in the mood to lose some guineas.' He bowed and wandered off.

He looked around. Why the devil hadn't Venetia stayed where he put her? She knew he was returning with refreshments. Irritated, he strode more swiftly to her side than he should have. He was aware of the curious glances people cast his way, but he really didn't care.

She glanced up at his approach.

'Everett.' She hesitated. 'Is something wrong?'

'I didn't know where you had gone.'

'Oh, but—'

The young woman beside her gave him a rather critical glance, her hazel eyes huge behind thick spectacles perched on the bridge of her large nose. Her pink tulle gown was the worst possible shade for her pale skin and red hair. Like Venetia, she wore a severe bun. On Venetia it showed off her beautiful bone structure, but on this woman, it merely emphasised her large nose.

'One can hardly get lost in Almack's,' the woman said, her tone sarcastic.

He handed Venetia her glass. He looked down at the young woman. 'I do not believe we have been introduced.'

The young woman narrowed her eyes as if judging him lacking.

Venetia frowned at him. 'Gore, this is Miss Wells, my friend. I told you about her.'

He bowed. 'Miss Wells, a pleasure to meet you this time.'

'You do not sound particularly pleased,' Miss Wells said. 'Venetia was telling me you returned from India with some sort of ague. She says it recurs frequently.'

'Miss Wells is interested in medicine,' Venetia said swiftly. 'I was asking her if she was aware of any medications that would help with your condition.'

'I would not call it a condition,' he said rather more stiffly than he intended. He did not like the idea of his wife discussing such a private matter with others. 'But I thank you for your concern. Come, Venetia, there is a set in need of another couple. Good evening, Miss Wells.'

He took her drink and set it on a nearby table and ushered her towards the dance floor.

'Did you have to be so rude?' she muttered.

'Did you have to discuss my private business with a person unknown to me?'

'I am trying to help you, that is all.'

He wished he believed her. If she was a little more

honest with him, a little less secretive, he might have more confidence that her motives were innocent.

Now was not the time or place to clear the matter up. Therefore, it was better he remain silent.

They did not speak again until the dance was over, and then only to agree that it was time to go home.

He put her in the carriage and told the driver to deliver her to the town house. Too annoyed for rational conversation, he went to White's.

He would explain that this business of his ague was not something he wanted gossiped about. A man had his pride. And besides, now he was in England it would likely not trouble him any longer. The episode at Walsea was probably the last of it.

Chapter Fourteen

The next morning, Venetia reread the letter from Mrs Harper. Another wife was in terrible trouble with her husband, her life in danger if she did not escape. She would not have asked, if it was not a dire situation, Mrs Harper wrote. She promised it would be the very last time she would call upon Venetia's help, since she had arranged another way to aid these unfortunate women in future.

But she needed her aid this one last time and, to do that, Venetia needed to be at Walsea.

After some soul-searching during the course of a sleepless night, she had intended to apologise to Everett for discussing his business with a woman who was a perfect stranger to him.

While it might have been out of her concern for him, she should not have done it without talking to him first. She certainly would not like it if he discussed her personal matters with someone who was a stranger to her.

Then she had received this letter. Now, she wasn't sure what she should do. The trial they had agreed to wasn't over yet, not even if she counted the week he had spent with her at Walsea. She could not simply pack up and leave. Everett would have to agree. And likely he would not. Not without a good reason.

On the other hand, if she made him annoyed enough, he might be glad to see her go. For ever. Her heart ached strangely.

Had she, against her better judgement, begun to hope their marriage would not be so bad, after all? Her chest squeezed. No, she was not telling herself the truth; she had begun to hope it might be better than that, much better.

She wanted to make love with him again. She wanted to have children. She wanted him to see her as more than an obligation.

The letter from Mrs Harper crumpled in her clenched hand. She relaxed her fingers. Smoothed it out.

The girl's life was in danger.

Everett strolled into the drawing room.

Venetia stuffed the note into the little bag containing her embroidery silks and tried to look unconcerned.

'Good morning,' he said, his voice pleasant, but his gaze dropped to her sewing bag, then returned to her face with an expression of anticipation. As if he expected her to say something about the note.

How could she?

She pretended not to notice.

'Good morning, Everett.' She kept her voice cool. After all, they had been at odds the previous evening.

He gave her a sharp look. 'You missed breakfast.'

For the past few mornings they had breakfasted together before he went for his morning ride.

Now he was acting as if she had missed some sort of required appointment.

'I overslept,' she said, lifting her chin.

'May I?' He gestured to the seat beside her.

'Of course.' What should she do? What should she say? She desperately wanted to apologise for upsetting him the previous evening. She bit down on her words. He was the one who had stormed off. He should apologise.

He took a deep breath. 'I wanted to talk to you about what happened last night.'

Her chest squeezed painfully.

Her hands shook. Her voice caught in her throat. *Her life is in danger.* 'Why did you make such a mountain out of a molehill?' She huffed out a breath, steadying her voice. 'Why, Augusta might even come up with a cure for what ails you.'

He stiffened. 'I have medicine.'

She waved a dismissive hand. 'As far as I saw, it does not work at all well. Augusta writes to a great many people all over the Continent. One of them—'

'Enough.'

It wasn't quite a shout, but it was close and the skin on his face darkened. See, she was right. He would bully her if things did not go exactly the way he wanted.

The bottom fell out of her stomach.

'Enough,' he repeated, more quietly. 'I have consulted with experts on this illness. They recommended England's air. Therefore, there is absolutely no reason for your friend to concern herself, let alone go writing to people all over the world on my behalf.'

Why did men always assume they knew best? Why couldn't he, for once, listen to her opinion? Once more he was treating her as if she did not have a brain in her head. This was how marriage to him would be. He would rule the roost and she would obey. She was a fool to think it could be any different.

She offered him a pleasant smile. 'I assure you, it is no trouble for her. She does it all the time. She really likes a puzzle. She was fascinated by your case.'

He glared at her, clearly astonished at her persistence. 'You will write to your friend and tell her to cease and desist her enquiries on my behalf, I insist.'

'You cannot tell me what to do.'

'I am your husband.'

She glared back. 'Well, I liked you much better when you were my husband in India who never once communicated with me. You come marching back to England and assume you can order me about. It is most annoying.'

He stared at her for a long moment. 'You are most annoying, madam. You do not even try to be a proper wife. No wonder no one wanted to marry you.'

A pain pierced her heart. There was the truth. What he really thought. This marriage could never work. Not for her.

'Marriage to you is the last thing I wanted. I was forced into it because your grandfather paid a fortune to my father, so as not to cause a scandal. You kept me in poverty for five years and now just because you have a title you think I should jump to obey your every demand. I never needed a husband. I proved that after you abandoned me the same day we wed. I certainly don't need one now.'

He looked horrified.

'Dammit it, Venetia. I did not abandon you. My passage to India was booked months before. I made arrangements—'

'Do not curse at me, sir.'

'You are impossible.'

'This whole marriage is impossible. I am returning to Walsea first thing in the morning.'

'Good riddance.'

He rose to his feet; at the door he stopped and turned. 'Do not expect me for dinner. I shall eat at White's.'

'Then let me bid you farewell, sir, for I doubt I shall see you again before I leave.'

He slammed the door behind him.

Venetia sat, rigid, listening to the sound of him leave the house. She would not cry. She would not let the burn at the back of her throat turn into tears. He did not deserve her tears.

This was for the best.

Everett was hot, shivering and nauseous. And lying in bed.

Another bout of the ague? Surely not so soon. He looked around him.

He didn't even know where he was. Nowhere good, from what he could see of his surroundings, dingy walls, a window covered by a curtain that drooped sadly, a spider's web in the corner of a ceiling marred by cracks and stains.

He groaned and tried to raise himself off the grimy sheets. His head spun and he sank back.

A woman he had not noticed on the other side of the bed leaned over him.

'Feeling better, are you, dearie?'

'Where the devil am I?' He sounded a whole lot weaker than he expected.

She touched a hand to his brow and shook her head. 'The Crowing Cock, off Fleet Street. Came in early this morning with a fellow who paid your shot in advance and left you here.'

Everett wracked his brains. Who the devil would have brought him to a place like this?

And why?

The previous day's event came back in bits and pieces through the haze of his aching head. He'd been at White's and then moved on with someone to a hell. Grant. He'd gone there with Grant to one of his brother's old haunts. Then someone had brought him here. But who?

Then he remembered his argument with Venetia, the way she had goaded him beyond endurance and the way he had flung out of the house, like a twenty-year-old rather than a mature man of thirty. The woman had him head over heels in confusion.

And he'd drunk too much.

He clenched his teeth when he remembered the words he and Venetia had spoken. She seemed to be going out of her way to make him angry.

A pain shot through his head. He groaned and lay back down on the pillow.

'The gentleman said as how he'd be back in a jiffy,' the woman said.

Everett shivered. What gentleman?

The next time he came to, it was to someone forcing liquid down his throat.

'Come on, Gore, swallow the damn stuff. My valet's secret recipe. Always makes me feel better in the morning.'

Paris. It was Venetia's brother. Paris. They had met in that damned hell when he was already half seas over.

Paris had told him things about his father, and Venetia. Things that had made him feel as guilty as all hell.

If only he could think.

He swallowed the stuff being forced between his lips and recoiled at the taste. 'Oh, my God, what is that?'

'Stuff that will make you feel better,' Paris said. 'For God's sake, clean up the mess.'

Paris wasn't talking to him. He must be talking to the woman. Everett recalled being violently ill, into a bucket. Dammit all

'Feeling better, old chap?'

Everett opened his eyes to see Paris leaning over him. 'Yes,' he croaked. 'Well, somewhat. I think. I could drink some water.'

The woman left the room with the bucket.

He pushed himself up to sitting and Paris held a glass to his lips. He swallowed the cool refreshing liquid. 'Why did you bring me here?' he asked once his throat felt less dry.

'Because I couldn't carry you any further and you were legless, old chum.' Paris sat on the edge of the bed. 'Your coachman will be here shortly to take you home. I didn't want to wait for him to put the horses to, in case you cocked up your toes. I don't think I have ever seen a man so ill after a couple of bottles of brandy.'

Everett heaved a sigh. 'It was more than a couple.' And he should never have drunk so much after his bout of ague only a few days before.

Paris leaned closer. 'I have been thinking about what you said about India last night.'

He had no idea what he had said, but he could hear a note of hope in his brother-in-law's voice.

'You want to go?'

'I thought I might travel. See some of the world. I thought I might wander around the Orient for a bit. Is it possible to ask you for some letters of introduction?'

If only his head didn't hurt so much, he might be able to form some sort of coherent answer. Right now, all he wanted to do was sleep. 'I'll be happy to talk to you about it in a day or so.'

There was the sound of horses below and a bit of a commotion. 'Sounds like your man has arrived,' Paris said.

Everett groaned. All he wanted to do was sleep. 'I am not sure I can.' He could not remember the last time he had drunk so much. How could he have been such an idiot? He should never have let Grant talk him into going to that hell. The stupid thing was that he had the devil's own luck and had come out richer than he went in.

'Sorry, old fellow, you cannot stay here. It's a filthy hole.'

He forced Everett out of bed, helped him into his coat and down the stairs to the waiting coach.

With the help of the coachman, Paris got him inside.

'I'll send you a note when I can meet with you to talk about India,' Everett managed to say, once he was propped up in the corner of his coach.

'I look forward to it.' Paris shut the door of the carriage and it pulled off.

Paris desperately wanted to get away from his father, Everett recalled from their conversation at White's. Because…because… Oh, God, he was going to be ill again.

He held on to the hand strap and by force of will did not cast up his accounts before the carriage halted outside his house.

To his chagrin, two footmen had to help him out of

the coach and up the stairs to his chamber. 'Where is my wife?' he muttered as his valet undressed him.

Godfrey looked at him askance. 'She left this morning, my lord. I understand urgent business required her presence at Walsea? You knew about it, did you not?' Likely they would all have heard, or heard about, his and Venetia's argument.

His heart felt strangely heavy. 'Ah, yes, now I recall.' He recalled how kind she had been when he had been ill at Walsea. He was going to miss her. He had to find a way to make her see he wasn't a complete ogre. All he wanted was for her to respect his wishes. It wasn't too much to ask of a wife, surely?

He closed his eyes and slid between the cool sheets. They would not be cool for long but he revelled in the chill against his skin.

He needed rest. Tomorrow would be time enough to decide how to handle his wife.

Somehow or other they would have to discover a way to get along.

They could not continue on in this way.

He had a duty to the title to fulfil.

The girl who arrived at Venetia's door was impossibly young. No more than sixteen in Venetia's estimation. Wide-eyed with anxiety, pretty as a picture with dark hair and eyes and far too young to be wed. What was wrong with her parents?

'Come in,' she said, taking the girl's valise. 'I am Lady Gore. Do not fear, no one will ever look for you here. You may rest here until it is time for you to board ship, tomorrow or the day after.'

Mrs Harper had promised her guest would not stay

more than a night or two. It was too dangerous. Everett had every right to follow her here, despite him saying she could return.

The girl gave a little moan. 'What if the boat sinks?'

'None of them have sunk so far, my dear. Come, I will show you to your room.'

As usual, she lodged the girl in the room the other women had used while they waited for their chance to leave England. If anyone did come looking for them, there was a set of servants' stairs leading off from a hidden door that led down to both a small side door at the bottom of the steps or, if one continued on down to the cellar, one could leave by way of the root cellar which emerged in the kitchen garden.

She would explain all of that later. Once the child had calmed down and settled in.

'While you are here, I will call you Mrs Mary Smith,' Venetia said.

'My name is—'

Venetia shushed her with a finger to her lips. 'It is better for you if I do not know your name.' It would be better if her guest did not know her name either, but after trying it with the first woman, Venetia had realised the circumstance of tradespeople calling and John's presence made it impossible. And since the women departed for the Continent, there was little chance of them revealing her secret. Not to mention that before Everett returned home, there was no one to care what she did.

She winced inwardly at the thought of Everett. He had been so angry with her the day before she left she hadn't even come home that night.

He'd abandoned her the way he had abandoned her after her wedding.

She shivered.

Clearly, Venetia would be better off without Everett. The delicious feeling of Everett caressing her feet, the astonishing sensations he had wrought when they joined together, crept into her mind, no matter how hard she tried not to think of it. Worse, every time she was alone, she remembered his smile over the breakfast teapot and the way he had teased her until she agreed to ride out with him.

And then he'd surprised her with the loveliest day she had ever had in her life, only to ruin what she had hoped was a new understanding by losing his temper over a triviality and walking away. Again.

A pang of sadness stole her breath. If she hadn't also been so intent helping this young woman, might she have better explained her motives for speaking to her friend about his condition? That she had done it because she cared?

Instead, she had goaded him, deliberately. Anyone would lose their temper after the way she had behaved. And he could have done a whole lot worse than walk away. If Lucy hadn't asked for her help, likely there wouldn't have been any sort of argument at all, because as she had discovered on a couple of occasions, Everett was actually prepared to listen to reason.

Overcome by a sense of loss, she placed the girl's valise on the bed. 'I will see you downstairs, when you have unpacked.'

She fled for her chamber. Finally, away from the possibility of prying eyes, she fell face down on her bed and let herself weep.

Life was so unfair.

To have come so close to having what she had always

thought could never be hers, a kind husband, a life of comfort and ease, the hope of children—if only the call from Lucy hadn't been so urgent...

It was too late for regrets. She'd made her decision.

The tears started to flow again. Determined to pull herself together, she got up and went to the mirror to tidy herself. The reflection that stared back at her, her red eyes, red nose, hair in disarray, reminded her of the way she had looked as a child when she realised she was ugly.

No wonder Everett had been so shocked when he saw her the first time. And yet, somehow, these past few weeks she had felt beautiful when they were together. His compliments had made her insides glow with happiness. She had felt confident by his side.

The hope that her dreams might indeed come true had seemed almost within reach. She had let it slip through her fingers.

Well, she could not continue mourning as if she'd lost a beloved.

She took a deep breath. She had a woman in her charge whom she must help escape. She needed to focus on what must be accomplished.

She poured water from the ewer into the basin and splashed cool water on her face. It was time to get on with more important things.

Downstairs, she found her guest sitting in the drawing room looking uncomfortable.

'Would you like a cup of tea?' Venetia asked.

'Yes, please. I rang the bell, but no one came.'

'I am here now,' Venetia said calmly.

The young woman looked confused. 'I meant a servant.'

'I do not have any servants.' John had returned to his

father's farm. She had not yet sent for him. She had decided not to do so until after her guest left. She did not want him to get into trouble should anything go wrong.

'Oh. I see.' The girl's face brightened. 'Then perhaps I can help you.'

Pleased at her response, Venetia gave her a warm smile. 'Certainly, you may.'

Why was it that these lovely young women were treated so badly by their husbands? They deserved happiness, not abuse.

'This way to the kitchen, Mrs Smith.'

'Would you mind calling me Althea, my lady?' the girl said. 'I feel lost as Mary Smith. And my husband—' she winced '—only ever called me "girl." I don't think he even knew my name.'

Venetia had made it a point of not knowing these young women's names. The girl looked so sad she could not refuse. 'Very well, Althea. And you will call me Venetia and we shall be friends.'

Gratitude shone from the girl's eyes. 'You don't know what it means to me to have a friend.'

'How old are you?'

'Seventeen, nearly eighteen. He married me two years ago.'

Not quite as young as she had thought, but still very young. She didn't like to ask the age of the husband. Not today anyway. The girl looked close to tears and if she started crying Venetia might well find herself weeping too.

'Let us make tea. We will both feel more the thing and then we can start planning for the next stage of your journey.'

Chapter Fifteen

It took a whole day for Everett to start to recover. A day wasted feeling dizzy and ill, but he'd awoken this morning feeling like himself. He'd even felt well enough to go for an early ride that had cleared out the cobwebs.

On his return, he headed for his study and sat down before a stack of papers his man of business had left for him the previous day. Those must be dealt with. He also must send word to Paris to arrange a meeting as he had promised.

He really did not like that Paris had been forced to take care of him. Now he was in debt to Venetia's brother.

Some of their conversation from that evening pushed into his memory. A bitter taste filled his mouth.

Apparently, at the time of the debacle, Venetia had point-blank refused to marry him. She had only consented because her father threatened to make her siblings' lives miserable.

According to Paris, their father was a bully and not above some pretty nasty behaviour. They had all had more than one beating. As had their mother.

He had felt physically ill at what Paris had revealed.

Guilt swamped him. She should never have been forced to wed. It wasn't as if they had been having an affair and she had actually been ruined. He had just wanted to appease his grandfather, who had only wanted the best for the family name.

So, he had done what he thought was his duty to the family and then he'd continued on with his own plans without a thought for the woman he'd married and how she would go on. And then his stupid brother had stolen the money intended to keep Venetia in prime style.

Why in the devil's name hadn't she written to him to demand the support to which she was entitled?

It seemed out of character that Venetia would accept such dreadful treatment so meekly.

There was no sense in going over old ground. All they could do now was move forward.

To stop himself from thinking about how badly Venetia had been treated, he focused on his paperwork. By the middle of the afternoon, after a lunch of bread and cheese at his desk, he had ploughed through most of the pile.

Clearly, things had accumulated before he returned to England, and it seemed that Simon had also not attended properly to a great many matters related to the estate. He'd been too busy enjoying the fruits of his ancestors' labour and getting himself killed by falling drunk out of a balloon.

Everett tamped down his resentment.

Simon hadn't changed. He'd just become more like his real self once Grandfather wasn't around to rein him in. And Everett hadn't been there either. Not that Everett was sure he could have stopped Simon once he had the title.

He leaned back to ease his aching shoulders and to sharpen his quill before writing to Paris. He snapped the end off the nib.

Dammit.

He poked around in the top drawer for a fresh one. Nothing. No doubt Simon rarely sat at this desk. He opened the bottom drawer. It was empty apart from the small wooden chest Everett had noticed the last time he sat here.

Curious, he lifted it out and set it before him. He found the key in the top drawer. When he opened the lid, he discovered it was full of letters.

The top one was addressed to Simon, but the return address was Walsea.

Why was Venetia writing to Simon when she had never written to her husband?

And why had Simon apparently not opened it, since the seal, a plain little blob of red wax, remained unbroken.

Should he read it or not? Well, it was addressed to the Marquess of Gore. And that was now him. He slipped a paperknife beneath the seal.

Out of it fell another sheet. Addressed to Everett.

Astonished, he stared at it. The contents nigh on broke his heart.

Dear Husband,

Since I have written to you for over two years without receiving the courtesy of a reply, I shall not trouble you again with regard to my difficulties here at Walsea. I have discovered a talent for

*raising chickens and gardening, so you need not
concern yourself about my welfare. Not that you
ever did.*

*If by some strange chance you should decide to
respond to this missive, anticipate no reply.*

*Yours faithfully,
Venetia Lasalle*

He reread the note with growing horror. What the
devil did it mean?

Slowly and with an increasingly heavy heart he read
the rest of the letters. She had pleaded with him to assist her with the maintenance of Walsea right from the
start of her sojourn there.

The first few notes were open. The rest some twenty
letters ignored, tossed in this little chest and forgotten.

He opened the earliest one. It contained a few words
addressed to his brother.

Dear Gore,

*As instructed, I am sending my communication
to my husband in the care of your man of business. Please forward his replies at your earliest
convenience.*

*Your sister-in-law,
Venetia*

If Simon had been alive and within reach Everett
would have strangled him.

Beneath her letters he found one or two of his own,
addressed to Venetia by way of the estate's man of business, Bucksted.

No doubt passed to Simon for delivery to Venetia as per Everett's request.

He recalled his disappointment that his wife had never responded to his correspondence. How quickly he had given up, while she had persisted for what looked like a period of two years.

He felt physically ill.

The letters showed how hard her life had been as she tried to make sense of her circumstances. How carefully she had eked out the few pennies she received as pin money from the marriage settlement, heating only one room, digging her own garden, cooking her own meals.

He struck the desk with his fist.

And started at the loud crash when the inkwell shattered on the floor.

Dazed he got down on his hands and knees and picked up the tiny fragments of glass. A sting of pain said he had cut his hand.

He stared at the blood oozing from his palm.

Damn Simon.

Damn himself for not doing his proper duty as a husband. Why would he have imagined that Simon would do the right thing, when he had never once done anything sensible in his life.

Somehow, he had to make it up to her.

His gut felt empty.

According to Venetia, the only thing he could do that would make her happy was to let her go her own way.

So be it.

This time he'd damn well make sure she lacked for nothing.

He closed his eyes. He'd have to talk to his cousin

about the future of the title, because it seemed he wasn't going to be the one providing the heir.

Unless, at some point in the future, Venetia took a lover. He groaned.

Oh, God, what a mess.

A full day had passed and rising from her bed at dawn the next morning, Venetia began to worry. She had heard nothing from Mrs Harper about a ship to take her charge to the Continent.

After breakfast, she would have to decide whether to send her a message. She got dressed, went downstairs and took her basket out to the henhouse to collect eggs for breakfast.

As always, collecting the eggs seemed to calm her thoughts. She felt ready to face the day. When she emerged into the sunshine, it was to see a man, knocking on the back door.

'Hello,' she said. 'May I help you?'

He spun around. It was Lucy's son.

'Thank God,' he said. 'Mother sent me. We have a problem.'

She hurried to bring him into the kitchen, out of sight of any prying eyes that might pass by in the lane.

'What is the matter?' she asked. 'Can you not acquire a berth on a ship?' She poured water into the kettle and stood it on the stove top.

He shook his head. 'Worse than that.' He made an odd grimace. 'Where is Mrs, um, Mrs...'

'Smith,' Venetia provided. 'Not yet awake. She is not used to country hours. I will take up some tea in a couple of hours.'

He inhaled an unsteady breath. 'Her husband is dead.'

'What?'

He looked ill. 'He was found dead in his bed, by his valet, on the morning she left. With her disappearance, there is talk of poison and murder. They are saying she killed him.'

Horrified, Venetia stared at him. 'I do not believe it. She is not that sort of girl.'

'Mother doesn't believe it either. But the hue and cry is on. I have a friend at Bow Street. He told me about it.'

'Then we have to get her on board a ship right away.' She warmed the teapot and added tea leaves and boiling water and brought it to the table. She set out a pair of mugs and went to fetch milk from the pantry, while he continued talking.

'That is what I said, but... But Mother says if she is innocent, we need to prove it.'

Venetia paused on the threshold to the pantry with a jug of milk in her hand while she absorbed this piece of information. She nodded. 'Your mother is right.'

As a widow, the girl would not have to leave England. She would be free to do as she pleased. Marry where she pleased. If she was innocent. She brought the milk to the table.

'What if we can't prove it?' he said. 'It is too dangerous. I do not wish to risk her life.'

He sounded completely distraught.

Surprised, she poured them each a cup of tea. When she glanced up at his face, she understood.

'Mr Harper, does Althea mean more to you than simply another woman you are helping escape a bad marriage?'

He paled. 'I love her. I fell in love with her the first day I saw her. Mother had heard that she was not happy in her marriage and invited her for tea, as she always does when she hears of such cases. I arrived just as she was leaving. She is so sweet. So pretty. I was determined to help her.'

Venetia handed him a cup of tea. 'I see. What does your mother say about that?'

'I never said anything to Mother. How could I? Althea is married.' He looked stricken. 'Was married. I cannot allow anything to happen to her.'

Her heart went out to him.

'Althea does not know of your feelings for her?'

He shook his head. 'She knows I like her. She thinks of me as a friend. Nothing more.'

'Drink your tea. We have to think what to do.'

'I know what to do. Mother is wrong. The only thing to do is to get her away. Find a ship and get her to Italy.'

How wonderful that he cared for this young woman so deeply that he instantly believed in her innocence. Even if he was misguided. 'And leave her to be branded a murderer in her absence? What if you and your mother's role in helping her escape is discovered? You could be charged as accessories to murder. It is one thing to help a wife escape her husband, but to help a murderer escape—'

'I won't have Althea put in prison.'

'Why would I go to prison?'

They turned to see Althea, pale and glassy-eyed, standing in the doorway.

Mr Harper shot to his feet.

'I— You—'

Venetia got up and led her to a seat at the kitchen table. 'Let me get you a mug and we will explain.'

'There is no need—' Mr Harper began.

'There is every need. Althea needs to understand and make her own decisions.'

She handed the young woman a cup of tea. 'It seems that around the same time you left your house, your husband died. He was found dead in his bed and, with you gone, there is a suspicion that you might have had something to do with his demise. Did you?'

Althea blinked. 'Of course not.' She turned to Mr Harper, her eyes welling up with tears. 'You think I killed my husband?'

He gazed at her with indignation in his expression. 'I do not think any such thing. It was his valet that suggested it to the coroner when he was sent for. And of course they sent to Bow Street for a constable.'

Althea looked troubled. 'I don't understand. His health was not good. The doctor came almost every day with different medicines. That was why he was so anxious to have an heir. I may not like him—' she gave a little shudder '—but I never thought to kill him. I wouldn't know how. I do not understand why they would even think such a thing.' Tears ran down her face.

'I know you wouldn't,' Mr Harper said, sounding anguished. 'We all know that, but his valet—'

'Parks?' She wiped a hand across her eyes. 'That mean old man. He didn't like me from the day I arrived. I caught him stealing a silver candlestick. Had it under his coat he did. And I don't think it was the first time either. From then on, he was always saying bad things about me to my husband. If anyone killed him, it was Parks. By now, he's probably run off with the rest of the silver.' She gazed at Mr Harper. 'Oh, no! Do you think they will hang me?'

'I won't let them.'

'I think we must prove her innocence,' Venetia said.
'But how?' Althea wailed.

Everett had stayed overnight at the closest decent inn
to Walsea. Unable to sleep, he arose at six and drove his
curricle the last five miles to confront his wife. To tell
her of his decision with regard to her future.

He wasn't happy about it, but he was hoping that she
would be satisfied.

He was surprised to see a post chaise waiting in the
lane. The post boy touched his forelock as Everett drove
up.

Was Venetia going somewhere? 'Waiting for someone?' he asked cheerfully.

'Yes, sir. I come with a gentleman who said as how he
would be back shortly. Been in there a good half hour.
If he don't come soon I is going to knock on the door. I
can't keep these nags standing around all day.'

A gentleman? Everett had a bad feeling in the pit of
his stomach. 'Hold my horses, would you? I'll find out
why the delay.'

The lad took his horses' reins.

Rather than go to the front door, Everett went around
the back. He wasn't going to hang around waiting to be
let into his own house.

The little group in the kitchen stared at him aghast
when he entered. His wife, and James Harper, who was
comforting a tearful young lady he didn't recognise.
What the devil was Venetia up to?

Assisting an elopement?

He folded his arms across his chest. 'What do we
have here?'

Venetia placed herself between the young couple and

himself, like a mother hen defending her chicks, clearly ready to do battle on their behalf. God, he admired her spirit. He waited to hear what she would say.

'Why have you come, Everett?'

'I came to see you. I had something I needed to tell you. It seems I have arrived at an inopportune moment.'

'You have. And I thought we said all we had to say.'

This was getting them nowhere, but there was a sense of panic in the room he found concerning. 'Are you in some sort of trouble?'

'Yes,' Venetia said. 'Serious trouble.'

'Tell me what the problem is. Perhaps I can help.'

'You will not like it. It is better if you do not become involved.'

He raised an eyebrow. Was she trying to protect him? It certainly seemed so. 'Whatever the problem, I cannot help but be involved. I am your husband. Surely, you understand this? Let me help you.'

He would do his damnedest, whatever it was. He just wished she would see that and trust him. It would be difficult for her, he realised, after he had let her down so badly in the past. 'I promise you, if I can be of assistance, I will. As long as no one has committed some terrible crime.'

They looked at each other.

His stomach sank. 'Venetia?'

Her expression lightened, as if some great weight had been lifted from her mind. 'I promise you, no one has committed a crime,' she said softly, hesitantly. 'But there has been an accusation.' She took a deep breath and glanced over her shoulder at Harper. 'We must tell my husband the whole story. If he cannot find a way out of this conundrum, I am not sure who can. Please, everyone sit down.'

If he had felt pride before, now he felt humbled by her show of trust.

Finally.

Everett helped her to sit, while Harper assisted the young lady to a chair. He stared at the three of them one by one. 'I am all ears.'

When Venetia had finished explaining, not just the incredible story of the young woman seated at the table, but a tale of wives leaving their husbands and fleeing to the Continent, he was flabbergasted, somewhat shocked and hugely impressed with his wife's courage and fortitude.

She looked at him anxiously at the end of her story. 'I am sorry, but I do not see what else I could have done.'

'Nor do I,' he said.

For a moment she looked perplexed, then an expression of relief crossed her face. She nodded. 'I apologise for doubting you.'

He had given her many reasons to doubt him. And because of that, he could quite see why she might not have trusted him with this sort of secret.

And that made him feel a terrible sense of loss.

Because he loved her madly.

His heart stilled at the realisation.

But now was not the time to think about his feelings. The problem before them was urgent.

'We need to think fast. That post boy will not wait much longer,' he said.

Harper turned red. 'I had forgotten all about the post boy.'

Only one alternative seemed possible. 'We must all return to London.'

Harper clenched his fists. 'You are not taking Althea back to that house to be accused of murder.'

'If she runs away, she will look as guilty as hell. But I wasn't thinking of her going back to her own house. Althea, did you give any reason for leaving when you did? Or did you just disappear from the house without a word?'

The girl's eyes widened. She shook her head. 'When Mrs Harper told me it was time to go, I just left. I might have said something about going shopping.'

Venetia frowned. 'Could we say we are old friends and met in a shop on Bond Street? I invited her to come for a visit for a day or two. Of course her husband knew. We sent a servant round to tell him.'

Everett's stomach dipped. 'I had thought to try to keep you out of this, in case something goes wrong.'

Venetia lifted her chin. A militant glint entered her gaze.

'But it is the perfect answer,' he added swiftly. 'Two old friends getting together for a gossip. However, we have to get you both back to Town without anyone seeing you.'

He got up and paced around the table. 'I have it. Lady Gore and I will travel back with the post boy.'

He turned to Harper. 'Can you drive a curricle?'

'I can.'

'Then you will drive to the Red Lion at Colchester. It is a posting house. There you will leave my horse and carriage and rent a post chaise under a false name. You will need money.'

Harper stiffened. 'I have money, my lord.'

Everett grinned. 'Good. You will travel as a married couple using another name and Althea can try to stay out of sight.'

'I have a hat with a veil she can use,' Venetia said.

'We will drive to the Swan with Two Necks and part with our post boy there, so he remains unaware of who we are. We will all arrive after dark, so we should avoid unwanted attention. I will have my carriage retrieved in a day or so. You will need to leave some funds for the care of my horses.'

'It's perfect,' Harper said. 'I will tell the post boy we won't be much longer.' He strode off.

Althea was staring at Everett as if he was the hero out of some dreadful novel. That would not do.

'You are fortunate Mr Harper came to warn you,' he said to her. 'His quick thinking made all the difference.'

The girl nodded. 'Oh, yes. He is wonderful, isn't he?'

Venetia smiled. 'He is clearly worried about you.'

Harper returned. 'He said he will wait ten more minutes. No longer.'

The girl gave him an admiring glance.

Harper grimaced. 'Lord Gore, you will have to say Althea arrived at your house the day before her husband died.'

'You can say it,' Althea said. 'But I'll wager Mr Parks will give us the lie.' She wrung her hands. 'He would do anything to get me in trouble. And your servants will know the truth.'

'Our servants are loyal and discreet. It will be their word against his,' Everett said.

'We must not give this Parks fellow time to get rid of anything he has stolen since your husband died,' Venetia said thoughtfully. 'We need to discredit his word in a way the authorities will understand. It must be proved that Parks is acting in his own self-interest. For nefarious reasons. To accomplish this, we must leave for London immediately.'

'My friend Alex, who is a magistrate, will assist us,' Everett said, 'provided he is convinced of Althea's innocence. And if I am, then I am sure he will be also.'

It was not long before they all set off on the road according to the plan.

Chapter Sixteen

The post chaise streaked through the English country-side and morning turned to afternoon and then to dusk. In accordance with Everett's instructions, the post boy changed the horses in minimal time at each stop and they got out only once to order meat pies they could eat in the carriage and to use the necessary.

Venetia held tight to the hand strap to prevent being thrown about when they hit the odd rut; she pondered the strange turn of events that had turned her husband into a co-conspirator.

She was still stunned by his reaction. She had expected him to be furious.

'I am sorry I dragged you into this affair,' she said.

Braced in the corner, Everett looked amused. 'It is the most excitement I have had for ages.'

'I should have thought India was pretty exciting.'

'It had its moments, but for the most part I was hot, uncomfortable and stuck in a room with a lot of dusty ledgers.'

She frowned. 'What did you do there?'

'I worked for an old fellow whose company shipped

cotton to England. I worked my way up from lowly clerk to being second only to the owner.'

'But surely you had no need to work? Not with your wealth and position.'

He shrugged. 'I was tired of being my brother's keeper. I wanted to make my own future. I learned a great deal. I was on the cusp of becoming a partner in the business when I was called home.'

'You did not wish to return?' The hurt in her voice made him wince.

'I always planned to return at some point. I certainly did not want or expect to end up with the title.'

She gazed at him for a long moment. 'You are nothing like your brother, are you?'

He wearily shook his head. 'No. Simon's only goal was to please himself. He was always in some scrapes or another and I was always rescuing him from the worst of his follies. He thought it a great jest that I, the person who was always lecturing him about his behaviour and saving him from the consequences, was the one forced to wed.' His lips thinned.

He shook his head slightly. 'It was one of the reasons I was so furious about what happened. Especially after the bear-garden jaw I received from Grandfather before we left for the church. That and Simon telling me you had trapped me nicely. Simon made it sound like you had plotted the whole thing, which I know now you did not, but looking back, I can see I was always a fool where Simon was concerned. I always wanted to believe him to be better than he actually was.'

He took a deep breath. 'And I am sincerely sorry that you were dragged into my brother's stupid scheme.'

'So am I.' But it was water under the bridge, wasn't it?

His mouth tightened. 'I will see to it that you have the freedom you desire. It will take time to arrange a divorce. But I will set the wheels in motion.'

Her heart seemed to twist painfully.

Now that she had learned that she could trust him, that he wasn't anything like her father or his brother, that he was a good and kind man, he intended to be rid of her.

Why would she be shocked? After all, she told him, more than once, she never desired this marriage any more than he had. Now he thought he was giving her what she wanted.

She could not see forcing him to remain in a marriage he did not want.

'Thank you.' She realised she did not sound quite as grateful as she should have done. She wasn't grateful. She had the same disappointed feeling she had had all those years ago on her wedding day. But she had been young then, and naive.

Now she was neither.

'It is what you want, isn't it?' he asked, clearly surprised by her lack of enthusiasm. 'Your independence. You mentioned it in your letters repeatedly.'

She lifted her chin. 'You read my letters? Then why did you never reply?'

'I only discovered their existence yesterday. I found them in Simon's desk.'

He had never received her letters? 'Did your brother hate me that much?'

'I doubt it was anything to do with you. Or me. He was only thinking of himself. Of his need for money.'

She tried to recall exactly what she had said in those letters. She did recall that she had been extremely cross with her husband when she wrote them.

'I see.'

He gave a slight sigh. 'Once we are past this little debacle, you will have your precious independence.' He frowned deeply. 'I would, however, ask you to promise not to continue with these activities. It is far too dangerous.'

'Rescuing wives from their horrible husbands, you mean?'

'Yes.'

She shook her head. 'I am sorry. I cannot make that promise. All I can think of is the way my father treated my mother and what an awful life she led. If I can help women like her, then I will.'

He gazed at her, and there was understanding, perhaps even sympathy, in his expression. 'Very well. Then do this instead. Take care you do not get caught. I would not have you end up in prison. I might be able to help save this girl today, but you might not be so fortunate in future, and I dread to think of the consequences you might face.'

Prison. Or deportation. Or perhaps worse. He dreaded to think of them? He was worried about her? He looked worried. A pang in her chest stole her breath.

'I will not take unnecessary risks, I promise.'

'Thank you.'

Divorce. The word echoed in her mind. If anyone had told her a month ago she could have anything she wanted, she might well have asked for a divorce. Now the prospect looked less than inviting.

Everett paid off the post boy and organised the retrieval of his carriage while Venetia went indoors and made the necessary arrangements for the arrival of their guest.

Everett shook his head at the circumstances in which he found himself. Of all the things he could have imagined, helping wives escape their husbands was not one of them. And yet, after what he had learned about her this past week or two, he should not be surprised. She was a woman who had never let life's hardship steal her courage. And nor would she stand by and let others suffer if there was a way she could help.

All these years, he'd had a treasure under his roof he had not appreciated. Worse, he, who prided himself on his sense of duty and honour, had let her down badly. He clearly did not deserve her.

He watched his groom mount up. 'You will find the team at the Red Lion in Colchester.'

The groom touched his hat and trotted out of sight.

The next step in his plan was to visit his magistrate friend, Alex, but first he needed to bathe and have something to eat. He was starving.

He trotted upstairs.

By the time he was ready to go downstairs again, he had been informed that Venetia had ordered supper to be served to them in the breakfast room. She was waiting for him when he entered.

He sat down and looked at the spread before them. A meat pie, a cold leg of roast beef, a plate of steaming mashed potatoes and a blancmange with custard.

'You are a miracle worker,' he said.

She smiled, looking pleased. 'Would you like tea, or something stronger?'

'Tea will be the best. I don't want to drop off to sleep before I complete the rest of my plan tonight.'

At her puzzled look, he explained, 'I will visit Alex before I go to bed. I believe we do not have a moment to waste if we are to bring this off successfully.'

'It is very good of you to take so much trouble for a girl you do not know.'

'Not really. To be honest it makes me furious to think of these men who treat their womenfolk so badly. They deserve a good hiding.'

Surprise shone from her eyes before she looked down at her plate, hiding her thoughts from him. 'According to the law, they have every right to do what they do.'

'Then the law needs changing.'

She put down her fork, finally meeting his gaze full on. 'Do you mean that?'

'Of course. Men are supposed to protect the ladies in their care, not cause them harm.'

Disappointment replaced surprise. Her voice turned cold. 'I see.'

Now what had he said? He was agreeing with her, wasn't he?'

Every time they had one of these conversations they ended up in this state of chilly silence. The only time that had not happened was the one time they had made love. But on that occasion they hadn't talked at all.

His body hardened.

He cursed inwardly. She was the only woman he had come across since his teen years who could make him react that way with a simple thought.

Better to stop thinking. They were going to part very soon. He wasn't looking forward to making the arrangements. She had said she didn't care about her reputation, but he wasn't going to have her ostracised through no fault of her own. He would have to talk to her brother. He would have to find a way to have the blame placed squarely on his shoulders.

The thought of a trial in the House of Lords sent a cold feeling down his spine.

Also given that they had made love, they would need to be sure there were no consequences before moving ahead. Which meant they could not allow the attraction between them to overcome their good sense.

And since these thoughts were beginning to give his body ideas, it was time he left.

'Thank you for supper. I really must go to see Alex before he retires for the night. You must be tired after such a long journey. Let Mrs Kraft look after Althea when she arrives and take yourself to bed.'

The thought of his wife in bed was too much.

Venetia shook her head. 'I think she will be less nervous if I am here to greet her.'

'Then I will leave her in your capable hands.' He bowed and left before he suggested a different way to spend what was left of the evening.

A brisk walk to Alex's house would set him to rights. He hoped.

When the butler showed him into his friend's house, he found Alex in a small cosy room set in the back of the house, cigar in one hand and a brandy in the other.

He grinned when Everett strolled into the room. He waved a hand. 'Have a seat, old fellow. Smithers, give Lord Gore a brandy and take yourself off.'

Everett winced. His friend was a couple over the eight apparently. He might not be of much help in this state. But the matter really could not wait.

He took the brandy from the butler, who made his escape with alacrity.

'What brings you here at this time of night?' Alex asked once they were alone.

'I need your advice. And your help.'

'Anything, old chap. Name it.'

Everett had been tossing over in his mind just how to approach such a delicate matter, but given his friend's state of drunkenness he decided plain and simple was the best approach.

'A friend of my wife's has got herself in some hot water.'

Alex straightened in his chair. His gaze sharpened. 'What sort of trouble is she in?'

Everett grimaced. 'She is accused of murder. Which I believe she did not commit,' he added hastily at the look of shock on Alex's face.

He explained the details and sat back, waiting for Alex to process the information.

'We need to question the valet.'

'Yes.'

'Do you know who is investigating the case?'

'I do not. I only heard about it this morning and, as bad luck would have it, I wasn't in London and had to drive back post-haste.'

'Where did the crime occur?'

Everett provided the address.

'Hah, you are in luck. I have friends in that ward. Let us go and see what sort of ants' nest we can stir up.'

'Are you sure you are in any fit state to go tonight?' Everett asked, surprised by the burst of energy displayed by his friend.

'It is just what I need to get me out of the dumps, old fellow.'

'What has put you in the dumps?'

'A woman. What else? But it's a long story with a sorry ending. Not something any man of sense needs to hear. So, let us be off.'

Althea's arrival had gone without a hitch the previous evening to Venetia's enormous relief.

She headed down for breakfast.

It was strange that she had not heard a word from Everett this morning. Likely he was sleeping late; she had heard him return to his room at around three in the morning.

She had been very tempted to satisfy her curiosity right then and there, but she had decided against it. If there was something wrong, she was sure he would let her know immediately.

And besides, entering his room in the middle of the night was fraught with too many dangers, now they had agreed to separate.

The tightness in her chest increased. It had been doing that since the moment he suggested they divorce. When her father found out... She shivered.

'Good morning, my lady,' the footman at the bottom of the stairs said. 'His Lordship's compliments, he asked if you would join him in his study after breakfast.'

Clearly, Everett was up already.

Her mouth dried. Was something wrong? She would not be able to eat for worrying. She went straight to the study where she found him closeted with a gentleman she thought she recognised. One of Everett's friends to whom she had not yet been introduced.

The two men rose as she entered. Everett looked so handsome, despite his obvious tiredness. Tired because he was now embroiled in her scheme and surprisingly willingly. Knowing he was prepared to help gave her a warm feeling in her chest. 'Good morning, Gore.'

'Venetia, this is a good friend of mine, Alex Paxton, the magistrate friend I spoke of.'

She greeted Mr Paxton, and Everett gestured for her to take a seat.

She hoped she did not look as worn down as he did, though after such a restless night, there wasn't much chance.

'You have news?' she asked.

'We do.' Mr Paxton looked very pleased with himself. 'A great number of items were found in the valet's dwelling. And not just from his current master's home. It seems he has been doing this for years. Why he would steal so many items and then keep them, I do not understand.'

'It gave us the upper hand, however,' Everett said.

Paxton nodded. 'To save himself from prosecution for theft he admitted that when he saw Mrs Wren leave the house with her valise, he immediately told her husband of her departure. The old gentleman was furious. Wren put plans in motion to have her found and brought back before retiring for the night. He was perfectly well when the valet helped him to bed. It is the doctor's opinion he simply died of old age.'

'Is it possible that she will be accused of leaving poison in his nightcap or something?' she asked. 'Poison he drank after she left?'

'We thought of that,' Everett said. 'There was a glass of water beside the bed. The doctor after smelling and tasting it confirmed that it was nothing but water. I even went so far as to take a sip with no ill effects.'

'You what?' Appalled, she stared at him. 'How could you? The valet or someone else could have put something—'

'I doubt it, Lady Gore,' Paxton said. 'The death of his master was the last thing Parks wanted. There were still a great many valuables left in the house for him to pilfer, something he could not do once his master died. It seems he had begun to think of those things as his own. He finally admitted his mistress had caught him stealing and he suggested she poisoned her husband as a means of revenge.'

'Unconscionable,' Everett said.

'Indeed,' Alex said.

'What happens now?' she asked.

'Alex will accompany Mrs Wren home to explain her absence to the magistrate in charge of the case. The valet has been dismissed, having been required to return everything he stole, and Mrs Wren can go about her day as usual. But as a widow not a wife.'

'Althea, Mrs Wren, will be thrilled at this news,' Venetia said. 'Thank you. I will bring her down to you.' She got up.

Alex and Everett stood as she left.

Her mood plummeted. Now there was absolutely no reason for her and Everett to remain together. Really? Was she thinking of herself at a time like this? How selfish. The most important thing was that Althea was safe.

She ran upstairs. The young woman was sitting up in bed with a tray on her lap. It looked as if she had barely touched a morsel of food.

She gazed at Venetia anxiously. 'Have they come to arrest me?'

'No. Do not worry, my dear. Everything has been sorted out and your husband's valet has admitted to fabricating the whole thing. You may go home in peace.'

Althea burst into tears.

Venetia sat beside her on the bed and put her arms around her. 'There, there. It is over. You are perfectly safe.'

Slowly, the young woman ceased her sobbing and dried her eyes. She gave Venetia a rather watery smile. 'I cannot thank you enough for all you have done for me.'

Venetia patted her hand. 'It is my husband who has done the most, my dear. He has helped prove your innocence without a doubt. Now, it is time for you to dress and go home.'

She rang for the maid and soon Althea was on her way home with Alex and Venetia's maid as her escort.

Venetia took a deep breath. Everything had ended far better than she could have hoped, thanks to Everett's help.

He was a kind and honourable man. And she was going to miss him terribly.

Chapter Seventeen

Everett took a deep breath and entered the drawing room where he had been informed by the butler he would find his wife.

As she was so often, she was absorbed in her needle-work. She looked up upon his entry and smiled. 'Will you ring down for tea?' She glanced at the clock on the mantel. 'It is about that time.'

'Tea would be excellent.' He rang the bell and sat beside her. 'What are you working on?'

She coloured. 'A pair of slippers. A gift.'

Slippers for a man, judging by the dark colours. 'Who are they for? Your brother?'

'Paris?' She sounded surprised. 'No, I was making them for you. I noticed that the ones you wear are quite worn out. I thought you might like new ones.'

'For me?' That he had not expected.

'I had intended them as a surprise, but perhaps it is better that you know about them, so you do not buy any.'

'It is a surprise,' he said. 'A very nice one. Thank you.'

Her smile in answer held sadness. For some reason

his heart gave a little skip of hope. He cursed the foolish organ.

The butler entered, set the tea tray down before her and left.

The tea she handed him tasted perfect. After a restorative sip, he braced himself to address the matter that had brought him here. 'We need to discuss our next steps.'

'Next steps?' There was an odd nervousness in her voice.

'How to proceed with our separation. Our divorce. It will not be easy. After an incident of infidelity, which must be witnessed, there will be a trial in the House of Lords. None of this will happen very quickly.'

She looked anxious. 'I suppose it will create a terrible scandal.'

'A horribly messy one. Neither of us will come out unscathed, but I shall do my best to shield you from the worst of it.'

'You think divorce is necessary?'

'If you want the freedom to live your life the way you see fit.' He shrugged. 'I will set things in motion the moment we are sure our…lovemaking did not result in progeny.'

'Oh, my goodness. I had not thought about… Do you think it might have?' Her eyes were wide with worry.

He had not expected her to be quite so innocent of the consequences of their passion.

But then how could it be otherwise when she had barely had any experience as a wife and had been locked away in a backwater for years? Guilt wracked him.

He prayed his lack of control wasn't going to ruin any chance she might have for the happiness she deserved.

'It is certainly not impossible. I regret…'

The surprise turned to dismay. She looked down at her hands pressed tightly together in her lap.

'Venetia. My dear. I do not regret what we did together. It was more than lovely. I simply do not want what we did to ruin your hopes for your future.'

'Oh,' she said softly. 'I see.'

'As my marchioness, you certainly would not be able to continue to help women like Althea to escape their husbands.'

'I am glad you agree it is important work.'

'Without a doubt, though I fear you will find yourself in hot water if the authorities ever discover what you are doing. To be honest, I am infuriated at the thought of these men getting away with the abuse of their wives. They are the ones who deserve to be punished. If such a thing could be accomplished within the confines of the law. Though it will not happen quickly, I plan to work to see it done.'

'You do?'

'Of course. For any man to harm the woman who is his to care for, well, it is wrong. I become angry thinking about it.' He took a deep breath. 'When I think of how badly you were treated…' He hung his head. 'You cannot know the burden of guilt I bear. I will do everything I can to make up for the wrong I did.'

She did not look happy. 'I shall return to Walsea tomorrow.'

He shook his head. 'If you would not mind waiting a day or two, I would like to rest my horses before they make the journey.'

'Oh, you do not need to concern yourself with that. I can go by mail or stage. I have done it before.'

'I am not having my wife, and you are still my wife, travelling by common stage. It is not safe.'

She stiffened. Her chin came up.

'I would only worry the whole time,' he said hastily. 'Indeed, I would have to travel with you, if you choose that mode of transport.'

She relaxed and there was a gleam of mischief in her eyes. 'Shall I arrange for the tickets, or will you?'

He laughed. 'Don't be brattish.'

She chuckled. 'Very well, I shall do as you ask and wait for a few days.'

'It will give you time to shop and time to pack.'

She frowned. 'Oh, dear, there are all these clothes I bought for the Season. I am sure I will not need them at Walsea.'

She intended to return to her hermit way of life. It made him feel sad. 'Take them. You might find a use for them in time. I will see to any repairs required for the house and there will be sufficient funds for you to pay the staff John has been busy hiring.'

'You have thought of everything.' She seemed disappointed. Perhaps she thought he was interfering too much.

'If you prefer, you can meet with Bucksted yourself. Tell him what you else you need. You will find him very competent.'

'Oh, no. I am sure everything you have arranged will be perfect.'

He nodded briskly. 'Then it is settled. All we need is confirmation that there will be no child.' He had decided not to ask her to reconsider her departure. He did not want her to feel under any pressure. Struggling to hold the words back, he strode for the door.

He paused on the threshold. 'Would you care to go to the theatre this evening? I know it was the one thing you were actually looking forward to attending.'

She looked puzzled. 'Are you sure you want to?'

'I would like to go, if it would please you. You have done a great many things to please me.'

She beamed with delight and as always when she smiled, her loveliness shone through. 'Then yes, I would like to go.'

His heart warmed at her pleasure. 'Excellent. I will see you at dinner.'

He wasn't sure he could wait until dinner to see her again. But he must. The hope he had felt earlier forced its way into his mind. Perhaps they could enjoy a nice evening together. It would make for a good memory after she left.

After a day closeted with the two men his brother had employed to run his affairs, one with regards to the estate and the other to deal with his less savoury activities, Everett had come to an agreement with both of them. He had paid off the second and moved all responsibility to the former, Mr Bucksted.

There were still some loose ends left over from some of his brother's escapades but Bucksted, despite his distaste, had agreed to deal with them with great discretion and kindness.

Including looking after the well-being of his wife.

He had had a rather uncomfortable meeting with Bucksted after Week had left. The old gentleman had been appalled about the plan but had been forced to agree that the treatment of Venetia had been shocking and he would do all in his power to assist with rectifying the matter.

And now Everett was looking forward to spending an evening in her company with the clear conscience of a man who knew no women were left destitute and no children left without a decent future. Something he had discovered, to his horror, that Simon had not been able to say.

Although there was an underlying sadness that this would likely be the last time they would spend an evening together as husband and wife.

He entered the drawing room. The footman poured him a glass of sherry. He nodded to the fellow. 'Thank you. No need for you to stay. I will pour for Lady Gore.'

The footman bowed and left.

He did not have to wait long for his wife. She looked stunning in a gown of mint green embroidered with birds of paradise and adorned with lace. Her hair had been dressed in a most fetching fashion, unlike her usual neat plain bun, and at her throat she wore the yellow diamonds. She looked regal yet somehow vulnerable.

'You look lovely,' he said. 'I shall be the envy of every man at the theatre tonight.'

She coloured delightfully and shook her head. 'You are very kind.'

'May I pour you a glass of sherry?'

'Thank you.'

When he handed her the glass he felt her hand tremble slightly.

'Is something wrong?'

'Oh, no. Not at all. Why do you ask?'

'You seem a little nervous.'

'As to that, I suppose I am. I feel a bit of a fraud, to

be honest. Knowing that we are soon to part and yet we are going about as if nothing is wrong.'

'We are going about as friends. What is wrong with that? And besides, it is no one else's business what we plan to do. The present is all that counts.'

She sipped her sherry thoughtfully. 'I suppose you are right. We have become friends, have we not?'

The words hurt more than they should have. Because he should have been so much more than a friend. He drew in a breath. 'I will always be your friend, Venetia. Always. If you ever need anything you may always rely on my assistance.'

She looked away. 'Thank you,' she said softly.

Dash it, now what had he said to upset her?

'Dinner is served, my lord,' the butler announced.

They walked into the dining room arm in arm. Her hand was not shaking at all now.

He felt a sense of pride that he had managed to settle her nerves.

When they were seated, he was pleased to see that she had arranged for them to be at one end of the table and beside each other on the corner.

Once the dishes were placed on the table, he dismissed the servants. 'We can manage to serve ourselves,' he said to Potter.

She looked pleased. 'The servants will be glad. It will mean they can have an early dinner.'

'*I* shall be glad. I will have you all to myself.'

Puzzlement filled her expression. 'Was there something else we needed to discuss?'

She didn't have a flirtatious bone in her body. He wanted to kick himself for acting like a lovesick fool. 'No. I simply enjoy your company.'

She blushed.

Perhaps she wasn't completely immune to a bit of flattery. They filled their plates with roasted chicken, peas, boiled potatoes, a fish in creamy sauce and assorted vegetables all cooked to perfection.

She picked up her wine glass and sipped the white wine he had poured.

She gave him a quick glance and there was uncertainty in her gaze. 'There was something I wanted to talk to you about. I wasn't sure if I should.'

It served him right that she did not feel comfortable saying what was on her mind. 'I am all ears,' he said with an encouraging nod. He savoured another mouthful of the fish. The chef had excelled himself. With the help of his wife, of course, for she would have chosen the menu.

'I mentioned Miss Wells's interest in all things medical.'

She cut and ate a small portion of the chicken.

'You did. And I reacted badly. I shall not do so again.'

He took a sip of his wine. He would let her unfold her story at her own pace, since beneath her calm words he sensed some sort of tension, excitement, perhaps.

'One of them, a Professor Gomez in Portugal, indicated he thought he might be close to making a new medicine for the sort of ague from which you suffer.'

This again. She looked so animated, so pleased, he tamped down his irritation. She was trying to help him and he ought to be grateful. As she had so rightly pointed out last time, he wasn't the only person who suffered from this debilitating affliction.

'He has discovered a cure?'

'He believes he has isolated crystals from fever tree bark that, produced in its purest form, may well be a cure. I have asked her to ask him if it can be purchased. Of course, I asked her not to reveal your name, or indeed make any commitment to buy, until I had spoken with you.'

Could this indeed be the medicine he needed? The one supplied by his doctor helped, but it was not a cure. 'I was wrong to take you to task for discussing my illness with your friend, Venetia. You meant for the best. And if this proves to be a cure, it will be marvellous for me and many others who suffer.'

'It would be. I will keep you informed, shall I?'

'I would be most grateful if you would.'

Her obvious delight in his reply pleased him no end.

Dinner had been excessively enjoyable. Venetia had been glad she had taken her courage in hand to address the issue of the possible new medicine.

Now, sitting beside Everett in his Covent Garden theatre box, she felt more contented than she had felt in a long time. Not to mention it was the first time she had seen *Hamlet* performed.

She glanced over at him, lounging in the seat beside her, and was surprised to meet his gaze.

He leaned forward and whispered, 'Are you enjoying it?'

'I most certainly am.' She turned back to the performance. But for a few minutes she was very aware that his gaze seemed more focused on her than it was on the stage. Gradually, she became so absorbed in the play, his regard no longer caused a distraction.

The curtain fell on the last act and the audience applauded loudly.

'Do you want to stay for the farce?' Everett asked. 'If

so, I will obtain some coffee for us, but we can expect to be inundated with visitors during the intermission.'

Something she did not want to face. The thought that once their divorce proceedings started, these same people would revile her and possibly Everett did not sit well in her heart. For herself, she did not care, but it was bound to cause Everett some heartache, she was sure.

She had very carefully avoided catching anyone's eye during the performance, but she had felt their critical eyes upon her from the boxes on the other side of the theatre. No, she had been enjoying herself. She did not want to spoil the evening.

'I would rather go home,' she said.

He grinned that charmingly boyish grin that sometimes appeared when he was flouting the rules. Her heart missed a beat and she smiled back.

'Yes, I would sooner go home too,' he said.

They departed from their box. Already the corridors and the saloons were filling with people eager to get a cup of tea or coffee and a slice of cake.

Everett easily cleared a path for them, and they returned home in their carriage, while having spirited discussions about the play and its actors.

'Perhaps you would join me for tea in the drawing room before we retire,' she said. 'I don't feel at all sleepy.'

Everett handed his coat to the butler. 'I will join you, but I would prefer something a little stronger. Bring the brandy to Her Ladyship's drawing room along with the tea, will you please, Potter.'

'Yes, my lord.'

They climbed the stairs to the first-floor drawing room and sat facing each other across the hearth. 'So, you have no sympathy for Ophelia,' Everett said, continuing their conversation from the carriage.

'None at all. Had she had a bit more fortitude she might even have saved Hamlet from dying. It was her pride that caused her death. Too much death altogether, I have always thought.'

He chuckled. 'But then we would be looking at a very different sort of a play.'

Potter arrived with the tray, which he set in front of Venetia. He poured a glass of brandy for Everett before he left.

Venetia poured tea for them both. 'Yes, I suppose it would be a different kind of play,' she said. 'But it would also be much more satisfying. Although, I suppose, given his heroism, Fortinbras is ultimately the most deserving of the title of King.'

'As in real life, it is not always the most deserving who inherit the title.'

'Are you thinking of yourself and your brother? In my opinion, it is finally right.'

'Why, thank you, my lady. I take that as a compliment.' He tossed off his drink.

'A deserved one.'

He gave her a long look. The air seemed to heat. Her skin prickled all over. She put down her cup lest she spill it, her hand trembled so hard.

'I think it is time I retired,' she said, suddenly breathless.

He closed his eyes briefly and nodded. 'Yes. It would likely be a good idea.' He rose and bowed. 'Thank you for your company this evening. I cannot recall when I have enjoyed the theatre more.'

She dipped a curtsey and fled.

When she entered her room, Green was waiting to help her to bed. Once in her nightgown she sat on the dressing room stool and the maid brushed out her hair. The rhythm of the gentle strokes allowed her mind to wander free.

She recalled the way Ophelia's hair had also hung free and beautiful in the play. Venetia's hair had always been her only beauty. Her one source of feminine pride. It was why she kept it severely dressed, she realised. She didn't want to hear any criticism of what she considered her only attribute.

She also recalled there was something she ought to tell Everett, which if she had not been too proud she would have mentioned during their talk about the future.

It wasn't that she had lied to him, but she had let him think something that she should not have.

She already knew that she was not with child. But to say it right then and there meant she would have made the end of her marriage seem that much closer. Which was ridiculous.

She had to tell him the truth. Because the longer she was in his presence, the less she would want to leave, and where would she be then?

Married to a kind and generous man.

It was too late for that. She had repeatedly told him she wanted her freedom. How would it look if she changed her mind? He would think she was after his title or his money or something.

Her thoughts went back to her earlier words about Ophelia. Was she, Venetia, making the same mistake? Was it her pride that refused to allow her to acknowledge that she didn't want to leave her husband? Pride that refused to let her admit she was wrong?

Venetia took a deep breath. 'That will be all, thank you, Green.'

'Your Ladyship does not wish me to braid your hair tonight?' Green asked.

'Not yet. I have a bit of a headache. It will feel better loose.'

'May I fetch you a powder or a tisane, my lady?'

It wasn't a powder or herbal tea she needed. It was something completely different.

And she wished the dashed maid would stop offering to help and go away.

Chapter Eighteen

After his wife left the drawing room, Everett poured himself another glass of brandy. A portrait on the wall caught his eye. A family portrait of his mother, father, brother and himself. He must have been about eight at the time. It was typical of many portraits he had seen over the years of noble families. It all looked perfect.

He took a swig of his drink.

It had likely been the last perfect moment. His mother had died, followed a couple of years later by his father, leaving him and his brother to be brought up by their grandfather.

Now they were all gone, except him, and he had made a right royal mess of his marriage.

He finished the brandy in his glass and poured another. He sprawled on the sofa and stared into his drink. If he drank this one he was going to be nigh on half seas over.

He groaned. There was too much to do. Too many responsibilities for him to be getting drunk and sleeping the day away. He put the glass on one side and made to rise.

The drawing room door opened and admitted his wife, looking like a siren with her hair around her shoulders and wearing a loose flowing nightgown. Was it some sort of dream? Was he more drunk than he had thought?

'Venetia?' His voice sounded like a frog croaking.

'It is I.'

'I thought you went to bed.' He shook his head to clear it. He wasn't making any sense.

'I did. I recalled something I needed to tell you.'

She drew close and the scent of lavender invaded his nostrils. Her hair hung down her back like a river of bronze. He could only think of that night two weeks ago when he had seen her hair down.

'Can it not wait until the morning?'

She flinched slightly.

Dammit. 'I mean, you are standing there looking for all the world like some nymph from another world, as tempting as the devil, and I am not sure I can control my baser urges. In truth, we already know I cannot.'

Instead of running for the hills, she gave him a shy smile and stepped closer. 'That was why I came.'

A man did not need more of an invitation than that.

She was within arm's reach and to the devil with it; he caught her about the waist and pulled her close, inhaling her scent and rubbing his cheek against a silky ribbon of hair.

She raised her face and put her arms around his neck. He kissed her deeply and long until his head spun. With desire. With longing. With hope.

He tilted her face up to meet his gaze. 'This is why you came?'

She nodded, her gaze hazy and soft. If he took her upstairs, she might well have time to think better of what they were doing; indeed, she probably should, but—

He scanned the room, picked her up, carried her to the sofa and sat down with her astride his lap.

She looked surprised.

Well, she would. His wife was an innocent, more or less, but there was no sense in not expanding her education. As long as she felt comfortable.

'Say stop anytime you want,' he said, pushing up her nightgown's flowing fabric.

He released his erection from the confines of his falls. She gasped.

He glanced up at her expression. She licked her lips.

He groaned. Did she have any idea what an erotic gesture that was? If she did not know now, she likely would before too much time passed.

Only if they remained married.

He could not think about that now.

He grasped her hips and lifted her up on her knees. She tipped forward, grasping his shoulders, and he nudged her into position over the head of his phallus.

'Oh,' she whispered, as if some secret was revealed, as the tip of him entered her hot, wet and indefinably silky channel.

Desire sent blood coursing through his veins in a hot rushing tide of lust.

He pressed down on her hip bones and felt her seat herself firmly on his lap, his shaft as far in as it would go, his balls up tight against her hot quim.

White light filled his mind.

After a moment's struggle, he regained some semblance of mental capacity and using his hands guided her to rise and fall as if she were posting on a horse.

The moment she got the rhythm she was off, and he let his hands fall lax to his sides, leaving her in control. Her expression filled with pleasure and delight.

'Oh, my,' she said, slowing her slide, then speeding it up. Her inner muscles tightened and her eyes widened with surprise, then softened with pleasure.

'That feels extraordinary,' she whispered.

He slid his hand beneath the hem of her silky gown, now hiked up to her waist, and cupped her small breasts in his hands.

She stilled.

He toyed with her nipples, tweaking them, rubbing them with his thumbs, enjoying how they fit so neatly within his palm.

She arched into his hands, bringing those beautiful tits so close to his mouth he could not resist temptation and leaned forward to suckle the jutting peak through the silky fabric.

She moaned her pleasure and pumped her hips. His bollocks tightened until the pain of denial was of the purest sharpest form of pleasure he had ever known.

To return the favour, he worked his hand down to where they were joined and used his thumb to pleasure the little nub deep in her slit. She made a sound of shock.

He froze.

'Don't stop,' she cried, circling her hips, seeking the pleasure from his touch.

The tightening of her core around his shaft sent his mind spinning out of control and he pumped his hips, thrusting deep into her body.

She cried out and shuddered, and his mind spun out of control. On some deep level he felt her fall into ecstasy and, released of restraint, took them both over the edge into bliss.

She collapsed against his chest.

Somehow, he shifted so they lay stretched out on the sofa in each other's arms. Hot darkness blotted out his mind and vision.

Everett slowly came to his senses. What the devil had come over him?

She stretched, then cuddled closer. 'That was lovely,' she said.

More than lovely. It was heavenly. And he should not have done it.

'It might be the end of all your plans,' he said brusquely.

'Why is that?'

'If you were not already expecting, you might be now.'

'That is why I came. I should have told you I am not with child.'

'You know this how?'

'A couple of days after we made love, the evidence arrived.'

He cursed softly under his breath. 'So it will be two weeks before we know...'

'But what a lovely way to procrastinate.'

His mind would not function. But somehow, he felt happy. No, not happy. Delighted. 'Are you saying you want to put off your departure?'

She rose up on one arm and kissed his cheek. 'No. That is not what I am saying.'

He lifted her up and set her on top of his chest so he could properly see her face. It was full of mischief, and yet, hope.

'Then... I do not understand.'

'What I am saying is that I do not want to leave at all.'

He wasn't sure he could believe his ears. 'You wish to remain with me as my wife?'

'I have realised what a kind good man you are, nothing like my father, nothing like the men from whom the wives I helped to flee. There are good men in the world, my brother, Paris, is one. So are you. And I would miss you terribly if we parted. Because, you know, I think, no, I am sure, I have fallen in love with you. I love you. If you still want me, it will make me very happy.'

His heart felt so full he couldn't speak for a moment. 'Want you? I want you more than anything I have ever wanted in my life. I love you with all my heart and I fear I am either drunk or mad, like poor Hamlet.'

She lay her head on his chest and stroked his arm. 'Neither drunk nor mad. I mean what I say. I love you.'

'After the way I treated you, I do not deserve such happiness.' He wished he could stop his tongue from relaying his thoughts. Any moment now she would realise he was right and decide to leave, after all.

'You deserve happiness more than anyone else I know,' she said. 'And I think I deserve some too. So let us say no more but continue on as husband and wife for ever and a day.'

'You really do mean it.'

'I do.'

As he stroked his fingers through her glorious hair, he had an idea.

'What would you think about us repeating our vows?' he asked. 'A small ceremony, to make up for the one I can scarcely remember I was so hungover. This time you would have a proper gown and bridesmaids and a big feast.'

She sat up and looked down into his face with a lovely and mysterious smile. She shook her head.

'No. We do not need all those people. We just need each other.'

The simplicity of it made him want to weep. He slid out from beneath her and got to his feet before helping her to stand. He straightened her robe and tied the knot in her dressing gown. He went down on one knee before her. 'Dearest, sweetest Venetia, you make me the happiest man alive and I promise to keep you safe and to love and cherish you for all the rest of my days.'

Tears ran down her face. 'Oh, my darling husband, I promise I will love you always, till death do us part.'

He stood up and they kissed as if they were one heart and one soul.

When they broke apart they smiled and then laughed.

He was grinning like a schoolboy, he realised.

'This,' Venetia said, 'is a much better ending than in Mr Shakespeare's silly old play.'

'Indeed, it is, my darling. Beyond a doubt.'

And he picked her up in his arms. 'And now it is time for me to carry you across the threshold of my bedroom and make love to you until the sun is high in the sky.'

'What a very splendid idea,' she whispered, snuggled up against his chest. 'Lead on, McDuff.'

He laughingly groaned. 'Enough of Mr Shakespeare, my lady.'

His lady. Yes. And he was her lord. And together, side by side, they would face the world.

* * * * *

*If you enjoyed this story, why not check out
Ann Lethbridge's other great reads?*

**The Viscount's Reckless Temptation
The Matchmaker and the Duke**

*And be sure to read her
The Widows of Westram miniseries!*

A Lord for the Wallflower Widow
An Earl for the Shy Widow
A Family for the Widowed Governess
A Shopkeeper for the Earl of Westram